FIONA'S HOMECOMING
Bradford Hall, Book Three

BARBARA MCMAHON

Prologue

Fiona Hunter dressed in the bad-ass attire that was so familiar—black jeans, black motorcycle boots, tight black T-shirt, spiky hair and an attitude she wore like a shield. She was going to the precinct, but to protect her cover, she dressed the part.

If anyone saw her, she'd bluff her way through by saying she'd been picked up. It'd happened once a couple of years ago. That, of course, had made it even easier for her to infiltrate that particular drug ring.

Working undercover vice was dangerous, but also exciting. Some days she wondered if she was risking death for the adrenaline rush. Mostly, however, she was not introspective, merely anxious to rid the Los Angeles streets of the vermin who preyed on the innocent.

Like the bastards she'd busted last night.

Arriving at the station early, she quickly climbed the worn stairs to the second floor, heading to the desk she shared with Jim Peterson. He worked vice, too, specializing in child porn. That was one vice she didn't want to get involved in.

Drugs was her area. Teenage pushers in the local high schools, to be specific. Fiona looked far younger than her twenty-eight years and passed for a high-school kid.

"Hey, Fiona, nice going on that bust," one of her fellow officers called out.

She waved and smiled, sitting at the computer and logging on. Jim had different hours. For the most part, sharing the desk worked. She pulled up the arrest records, scanned them, and then opened the word processing program. Fiona shut out the sounds of the bullpen and concentrated on writing her report.

An hour later, her shoulders ached from sitting at the computer. Being out and about sure beat working at a desk. Stretching, she decided a cup of coffee and chocolate would revive her, so she headed for the candy machine located on the first floor. Man, she hated doing reports.

A minute or two later she was studying the machine's selection—like it had changed in the past five years.

"Fiona? Fiona Hunter?"

She turned, suddenly on her guard. For a minute she didn't recognize the man. Handcuffed and being escorted by a uniformed officer, he was lanky and scruffy and obviously hadn't shaved in a day or two. Who...?

Then she recognized him.

"Denton? Jack Denton?"

For heaven's sake, it was a guy from her hometown in Mississippi. What were the odds of her ever running into anyone from home here in L.A., much less at the station?

"Hey, Fiona, looking good," he said, tugging on the hold the officer had. "Hold up, man. I know her."

Fiona glanced at the uniformed cop, no one she recognized. Hoping her cover would hold, she assumed her persona of street tough.

"I'd ask how's it going, but it looks bad," she said to Denton, motioning to his cuffs.

"What are you doing here?" he asked.

"Getting something to eat. They wanted me for questioning. No charge yet. I think the good cop is showing me what a fine dude he is to let me get some candy without someone breathing down my neck—like they don't have cameras everywhere watching my every move. I head for the door and watch the swarm."

She prayed one of her friends didn't happen along and call out to her.

"Hey, I know what you mean."

"What are you doing in L.A.?"

Fiona asked, hoping the policeman would have enough patience to allow Denton another minute or two. He was someone from home. Not a friend, not someone she'd ever have looked up, but suddenly that tenuous connection seemed important.

"This and that. This is a bum rap. I'll beat it. You ever get back home?"

Fiona shook her head. She'd screwed that up royally. There was no home to return to.

"I heard about Margaret beating you," Denton said. "Bitch. If there's one thing I hate, it's child abuse."

Fiona was surprised. She hadn't known Denton

very well. They'd dated a couple of times—on her part mostly to tick Margaret off. He'd been a big-time troublemaker back then, and it looked as if nothing had changed.

"Hear from my old lady now and then," he said next. "Thought you might want to know—Margaret Nunes had a stroke. She's not expected to make it. Payback time."

Denton seemed to brighten at the thought.

Fiona sucked in her breath. The words hit like fists. Margaret was dying?

"Let's go," the cop said, pulling Denton off balance enough that he had to take a step.

"Maybe we can catch up later," Denton said, smirking as his gaze ran down the length of her.

She couldn't answer, could only hear the echo of the words *not expected to make it.*

She remembered the last time she'd seen Margaret, the accusations she'd thrown at her. The anger and hurt and confusion that had filled her.

The wrong she'd done Margaret.

And Piper and Cassie.

Fiona felt sick. It had been years since she'd thought about that last day.

She turned and almost ran back to her desk. She had to get her reports done and talk to the lieutenant. She needed time off—needed to get home. To see Margaret and apologize. To talk to her one more time. She had to get to Bradford before Margaret died to see if she could make things right.

1

Fiona didn't roar into Bradford on her Harley. She drove a candy-apple-red convertible she'd rented at the New Orleans airport. The air blew through her short dark hair, giving the illusion of coolness until she stopped. Then the sultry Mississippi heat enveloped her, and the sun seemed to burn right through her hair to her scalp. Her skin glistened with perspiration.

She was no longer used to the humidity. L.A. heated up plenty in the summer, but it was a dry heat. She'd heard that so many times she couldn't count, but until today, she hadn't realized how true it was. She'd been gone too long.

Driving slowly down Main Street, she looked with interest at the town she'd grown up in. After the sprawl of Los Angeles it seemed tiny and quiet. The old brick buildings looked dirty and tired. For the most part, the cars were sedans, sedate and suitable for old folks. Who traveled far in Bradford? She didn't see the big SUVs that were so prevalent in Southern California, nor the "beater" cars gangs used, or the fancy foreign jobs seen rolling along Rodeo Drive.

People on the sidewalk stopped and stared. A

stranger still drew notice in town.

She resisted an urge to wave just to see what they'd do. But she wasn't here to stir things up. She'd come to make her peace with Margaret Nunes, if she wasn't too late.

As she glided by Ruby's Café, Fiona's mouth watered in memory. She'd spent a lot of time there eating burgers and fries. She wondered if they still tasted as good as she remembered.

As she drove away from the center of town, she caught the eye of a law-enforcement officer about to get into a car emblazoned with the sheriff's shield. Bradford wasn't big enough to afford a police force and so it used the same law enforcement the entire county did. The man getting into the patrol car didn't look anything like Sheriff Halstead, the man who'd manipulated things to suit himself and the good citizens of Bradford, and shipped Fiona off rather than deal with her accusations.

She should have come back sooner and set the record straight.

But who'd have believed her?

Nothing had changed in the interim. Now it was too late. The statute of limitations had long run out even if she could get someone in authority to believe her.

The man watched her as she went by. She'd toned down a few things about her appearance for this homecoming, but the black tank top that showed her tanned, muscular arms was as out of place in summertime Bradford as her black jeans and motorcycle boots. Her hair was slightly spiked.

She'd come back to make a statement, as well as apologize, she admitted. And if they didn't like it, too bad. No one had stood up for her in this town. She was going to show them she needed no one.

And if she shocked a few people, so much the better.

No one messed with Fiona Hunter when she was in battle dress, and she figured she needed all the help she could get.

When her friend Randy Jones had dropped her off at the airport in Los Angeles, he'd shaken his head and asked why she dressed like that when flying. Didn't she know what a red flag she was waving?

Since Fiona had never flown before, she hadn't a clue how uptight the flight attendants might get. Fortunately, she took some of Tyler's advice to heart and bought a colorful short-sleeved shirt at an airport shop to cover the black tank top. Coupled with softening her hairstyle and keeping her expression bland, she felt she more or less fit in with the other travelers.

Still, she had been wanded and her boots double-checked by security. And the flight attendants eyed her suspiciously the entire flight.

Continuing without another look at the cop, she headed for Bradford Hall. If Denton's story had been true, Margaret was most likely in the hospital, but Fiona needed to see the place, to sort of ground herself.

She was stalling and she knew it. But it wouldn't hurt just to see the house before she searched for Margaret.

She almost laughed when the cop pulled in behind her—keeping far enough back not to crowd her, but definitely on her tail. How predictable. Would he follow her all the way up to the house?

She turned onto the curved, crushed-shell driveway. The old house, hidden by trees and shrubbery, couldn't be seen from the road. She rounded the bend and the old Victorian structure came into view, so out of place in Mississippi, with its antebellum architecture. The windows looked empty and blind. Yet flowers bloomed in garden patches, the lawn was mowed and two vehicles were parked in the driveway near the back door.

She pulled to a stop behind one of them, a white van, and killed the engine. Glancing in her rearview mirror, she realized the cop hadn't followed her into the driveway.

She opened her car door, stepped out and looked around. The familiar scents filled her head with memories. The sticky heat wrapped around her just as it had all those summer days so long ago.

Fiona was surprised by the pang she felt. One of homecoming and welcome.

Stupid. There was no welcome for her here.

She heard a radio and the sound of a power saw from within the house, muffled slightly because of the closed windows. She could also hear the dull roar of the air-conditioning unit at the far corner of the house.

That hadn't been here before.

Was the house still Margaret's? Was she in time, or had the woman already died and the estate been settled? Denton hadn't told her much, and she hadn't followed up before coming as fast as she could.

Nervous at what she'd find, she stepped up onto the back porch. Wiping damp palms against her dark pants, she rapped on the door, remembering how she used to barrel into the kitchen after school, hungry for food and Margaret's approval.

She wasn't looking for that anymore.

Funny how some memories just popped into mind.

"It's open," a voice called.

Fiona turned the knob and pushed the door.

A familiar scene assailed her. For a moment she felt like a teenager again. Cassie stood at the stove cooking. The aroma of the bubbling sauce filled Fiona's nostrils and made her mouth water. Rock music blared from a radio in the room. And now the sound of someone hammering could be heard in the background.

Just as Cassie turned, Piper came through the door from the hallway.

"Honestly, if I ever reach her, I'm going to ream her out for not answering the frigging phone ever. This is so frustrating—"

She stopped and stared at Fiona.

Cassie turned and stared at her, too. For a long moment all three were motionless.

"Fiona?" Cassie said.

"Fiona, where have you been?"

Piper asked, rushing across the room to throw her arms around her. Cassie only two steps behind.

A lump gathered in Fiona's throat. She was home. And greeted with a welcome she didn't expect or deserve. Cassie and Piper were both here. She couldn't believe it.

"Fiona, we've been trying to reach you for days."

"How did you know to come home right now?"

"How are you?"

"What have you been doing?"

"Look at you!"

Fiona felt the suspicious sting of tears. She never cried.

"You look fantastic," Cassie said, standing back to look her up and down, a wide smile on her face. "Omigosh, I can't believe you're *here!*"

"We've been trying to reach you for days," Piper said. "Why don't you answer your phone?"

"I can't believe you're both here," Fiona said. "I thought we were scattered to the winds. If I'd known, I'd have come back sooner. I never expected to see either of you again."

Cassie and Piper had been Fiona's best friends for most of her growing-up years. They'd lost touch after that fateful day. Seeing them again felt as if nothing had changed.

"We *were* scattered to the winds. I was living in Boston until about a month and a half ago," Cassie said.

"And I live in Paris," Piper said, smiling happily. "I've been back a few weeks. And we finally tracked you down to L.A. That is you, right? Could we have been living farther apart? How did you know to come home? Instinct?"

Fiona shook her head, trying to assimilate all the news.

"You've been trying to reach me?"

"Yes, we got your phone number in L.A. At least we think it's yours." Piper rattled off the number.

Fiona nodded.

"I've been calling for days," Piper said again. "You're here now. I can't believe it. Come in. Let me shut the door. This heat is horrific."

She reached behind Fiona and started to close the door, then hesitated.

"Sam's here," she said.

Cassie looked over her shoulder.

"Sam Witt? Wonder why?"

Fiona turned and saw the sheriff climb out of his car.

"Probably making sure I'm not stealing the silver," she said, watching him as he approached the back door.

He was tall and nicely put together. His hair was dark, his eyes hidden behind sunglasses. The uniform was immaculate, despite the heat and humidity. He looked to be in his early thirties, much younger than the former sheriff.

Fiona's two old friends looked at her, and Piper

wrinkled her nose. "You do look like biker trash in that outfit. What's with all the black? It's not your best color."

Before Fiona could reply, Sam stepped up on the back porch and peered in through the screen door.

"Everything all right, ladies?" he asked.

Cassie stepped around Fiona and pushed open the screen door.

"Come in and meet Fiona. She just showed up."

Sam stepped inside, his expression guarded. He took off the sunglasses, and Fiona was surprised at the velvet darkness of his eyes. His assessing look, however, was one she was familiar with.

The good sheriff didn't trust her. He gave her a look law enforcement the world over knew. But if the mood took her, she could give as good as she got.

Right now, Fiona felt a spurt of amusement. She knew what he thought. She'd left her gun at home, not wanting to have to explain it at the airport. But she did have her badge and credentials, and courtesy demanded she tell the sheriff. An imp of mischief stilled her tongue.

"Mary Fiona Hunter, of Los Angeles?" he said.

She inclined her head.

"We had a hard time locating you."

"She ended up coming home without us," Piper said. "I never got an answer on her phone. She just showed up."

"I heard about Margaret," Fiona said quietly. "How is she?"

She held her breath, hoping she wasn't too late.

"Me, too," Cassie said. "That's why I came, because of her stroke. She's doing better. Then I found Piper's number and called her. We've been searching for you for weeks. It's so good to see you!"

Cassie reached out and rubbed Fiona's arm. Fiona remembered Cassie had always been a touchy person. No one had touched Fiona in friendship in a long time.

Fiona looked around the old kitchen trying not to get all sentimental.

"Not much seems to have changed. You're still cooking."

Then she looked at Piper, in a gauzy sundress that floated around her legs, and smiled.

"Fancy dress for lazing around the house," she said.

"Same old Fiona—two minutes getting dressed and then you're ready for the day," Piper replied.

Fiona laughed, then swung her gaze to the sheriff.

"I'm not here to cause trouble, Sheriff. I heard about Margaret and came back to see her."

She turned to Cassie. "Is she really doing better?"

"Recovering more and more every day," her friend answered. "She'll want to see you right away. We told her we were searching. She hired a private detective to find you and Piper a few years ago. That's how I located Piper, but the detective didn't find you."

"Mary Fiona Hunter," Sam murmured. "Everyone thought Fiona was your only name."

"Yeah, well, Mary is only used on official

documents," she said.

It felt odd to be standing in the kitchen, talking as if they hadn't been away for more than twelve years. She half expected Margaret to come in to ask if they didn't have something better to do than stand around wasting time.

"Oops, better check dinner," Cassie said, dashing back to the stove. "Bring in your suitcase, Fi, and plan to stay here. Piper and I are both already in residence. You won't believe what's going on. The house is being renovated, so it's a mess. We're planning a fund-raiser at the Independence Day fair for Margaret's medical expenses and help fund a home for pregnant teens. We have so much to catch up on! And after dinner, you can go see Margaret. She's doing a lot better than when I first saw her—she's walking with help and can sit up on her own. She can't talk very well, though."

"Aphasia," Piper said. "Scrambled lines between her mind and her mouth. But she understands everything—at least we think she does. And she can write, after a fashion, but it takes her forever to get a sentence down. There's hope one day she'll fully recover."

She turned to Sam. "Can you stay for dinner?"

"Thanks, but not tonight—I'm on duty," he said. "Is Adam coming over?"

"Of course."

Piper smiled at him and then at Fiona.

"I just got engaged!"

She waved a sparkling diamond in front of Fiona's

face. "To the most wonderful man in the world. When he isn't driving me crazy, that is."

Fiona grabbed her hand and looked at the ring. The solitaire looked feminine and delicate on Piper's slender finger.

"Congratulations. Anyone I know?"

"Adam Saunders, former correspondent for CNN and the department head for a new project starting next month. You'll meet him at dinner."

"And you'll see Matt again," Cassie said. "Remember him?"

"Sure. You two have a bunch of kids now?" Fiona asked.

"No. Things happened. Actually, before I came home a few weeks ago, I hadn't seen him since that day—"

Cassie stopped suddenly.

Fiona knew exactly what day she meant.

Into the awkward silence, Cassie waved her left hand again and announced, "But we're getting married—as soon as Margaret's able to attend. Sorry you can't stay, Sam. Another night, then."

"Count on it."

He nodded to Cassie and Piper and gave Fiona another thoughtful look before returning to his car and leaving.

Things were not what she'd expected, Fiona thought as Piper handed her a glass of iced tea and told her to sit at the table. She tried to grasp the various nuances.

The sheriff was a friend. Of course, he was nothing like the sheriff who'd held office when she was a teenager.

Piper lived in Paris. As in France? She'd have to get that straight.

It seemed as if a time warp had happened. Cassie and Matt were getting married—about ten years later than Fiona expected. She had a lot to catch up on.

"This will simmer for a while," Cassie said, putting the wooden spoon on a holder on the counter and turning back to Fiona and Piper.

"Let's get your bags and find you a room. The second floor is a mess. I figure you can have that back corner bedroom. I don't think they've started in there."

"It's pretty small," Piper said.

"I don't have to stay here," Fiona said.

She felt uncomfortable. They acted as if she weren't to blame for breaking them up. Didn't they know?

If not, she knew she'd have to explain the events that led up to their being sent to different foster homes twelve years ago. She was surprised the topic hadn't been the first thing out of their mouths.

"Of course you'll stay here," Piper stated. "Where else would you go? Besides, Margaret will be coming home before too much longer. Think how much fun it will be to have all her girls under one roof."

"I can't stay that long," Fiona said quickly.

They obviously didn't know. This welcome and friendliness was all going to vanish when she told them what she'd done. No use setting herself up for the fall.

"Well, for however long you are in town, plan to stay here," Cassie said. "Is your suitcase in your car?"

"Just a small one."

Enough for a couple of changes of clothes. How long could it take to apologize and make sure Margaret didn't need anything? She probably wouldn't want anything from Fiona even if she did need something. But there were ways to get around that.

"I'll get it," Cassie said. "Piper, find some sheets that aren't layered in dust."

"What's with all the construction?" Fiona asked.

"This house is going to become a group home for pregnant, unwed teenagers," Piper said. "It's Matt's idea, but one Margaret was all for. And no wonder. Oh, there's so much to tell you!"

"Wait until I get there," Cassie warned, heading out the back door toward Fiona's car.

Five minutes later Piper and Fiona were working together to make the single bed in the small upstairs room. It hadn't been used when the girls lived in the house. The windows looked over the backyard. The entire room wasn't much bigger than a closet, but it would be fine for one short-term visitor.

"Okay, so bring me up to date," Fiona said, sitting on the newly made bed.

"You first. Whatever in the world possessed you to tell Sheriff Halstead that Margaret beat you?"

Cassie asked, standing at the foot of the bed, her hands on her hips.

Fiona glanced at Piper, who also stared at her. They *did* know! She hated to talk about it but knew she had to offer some explanation. She glanced at her finger.

"Remember this?"

She raised the finger and showed her scar.

Cassie stepped forward and touched her finger to Fiona's.

"I have a scar, too."

"Me, too," Piper said, reaching over to complete the ritual. "All for one and one for all."

Fiona heard the echo of younger voices. They'd become blood sisters that day.

"I messed up," she said, slowly bringing down her hand.

"I'll say," Cassie concurred. "Why?"

"I told Margaret what happened and she didn't believe me."

Even after all these years, Margaret's refusal to believe her had the power to hurt.

"Accused me of lying, of trying to protect one of the boys from school, of trying to—"

Fiona stopped. The words would resound in her mind forever.

"Never mind. I need to talk to Margaret. I was punishing her by telling the authorities she'd beaten me. When I tried to tell the sheriff the truth later, he threatened to put me in jail for lying. I believed him."

"We wondered why nothing beyond sending us away had happened," Piper said. "Cassie had Sam look into it."

"I say we use the fund-raiser in July to set the record straight," Cassie said.

"What do you propose—a banner declaring Margaret innocent?" Piper asked. "Someone walking around with a bullhorn?"

"So she didn't get into trouble for my lies?" Fiona asked.

The fear that Margaret had gone to jail or lost her home or worse had always hovered over her.

Cassie sat cross-legged at the foot of the bed.

"Nope. We got sent away and that seemed to be it. And we don't need a banner. We just need to be ready to answer questions."

Piper nodded, perching on the other side of the bed.

"Sam told Adam that the whole thing was badly documented. There didn't appear to be any attempt to make an arrest. And who, even back then, would believe Margaret beat you up? You were taller, younger, athletic."

"What really happened? Who beat you?" Cassie asked softly.

Fiona looked at them, then shook her head.

"Let me talk to Margaret first. Then I'll tell you everything."

"She's at the convalescent hospital. We can go over now if you like," Piper said, reaching over to grab a pillow and stuff it into a case. "Or after dinner, so we can stay and visit longer."

"I need to go by myself," Fiona said.

The other two looked at each other and nodded.

"We know you didn't stay with your next foster parents," Piper said, tossing the pillow at the head of the bed and leaning back on the footboard. "What happened?"

Fiona flipped open her ID case and lobbed it onto the center of the bed. The golden badge gleamed. Her photo on the identification card stared up at them.

"You're a cop!" Cassie said, grabbing the ID and reading the card. "A Los Angeles police officer."

She burst out laughing and handed the card to Piper.

Piper grinned as she took it.

"We thought you might have been in jail somewhere, a criminal—not *arresting* criminals."

"A criminal!"

Fiona felt offended.

Cassie nodded, her eyes brimming with laughter.

"You were always getting into trouble—skipping school, hanging out with those guys who were bad news."

"Hey, Jack Denton is the one who told me about Margaret."

Not that his revelation was altruistic.

"Can you arrest whoever attacked you?" Piper asked, handing back the leather case.

"The statute of limitations has run out, and I'm not living in this jurisdiction. I'm here to apologize to Margaret, nothing more."

Though she *had* thought over the years how she'd like to make the man pay. Maybe something *would* come of her visit, but she didn't have high hopes.

"Mending fences is a good thing, especially now that we're all together again," Cassie said. "You'll have to stay for the fund raiser at the Fourth of July fair."

"And my wedding," Piper said.

"What are you talking about?" Fiona asked.

"Which, the fund raiser or the wedding?" Piper asked.

"You told me about the fund raiser. Are you really getting married that quickly?"

"As soon as Margaret's able to attend. Doesn't seem quick to me."

"And everyone in the county shows up at the fair, making it the perfect place for you to show your support by helping out, and making sure anyone who asks knows Margaret never beat you," Cassie said. "That's even better than we planned. Since you gave the false information, you can set the record straight."

"Like anyone's going to listen to me," Fiona muttered.

No one had twelve years ago.

"I bet people in L.A. listen to you," Piper said. "How else could you do your job?"

"They don't know the situation."

Cassie frowned.

"Well, I'm thinking we don't know it, either."

Fiona nodded. "Just let me talk to Margaret and I'll tell you everything—if it's okay with her."

Fiona leaned back on the pillow propped against the headboard and looked at the two women who'd once been closer to her than sisters.

"So tell me all that's been going on with you two," she invited.

In the time before dinner Cassie filled Fiona in on her move to Boston and becoming a chef. Piper regaled her with her account of becoming a model in Paris and then startled Fiona when she told her she'd been married twice.

But the biggest surprise was that Piper had just discovered Margaret was her biological grandmother.

Fiona listened, glad her friends' lives had turned out so well. She'd have felt far worse than she did if other lives had been ruined because of her. She'd always figured she deserved what she got, but Cassie and Piper hadn't.

They were still talking when Matt arrived. Cassie dashed downstairs the moment she heard his voice, though Fiona didn't know how she could distinguish it from the voices of the construction workers.

"Adam'll be here soon," Piper said, rising. "Freshen up and come meet him."

Spontaneously, she reached over and hugged Fiona.

"I'm so glad you're here!"

Fiona watched Piper go, closing the door behind her. She was back in Bradford, but nothing was as she'd thought it would be.

How amazing to find both Piper and Cassie here.

And both engaged to be married. When she'd allowed herself to think about them over the years, she'd always envisioned them married with the families they used to talk about having one day. In her case, she had no dreams of building a family. There was plenty to do on her job.

The fact she'd never met a man she felt she could trust also played a big part in her decision. She'd leave romance to Piper and Cassie.

Fiona went to the bathroom at the end of the hall. The construction crew had finally left. Dust wafted in the air. She peeked in the door of the room Cassie had always had and saw a new connecting bath between her room and the room she herself used to use.

She moved to the door of her old room and went in. Surprised to see everything almost as she'd left it except for the new door to the connecting bath, she studied the posters and announcements on the old bulletin board. Together they captured moments of time in a teenage girl's life.

At last she pushed away and went to freshen up. She wasn't that same girl. Time had moved along and so had she. After seeing Margaret, she'd have to decide if she would stay for Independence Day. Small towns had long memories.

Fiona didn't want to be the focus of gossip and speculation for days on end. Yet she owed Margaret. It'd be little enough to endure if the record were set straight.

Where was Allen McLennon these days? He and

Margaret had been dating for several months before Fiona's attack. Margaret believed Allen, not Fiona. Was he still lording it over people?

Wouldn't the town be shocked to learn the truth about the lofty town banker?

When she entered the kitchen a short time later, Cassie was dishing up some delectable sauce and spreading it over pasta. Piper poured iced tea into tall glasses. Matt Bennett was setting the table. He looked older, of course, and had filled out nicely. There was another man Fiona didn't recognize, undoubtedly Piper's fiancé.

"Here she is," Piper said, spotting her. "Come and meet Adam."

Introductions were made. Matt greeted her, and before long all were seated at the old table enjoying Cassie's cooking.

Fiona felt odd sitting with the two couples. Cassie and Piper bubbled with excitement at her arrival. Matt seemed as easygoing as always. Adam Saunders, on the other hand, studied her as if he didn't trust her.

No biggie. She was used to going it alone. And she didn't begrudge Cassie or Piper their happiness. She felt like a fifth wheel, however.

"Seen Margaret yet?" Matt asked.

"Going after dinner," she said. "She's still at the convalescent hospital, Piper said."

Matt nodded.

"Want a lift?"

"Thought I'd walk."

"We've been doing a lot of that lately," Cassie said. "It's nice to be able to walk so many places without needing a car."

"That'll be strange for an Angeleno, I expect," Adam said.

"Right. I always drive everywhere. Usually on my Harley."

Adam's eyebrows rose.

"Motorcycle?"

Matt asked with a grin. "Do you really have a Harley?"

She nodded.

"Traffic is a bitch, so I have a bike. I can weave through the stopped cars to get to where I'm going faster."

"Dangerous," Cassie murmured.

Fiona shrugged.

"So far so good."

She was a careful driver, but liked the mobility the bike gave compared to cars in the L.A. freeway traffic. When she'd first bought the bike, it was used, and the only thing she could afford. But she didn't need to share that—not with Adam looking like he wanted to dissect her every word.

"Tell me about Paris," she said, hoping to turn the attention away from herself.

She felt uncomfortable with everyone watching.

Piper took the bait and Fiona began to relax as she listened to her friend talk about her career, her apartment on the Left Bank, and the fun of visiting

European capitals on someone else's tab.

Dinner ended with strawberry shortcake eaten on the porch. The evening stayed light late at the end of June, and citronella candles kept the mosquitoes at bay. Fiona felt suddenly very grown-up, sitting on the porch as Margaret and some of her ladies' club friends had done. Talking with other grown-ups. What would life have been like if that night had never happened?

Once again she regretted not handling things differently. But it always got back to Margaret's not believing her, then her anger, and her fear.

Time ticked by. Fiona finished her coffee and put the cup down with a click. Conversation stopped and everyone looked at her.

"Guess I'll be heading for the hospital."

She felt like she was heading for an execution. But she couldn't put it off any longer.

"She's on the second floor," Cassie said. "She's going to be so happy to see you."

Fiona doubted that. But this was something she needed to do. To make amends if she could, to apologize at the very least.

She headed out, enjoying the evening air. It felt strange to be walking. Even stranger to see so few cars on the road. Where she lived in L.A., she couldn't even get to the store without driving through heavy traffic.

Fiona turned onto Main Street. It looked the same, except for a few changes in storefronts. Ruby's Café was bustling with teenagers and a handful of older folks. She'd have to stop in and have a burger before she left Bradford.

The ice cream store was doing a terrific business. Most of the other stores had closed at six. She wondered if there were any all-night places in town, then had to remind herself this was Bradford, not L.A.

Moments later Fiona approached the convalescent hospital. The parking lot was less than half full. The brick building was small compared to the hospitals she frequently visited in the line of duty. This one had been built to serve the county and was rarely filled to capacity.

She reached the wide double doors and stopped. Beyond the threshold she could see the brightly lit lobby, with a woman at an information desk. A couple sat near the elevators as if waiting for someone. A man passed her and held the door.

She took a breath and shook her head. She wasn't ready.

She'd come from California for this express purpose, and yet she couldn't make herself walk inside.

Fiona wasn't sure how long she stood outside the doors before turning and retracing her steps. She'd have to come back tomorrow. Tonight was impossible.

When she reached the town square, she found an empty bench and sat. In the playground area of the nearby park, children laughed and shrieked as they slid down the slide or were pushed higher and higher on the swings by indulgent parents. A woman walked her dog on the far side.

The scene was peaceful.

Unlike her neighborhood in L.A.

Fiona had a thousand memories of Bradford. Many good. She should focus on those. It had always been a quiet, sleepy, Southern town. Nothing inherently bad. All places had bad people living in them. She couldn't condemn an entire town because of one man.

"Taking a walk down memory lane?" a familiar voice asked.

She looked up and to her left. Sam Witt stood there. She hadn't noticed his arrival.

"Sort of."

He sat on the bench beside her.

"Nice time of day," he said, taking off his hat and putting it on the bench between them.

"Mmm."

She wasn't up to small talk with the sheriff. Her own badge was burning a hole in her back pocket. She should give him the courtesy of identifying herself. But right now to do anything seemed too much effort.

"Been to see Margaret?" he guessed.

"Went there, didn't go in," she confessed.

"Tough visiting someone sick," he said.

"I screwed up. I need to apologize."

She could never make up for the damage her accusation caused. Was it that thought that kept her from going in tonight?

Or fear of the repudiation she expected from Margaret?

She hated knowing she was just plain scared.

"I looked into your file, you know," he said. "Sloppy piece of police work. There was never a resolution to the crime. No charges were filed, no suspicions even noted."

"I'm sure there weren't. Sheriff Halstead didn't believe me."

"He didn't even report the person you accused," Sam said.

Fiona knew he was fishing. Maybe it was too late to do anything about the crime against her, but she hated that the man had gotten away with it. What could she do to let people know the truth?

Had he tried to rape other young girls since she'd left? The thought made her shudder. Yet when she'd told the law, nothing had been done.

She needed to talk to Margaret first, then she'd open up to Sam Witt. A sheriff ought to know what was going on in his jurisdiction.

Sam leaned back on the bench, wondering why he was trying to make conversation with a woman who obviously didn't want to talk. His effort wasn't all about trying to learn what really happened twelve years ago. He sensed an aloneness in her that was at odds with her attitude.

So now he was playing Dudley Do-Right? Trying to make everything okay for this stranger? Patty would say it was like him.

The thought of his wife brought the familiar ache into focus. Three years and he still missed her.

"Seem odd to be back?" he asked, refocusing on the situation at hand.

She nodded, not looking at him, her gaze on the children in the park.

"Staying long?"

Getting her to talk was worse than interrogating hardened criminals.

She turned and looked at him.

"I'm here for as long as I want to be. You have a problem with that?"

He recognized the cocky attitude as a cover-up. Touchy.

"Not as long as you don't cause any problems."

She reached in her back pocket and pulled out a leather wallet, flipping it open with practiced ease.

The gleam of the gold badge caught his eye. He took the wallet and read the identification card. Fiona was a detective with the LAPD. That did surprise him. He tossed it back to her and studied her for a moment.

Just to yank her chain, he said, "Still, don't be causing trouble in my town."

2

"Your town?" Fiona said, replacing the wallet.

"Adopted town."

"Where are you from originally?"

"New Orleans before here. Born in Baton Rouge."

"Quite a change of venue," she said.

"I worked in the Big Easy PD a number of years."

"Been here long?" she asked.

"A little over two years now."

"And compared to New Orleans, this is satisfying?" she asked.

"It suits me. I worked the narcotics detail. It's a never-ending battle."

"But it's a battle that has to be fought. I'm in drugs myself."

Sam knew what she meant. It even made sense, remembering the dossier he'd read on Fiona Hunter. Her mother was an addict. Kids often became crusaders against drugs—if they didn't start using themselves.

"If you're not going to the hospital, I'll give you a ride home," he said a few moments later.

She seemed at a loss and Sam's instincts rose. Part

of the job of a cop was to help people, not only to catch criminals. He wanted to help this young woman, even though she probably didn't feel she needed help. The attitude of hers would only cover so much.

She slanted him a glance.

"Won't that look great, first night home and already riding in a cop car."

He caught the hint of amusement.

"I'll turn on the siren if you like," he said.

She laughed at that and his breath hitched. She was lovely when she wasn't trying to look and act like a street punk.

"Are you in disguise?" he asked.

"Undercover detail. I infiltrate high schools. Classy, huh?" she asked in self-mockery.

"You look young enough for it. Any luck?"

"Oh, yeah. More than I want. Several busts in the past couple of years. So three high schools and a junior high are safe for a little while. Until the next slime ball starts up trafficking. It's a never-ending war, but one I'm willing to wage forever to rid the world of such bastards."

"I felt that way."

"Burned out?" she guessed.

Sam shrugged. Partially that, of course.

But Patty's death had been the final straw. He'd tried hard to make the world a better place, and lost his wife along the way. If he'd listened to her, they would have moved to a place like Bradford long ago, established comfortable lives, and Patty wouldn't have been on that road the night the drunk careered into her.

"I'll take you up on that ride, but back to Bradford Hall. Then I'll screw up my courage to see Margaret in the morning."

He rose.

"Sounds like a plan."

She stood beside him, coming to his chin. She was slender, almost boyish in figure. But strong-looking. Her bare arms were toned and tanned, probably from spending time at the beach in Southern California. He wondered what her hair looked like when it wasn't spiked. Shorter than he liked on a woman.

He shook off the thought. He wasn't interested in Fiona Hunter as a woman.

She climbed into the passenger's side of the car while Sam got behind the wheel.

"Was Adam over to dinner tonight?" he asked.

"Yes. He and Matt both. I felt the odd man out."

"Yeah, I know that feeling. Cassie's a great cook, and she's always asking me over, but then it's always the two couples and me."

"Well, if I'm here next time you're invited, you know you won't be the only odd man out."

"Staying long?" he asked again.

She wasn't coming on to him, was she?

"I wasn't sure how Margaret was. I thought she was at death's door. So I planned a flying visit to say I'm sorry. Now they want me to stay for the fund-raiser and to tell anyone who asks that Margaret never beat me. Then for Piper's wedding. Sheesh, I could end up staying more than two weeks."

"If you're saying Margaret didn't do it, who did?" Sam asked.

Fiona wasn't surprised at the question. He'd want to know. Everyone else would, too. Not that they'd likely believe her. Margaret hadn't twelve years ago, and she knew Fiona better than anyone.

"I have no problem telling everyone. But I want to talk with Margaret first. I wish the authorities had believed me twelve years ago. The bastard got away with criminal assault and I'm the one who got the shaft."

"From what I can tell about my predecessor, he had trouble finding the office every day. Not a sterling example of law enforcement. But you can set the record straight with a name."

She laughed softly.

Sam liked hearing it.

The trip to Bradford Hall ended too soon. One place wasn't far from any other in Bradford. He stopped near the front porch, still occupied by Piper and Adam.

"Come up for a minute," Fiona invited.

"I'll see if Adam wants a ride home. He's staying with me, you know."

"I didn't know that."

"We go way back. When he was injured by a land mine a few months ago, in the Middle East, he came here to convalesce. Said his folks were driving him crazy."

"Funny how a Parisian model and a world-class journalist met in Bradford, Mississippi," Fiona said. "I wondered how he got that limp."

"Just goes to show if something is meant to be, it will be."

He tried to tell himself that whenever he thought about Patty's death. It didn't make things easier, but he kept hoping one day it would.

"Thanks for the lift."

"Anytime, Detective."

She nodded and got out of the car.

Sam stepped out and leaned on the door.

"Adam, want a lift?"

"Sure. Give me a few."

Sam watched Fiona pass the couple on the porch and go into the house. He climbed back in the car and waited, trying not to watch as his friend kissed his fiancée.

He remembered kissing Patty, the long, slow, hot kisses that inevitably led to making love. He envied Adam that pleasure. Patty had been dead for three years, but sometimes it felt as if she'd just stepped out of the room. Other times, he could hardly remember being married, being in love. Until the pain hit.

He missed his wife.

"Rise and shine," Piper said, coming into Fiona's room the next morning early with a steaming cup of coffee.

"Is there a fire?" Fiona grumbled, and rolled over, pulling the pillow over her head.

"No, but the construction crew arrives at seven and it's chaos after that. Sometimes there's no water all day, so if you want a shower, you'd best get up now. Here. Take the coffee. It'll help."

Fiona didn't want to get up. She liked the dream she was having. But it was too late, it was gone. Just as well; she didn't think she should be fantasizing about a man she'd just met. It probably was because of all the engaged couples she was hanging around. She sat up, leaning against the headboard.

"Thanks," she said, reaching for the coffee cup.

Piper sat in the chair already dressed in another floaty sundress. Makeup on, hair just so, she looked prettier than anyone else Fiona knew.

"I like your clothes," Fiona said with a smile. "I guess you're as clothes crazy as ever. Maybe more so now, given your work."

Piper nodded.

"And in Paris I get to see everything when it's first designed. But my days are numbered. I'm thinking of other things I could be doing."

"Like what?"

"We didn't go into a lot of detail about the home Matt's establishing last night, but one of the things we're thinking of offering is classes for the residents, such as cooking, meal planning and fashion hints. I might find I'm back here sooner than I expect."

"I assume Cassie is doing the cooking bit," Fiona

said.

"It looks like she and Matt will settle here in Bradford. His construction company can be run from here, with him going into New Orleans when needed. Plus, there's more and more growth in this direction. I'm sure he'll get plenty of work. She wants to be near Margaret."

"And you?"

"If you'd asked me a month ago, I'd have said Bradford was the last place I'd want to visit, much less live. But now I'm back, it's kind of growing on me. My job and Adam's prevent us from settling here when we're married, but we've already discussed visiting often, and finally ending up living here when circumstances permit."

"I'm surprised," Fiona said.

And a bit nostalgic and envious, she didn't add. She and Cassie and Piper had always done things together when they lived here. Now it seemed as if the other two had picked right up where they left off. Fiona felt left out.

It was her own fault, she knew. But that didn't make it any easier.

"Get up and come help me plan the logistics of the fund-raiser. We have a fashion show planned. Adam has a couple of New Orleans Saints football players coming, which has lots of people excited, why I don't know."

Fiona laughed. Piper was such a girlie girl.

"I'll be right down."

Piper headed for the door, turning to say, "Please don't wear black. It's depressing."

"It's all I have."

Piper rolled her eyes. "We have to go shopping."

Fiona remembered how much Piper loved to shop.

"Later. I still have to see Margaret."

"You didn't see her last night? I meant to ask you when you got home how things had gone, but Adam was still here and—"

"I didn't make it in," Fiona said.

"Ran into Sam first, I bet," Piper said. "He's the one who found your phone number for us. And helped a bit when I was looking for my birth parents. I like him."

"You still haven't told me all the details about learning Margaret's your grandmother and how exactly you found out," Fiona said.

"We have time. See you downstairs soon. Those workmen are prompt."

Cassie had breakfast ready when Fiona arrived in the kitchen.

"Sit, eat," she said, dishing up eggs, grits and bacon.

"I've gained five pounds since I've been here," Piper said, pouring another cup of coffee. "But I never say no."

"When we finish, we'll all go see Margaret," Cassie said firmly, pulling out a chair and sitting with her own plate.

"I can go on my own," Fiona said.

"Maybe, but you're not," she said. "We've decided."

"Bossy."

Cassie grinned.

"You better believe it. But after that, you're Piper's slave for the day. She has to figure out where she wants everything so Matt's crew can build the runway for the models."

"And," Piper added, "we also need a changing area and makeup area, and then the chairs and all for the paying customers."

"We have a huge awning ordered that we'll use to keep the sun off the models," Cassie said. "It's going to be a big undertaking. Cops are good for crowd control, so you can make yourself useful."

Fiona swallowed hard.

"It's good to be back," she said.

By nine, they had cleaned up the kitchen. Piper insisted Fiona drive them so she could ride through town in a flashy convertible. Cassie then insisted on sitting in the front, to allow Piper royal status in the back.

When they set off down the driveway, Cassie turned back to Piper.

"Aren't you going to wave like the queen did?"

"Brat."

Piper sat tall, looking around regally and all three burst out laughing.

Fiona hoped the fun in the car masked her case of nerves. She wasn't going to get out of seeing her foster mother this morning.

Would it be better with the others?

Practicing what she planned to say, she tried to calm down. But nothing worked.

The trip was too short. They entered the lobby and went right to the elevators. Cassie and Piper explained that one or both of them came to see Margaret each day. They commented on her progress and prognosis.

"Full recovery, that's what we're counting on," Cassie said.

"It'll help when she can speak again," Piper said. "Sometimes I can understand a word or two, but mostly it's garbled. Frustrating for her and for us."

Fiona nodded, trying to remember all they'd told her about Margaret.

But the reality proved a shock. The frail woman sitting in a chair near the window barely resembled the foster mother she remembered.

"Hi, Margaret," Piper said, walking over to give her a kiss and hug. "Look who we've brought!"

Cassie gave her a quick hug, then stepped back. Fiona stared at the woman who had done her best to "raise her right." The woman who'd been there when her own mother had abandoned her responsibilities and left Fiona to flounder.

The woman she'd betrayed.

Her throat felt closed. She couldn't take her eyes off Margaret. She saw every nuance of expression when Margaret realized who stood there. Shock and dismay. Then the struggle to say one word.

"Fee."

Fiona's heart dropped.

"Hello, Margaret."

The words stuck. She knew what she wanted to say, but just couldn't.

Piper and Cassie stared at her, puzzled. She knew she must look like a fool, but her feet seemed rooted to the floor. Suddenly she wished she'd worn blue or pink, though she hadn't worn either color in more years than she could remember.

Black was for widows and old ladies, she remembered Margaret saying. The woman had obviously never been to New York or Los Angeles.

Stupid thing to think about when so much was at stake.

"We didn't even have to track her down. She heard you were sick and came right away, just like Cassie and I did," Piper said.

Margaret hadn't moved her gaze from Fiona. She tried to speak, but as the others had said, only garbled sounds came out after that initial word. Fiona could see Margaret was frustrated at her limitations. She obviously wanted to tell her something in the worst way. Fiona could just imagine what.

"I won't stay. My being here's upsetting you," Fiona said. "I came to tell you I'm sorry for what happened. I never meant to have us all end up scattered. I never meant to get you into trouble. I'm so sorry."

Margaret tried to say something else, then shook

her head.

Fiona only gave a half smile and turned to leave.

"Fiona," Cassie called after her.

She didn't want to hang around. She'd done what she'd come for, not as smoothly as she'd hoped, not as healing, but it was the best she could do. She headed for the elevator. Luck was with her: it was discharging passengers as she reached it. She slipped inside and punched the button for the lobby.

Walking outside a moment later, she stopped. The heat of the day was rapidly building. She felt the sharp contrast to the hospital's air-conditioning, but now she relished the heat on her skin. She felt chilled inside.

Dispassionately she reviewed the scene, disappointed she didn't feel better. Somehow she'd thought if she apologized, the guilt of what she'd done would lift. It hadn't. Of course a hasty sorry and abrupt leave-taking wasn't quite what she'd pictured, either.

She considered going back, but couldn't face Margaret. She wouldn't blame the woman if she never wanted to see her again. And that hurt. Far more than Fiona expected.

She yearned for the relationship she'd seen between Piper and Cassie and Margaret. Comfortable with one another. Loving.

Heading for her car, Fiona had to decide what to do next. Usually she had every bit of her life laid out— she needed to have plans and backups for the undercover work she did.

Now she'd accomplished what she'd set out to do.

Feeling deflated and unfulfilled, she wasn't sure what to do next. She wished she hadn't agreed to stay for the next few days. Heading back to Los Angeles seemed a brilliant idea right now.

She climbed into the bright red convertible, started the engine and peeled out of the parking lot. She headed out of town, going faster than was safe, as if she could outrun her demons.

She hadn't gotten five miles before she heard the wail of a siren. Looking in the rearview mirror, she saw the flashing lights of a police car. Great, just what she didn't need.

She checked her speedometer and discovered she was going way over the limit. She hit the brakes and slowly, gradually, pulled to the side of the road, resigned to get a ticket and probably a lecture from the deputy.

She could imagine the hoots and hollers of her friends at the department if they ever heard about it. Some of them routinely had tickets, speed acting as an adrenaline release. But she'd never had one before.

She looked in her side mirror as the man got out of the vehicle, lights still flashing. Fiona almost groaned when she recognized Sam Witt. He placed his hat on his head, hefted the ticket book and walked to the side of her car.

"Do things a bit differently in California?" he asked when he drew even with her.

"No."

"Speeding is against the law."

"So write me a ticket."

He held out his hand for her license. Fiona knew the drill, although she had only worked traffic for six months some years back. She held it out for him to take, then reached over to the glove compartment to withdraw her rental papers. She handed them over, as well, looking straight ahead, fuming.

Not at Sam—he was just doing his job.

She was mad at herself. She should never have expected things to change just because she offered an apology. Margaret couldn't even talk. Did she remember all the hateful words Fiona had flung that long-ago day? Why had she thought an apology would fix anything?

Sam studied her license. The face on the laminated card was unsmiling. He glanced at her.

Fiona gripped the steering wheel so tightly her fingers were white. Staring straight ahead, she didn't move when he returned her paperwork. He was surprised she didn't try to talk herself out of a ticket. Usually when caught speeding, cops tried to appeal to the brotherhood of the badge and get out of getting written up.

Not Fiona.

Sam almost wrote her up, but something held him back. Instead, the rigid way she held herself alerted him something was wrong.

He looked down the highway. It headed north, nothing on it for about forty miles.

"Out seeing the sights?" he asked.

She shook her head.

"I'm just driving."

"When you take off from here, are you going to keep the speed below the limit posted?" he asked, wishing she'd open up a little.

She nodded. Sighing softly, she looked at him wryly.

"I'll return to town. Driving isn't going to solve my problem."

"And what is that problem?"

"Nothing that can be fixed," she said. "Give me the ticket and I promise not to be caught speeding in your jurisdiction again."

"*Caught* speeding? Or won't speed again, period?"

"Whatever. I'm heading out soon."

"I thought you were going to help in the Independence Day fund-raiser for Margaret Nunes," he said. "And I know all about the wedding—I'm Adam's best man."

She eyed the ticket pad, then looked at him.

"I'll give a donation and send the happy couple a gift."

"Your *presence* is what Cassie and Piper want."

"Yeah, like that's going to help anything."

He tapped the closed ticket book against the edge of the car.

"Take it easy, Fiona. I'm giving you a warning. Don't speed in my county."

"That's it, no ticket?"

"Call it professional courtesy to a fellow officer."

"One who should know better," she muttered.

He could tell she was embarrassed and angry.

"What are you doing working traffic, anyway?" she said when he stepped back to let her go on her way.

"I'm not. I'm on my way to take a report of a break-in at a farm just up ahead. Saw you taking off like a bat out of hell so I stopped you."

"I was upset, which is a stupid time to be driving."

"Right. Not upset now?"

She squinted against the glare of the sun.

"I'm still angry, but I'll control my driving."

He touched the edge of his hat and turned to head back to the patrol vehicle.

"Hey, Sheriff," she called, leaning out of the window.

He turned.

"Thanks. I appreciate it."

He nodded, wondering again what it was about her that intrigued him. She wasn't his usual type, if indeed he even had one. He liked small, blond women who loved to cook and had the flesh on their bones to prove it.

Like Patty.

Not that he was interested in Fiona in a personal way. He still loved his wife and couldn't imagine moving on and opening himself up to a potential loss again. Still, if he never saw Fiona Hunter again, he thought he'd miss something.

He continued to the patrol car and got in. Fiona took off, driving just under the speed limit. He smiled.

That speed would probably last only as long as she stayed in sight.

He had work to do. Pulling away from the side of the road, he soon passed her. She waved but did not increase her speed.

Her speeding was stupid, and dangerous, Fiona thought as she watched Sam's car disappear into the distance. She knew better than most that excessive speed was the cause of most road accidents. She'd cleared her share of bodies from automobile crashes.

On impulse, she checked to make sure there was no traffic, then made a U-turn in the middle of the highway. Heading back to town, she made up her mind. She'd stay around and help out at the Independence Day picnic. She owed it to Margaret. And she wanted to visit with Cassie and Piper a little longer. She'd missed them so much over the years.

If Piper still wanted her to attend the wedding, she'd stay for that, as well. Any hardships, she'd view as penance for her sins.

When she turned into the driveway, she remembered abandoning Cassie and Piper at the hospital. Cassie's van was gone now. Obviously they'd found a ride home or walked.

Cassie had told Fiona about starting a catering business in Bradford. She sounded as if she had the credentials to work anyplace she wanted. Fiona couldn't believe she'd chosen Bradford. Some things still had the power to surprise her.

The sound of construction filled the air. She saw

that some of the windows were open, letting out the cool air and the sound. It would be another week or two before the crew finished.

Then the house was scheduled to be approved as a home for unwed, pregnant teens who had nowhere else to turn.

She slowly climbed the three shallow steps to the porch, the din in the house uninviting. Where was Piper? Had she come home with Cassie or gone off to see Adam?

For the first time since leaving Bradford all those years ago, Fiona wished she had someone special herself. Someone she could talk to about how she felt. Someone whose advice she could seek to help her decide what to do next. Someone who would accept her just as she was and like her.

A few minutes later, determining Piper wasn't around, Fiona was at loose ends. She headed back to town. Might as well while away the time walking around and reacquainting herself with Bradford. Maybe she'd run into an old school friend or two.

She cut over to the high school. The building was smaller than she remembered. The yard stood empty, only a single car in the parking lot. No one hung around during summer break, not even the teachers.

Continuing her walk, Fiona soon came to the main street of town. Ahead on the right was the bank. Acting on impulse, she entered the old building. The columns supporting the ceiling were made of marble, as was the floor. She found the old-fashioned ornate fretwork on the ceiling reassuring. At least they hadn't torn down the old building to make way for progress.

The object of her interest was not in view. Maybe he no longer worked here. It had been twelve years. Who knew what happened to people in that time? Maybe he'd attacked someone else who *had* been believed and he'd been arrested and sent to prison.

She walked around, unaware at first of the interest she was causing. When she caught the eye of the guard, she knew her attire set off internal alarms. Maybe Piper had been right, and all black attire with motorcycle boots was a mistake. Or was it the spiky hair?

She turned to leave when she heard the hated voice. Heading for the door, she glanced over her shoulder. Allen McLennon was escorting an elderly woman from an office. He spoke again. Fiona couldn't hear the words, only the smarmy tone of his voice.

Her stomach lurched. Her heart pounded. The man she'd hated for twelve years was only a yard away. What would happen if he saw her? Would he recognize her, or be more concerned about her less-than-conservative appearance? She couldn't take her eyes off him. He looked older. Had put on a few pounds. But he still looked fit and strong. Strong enough to beat a teenager who fought off his attempts at seduction, or worse.

"Can I help you?"

The guard had come up beside Fiona without her being aware. Such inattention in her normal life could get her killed.

She looked at him and shook her head.

"I'm just leaving."

He didn't say anything more, but watched her until she was out of the door. Once on the sidewalk, Fiona took a deep breath.

"Casing the joint?" Sam Witt asked.

She jumped and turned to see the sheriff standing behind her. How had she missed him when she left the bank? Gee, at this rate, she had better retire, or return to traffic detail.

"I thought you were headed off to do some incident report," she said.

"It's done. Didn't take long. What are you up to now?"

"Nothing."

She glanced back at the bank, almost tempted to go back in and confront Allen McLennon.

"Come with me,"

Sam said, taking her arm gently. He led her across the street to Ruby's Café.

"Coffee."

Fiona went along, not putting up a fuss like she normally might have. Maybe she wanted to hear what the local sheriff had to say.

Or was she in for another lecture?

Ruby's was almost empty so late in the morning. In a short time the lunch crowd would start arriving, but for now, they practically had the place to themselves.

Sam steered her to a booth near a window and sat

opposite her. A waitress hurried over, coffeepot in hand.

"Anything to eat, Sheriff?" the woman asked as she poured.

"Just coffee for me." Sam looked at Fiona. "What will you have?"

"The same."

The waitress bustled off.

Fiona added cream and stirred, then met Sam's gaze defiantly.

"Allen McLennon is the man who tried to rape me and then beat me silly when I was sixteen. I told Margaret. She didn't believe me, so in retaliation when I was questioned at the hospital, I said she'd beaten me. I was so angry and hurt. I didn't know what an uproar that would cause. Then that damned sheriff wouldn't believe me when I told him the truth. Was that in the report?"

Sam looked taken aback.

Maybe she should have led up to the revelation, but she felt anger boil up again after seeing that man at the bank living a life no rapist and child beater should live.

Her worst fear resurfaced. Had she been the only one? The sheriff and Margaret had both been told the truth. If neither acted on it, was Fiona responsible for any further violent acts the man may have committed over the years?

The thought bothered her. She should have come back at eighteen and made a stink. Or after graduating from the police academy. Or any time over the last decade.

"Serious accusations," Sam said.

"The truth, take it or leave it," she replied.

Fiona held her breath. She wanted someone to believe her. But the world wouldn't end if he didn't. She'd had years of living with others not believing the truth.

Sam sat back and studied her thoughtfully.

"And what do you propose to do about it now?"

She shrugged. No overwhelming vote of confidence from the sheriff.

"What *can* I do? The statute of limitations has run out. If he never bothered anyone else, no other charges would have been made. He gets off scot-free." She paused. "Then again, maybe I should take out a full-page ad in the local paper and let the good folks of Bradford know what a son of a bitch they have as banker."

"He's a respected member of the community. Your coming in here and throwing accusations around—"

"Might damage his precious reputation? Who cares? Not me."

Surprisingly, she was disappointed Sam didn't believe her.

"Might not be believed," he said.

"So let him sue me for libel."

"And he'd likely win. What can you do to prove it? It's his word against yours, and I'm here to tell you the record of the investigation never once mentions his name."

Fiona stared at Sam for a moment, thinking the implications through.

"The sheriff was in his pocket. Bastard."

She lapsed into silence. There was nothing she could do—except watch the man to see if he'd changed or was still coming on to young girls.

But how such behavior could be hidden in such a small town for any length of time was beyond her. Maybe he had just had the hots for the teenager she'd once been, tried to get it on with her, and when he failed, snapped.

She remembered how angry Margaret had been, convinced that Fiona was trying to cover up for Denton and put a spoke into Margaret's romance with the banker at the same time. She'd refused to listen to Fiona, turning her over to the sheriff for interrogation and investigation, convinced the sheriff would find the boy who'd done that awful deed.

"If I make a formal complaint, you have to investigate," she said. "Maybe I don't want to tip my hand yet."

"I can be discreet, you know. I'll make some quiet inquiries—if there's anything to go on," Sam offered reluctantly. "What can you tell me about the event?"

"I can tell you about every horrible moment."

"Come to the office later and give a statement."

"And you'll investigate?"

"I'm making no guarantees. Allen McLennon is the president of the town's bank. I've known him for the two years I've lived in Bradford. He's never had a breath of scandal attached to his name."

"In other words, screw off, Fiona," she said bitterly.

"I'm a firm proponent of the truth," Sam said. "But not in revenge."

"Revenge?"

"You've talked to Cassie and Piper. You must know McLennon tried to foreclose on the house when Margaret was first in the hospital. They were angry as could be about it. Leads to all sorts of speculation, you know?"

"And you think I'm making this up now to get back at him?"

Fiona was incredulous. She *hadn't* known about the attempted foreclosure.

"I said I'd look into it. You stay away from the case and the man you're accusing."

"I don't report to you," she said.

Fiona stood and fished out a couple of dollars, tossing them on the table. Maybe there was some investigative work she could do.

Sam's jaw tightened as he glared at her.

"Running away?"

"Regrouping. I'll find a way to hang the SOB."

She turned to leave.

"I asked you for coffee, so take your money," he called after her.

Fiona hesitated, then charged forward. He had not *asked* her to have coffee. He'd marched her into Ruby's as if he were the Gestapo or something.

Fiona always paid her own way. Ever since she'd

left the foster care in Meridian she'd vowed never to be beholden to anyone again.

She halfway expected Sam to come storming after her. But she reached the sidewalk alone. She turned and headed back for the house, plenty of thoughts crowding her mind.

Her quiet walk around town had changed things. Somehow there had to be a way to bring McLennon down. And she was going to prove to Margaret and everyone that these days Fiona Hunter could be counted on to tell the truth.

3

Fiona walked back to Bradford Hall and into the kitchen, wishing Cassie were there making something good to eat. She made herself a sandwich, poured iced tea into a glass, then went to sit on the front porch in the muggy heat. How anyone stood the racket the construction workers made was beyond her. Probably why both Cassie and Piper weren't here. Eating slowly, she tried to sort through her emotions.

As a teenager, she'd been full of anger when no one believed her about the man who'd attacked her. She'd spent long hours fantasizing about revenge—against Margaret, against the sheriff, even the social services worker who had taken her from her home.

She fantasized how the truth would come out and everyone in town would beg her to come back to live there. And she'd spurn them.

Those daydreams had helped her heal and given her the impetus to go into law enforcement. She never wanted to be a victim again.

She was a survivor. She had the battle scars to prove it.

But the reality was different from fantasy.

Sam was right. No one would believe her without proof. McLennon had had years to polish his image. Anyone who remembered her would recall a trouble-making teenager who'd turned on her foster mother.

The perpetrator was living life high on the hog, and no one really wanted her back in Bradford.

Maybe Cassie and Piper, but they both had new directions in life.

She was feeling sorry for herself.

Muttering an expletive, Fiona finished the last of her iced tea and took the plate and glass back inside. She wasn't going to have a private pity party. There were things she could do to find the facts to support her claim. If not, her belief in justice would be sorely tried.

Taking a deep breath, she tried to rationalize her plans. The first step was asking for an official investigation.

Fifteen minutes later Fiona walked into the sheriff's department. The dispatcher pointed her in the direction of Sam's office. When she arrived, she recognized his secretary.

"Marjorie?" Fiona said.

"Fiona Hunter. I heard they were trying to find you. No one told me they did and that you were back already. I'm so glad to see you."

She jumped up and came around to give Fiona a hug. Fiona awkwardly returned it. Had she forgotten how touchy-feely people were in the South?

"Goodness, Piper and I are on the phone all the

time," Marjorie said in a rush. "She didn't tell me!"

"I arrived yesterday. She'll be calling, I'm sure."

Fiona glanced around. The place hadn't changed much from the day old Sheriff Halstead had brought her in and listened to her account of the incident. Dismissing every word as a lie.

"Sam in?" she asked.

If he were, would he see her? Take her statement and really read it?

"Sure is. He's on the phone but should be finished soon. Have a seat. Where have you been all these years and what have you been doing?"

"I live in L.A.," Fiona said, sitting gingerly on the edge of one of the visitor chairs.

"Hollywood?"

Marjorie sat beside Fiona.

"Do you get to see movie stars all the time?"

Fiona shook her head.

"Sometimes I see one or two, but I'm not on that detail."

"You're a cop?" Marjorie guessed.

"Yup. Detective."

Fiona said it with pride. She'd fought long and hard to get where she was, and she was proud of it.

"Isn't that a kick? I bet Margaret's as proud as a peacock about that. She must be so happy to have all her chicks back. We're all pulling for her recovery, you know."

"Thank you."

Fiona was taken aback that Marjorie seemed to

discount entirely the cloud under which she'd left.

"You here to talk about that night twelve years ago?" Marjorie asked, voice lowered.

"The sheriff said earlier I could come in and make a statement."

"There wasn't anything in the file," Marjorie said, voice still low.

"You think Sam will let me look at the records?"

"Why, sure he will. He gave a copy to that Adam Saunders when he and Piper were hunting for you. There's not much. I looked at it myself. Sheriff Halstead wasn't quite the law enforcement man Sam is. I worked for Halstead for two years before Sam came. What a world of difference."

"What happened to Halstead?" Fiona asked.

Maybe she could tackle the man after seeing Sam.

"He died a couple of years ago—heart attack. That's what got Sam appointed to the job. Then he won the election last year. Otherwise I expect the good ol' boy network would have kept that old man in office forever. Oops, the line is free, which means Sam's off the phone," Marjorie said.

She rose and went to the door near her desk, knocked and stuck her head in.

A second later she pushed it open and gestured to Fiona.

For a second, walking into Sam's office felt like walking into the past—only nothing looked the same. The walls had been painted off-white, and there were citations and awards and photos on the long wall. The windows had wooden blinds, which added a touch of class to the government-issue decoration.

Sam had an old oak desk, scarred and aged. It suited the office and the man.

"Fiona," he said, rising.

"Hi."

She swallowed hard. She shouldn't have stormed away from Ruby's. This was as awkward as it got. She should apologize. Would it make a difference to his looking into things?

"I came to make that statement. And ask if I could see the file."

He looked at her for such a long time she was sure he was going to refuse. Then he nodded and asked Marjorie to get it. Gesturing to the chair across the desk from his, he indicated she sit.

Fiona did, her knees feeling wobbly.

"Thank you. Do you want me to type up a report? I'm good at that. Or I can just tell you what happened that night."

He sat and leaned back in his chair.

"I'd appreciate not having to write it up myself. You can use the computer in Marjorie's area."

She smiled. No one she knew liked writing reports.

"I hope you write reports better than Halstead did. There's nothing to go on in his. Just some mention of wild accusations from a teenager, no follow-up with either Margaret or anyone else. And he never mentions other possibilities."

"So Margaret didn't get into trouble? I heard

Halstead say they would take away her foster license."

"Maybe they did, but I don't have any information on it. As far as I know she never had other foster children after you girls were sent away. Yet she's part of this new home for unwed pregnant teens, and I haven't heard a hint of anyone opposing her involvement."

"Suspicious, don't you think?"

He shrugged. "Southern towns have loyalties to home-grown people."

"I was born here," Fiona said, refuting his claim.

Sam set her up at the extra computer in the outer office. It took Fiona longer to write the report than she'd expected. She could see every moment, and to write it all down took time. When she was finished, Marjorie printed it out and took it in to Sam. Fiona followed and sat in the visitor's chair.

She waited in silence while he read. She fidgeted a little, feeling nervous and unsettled. She looked at Sam, found his gaze on her and looked away, feeling butterflies in her stomach. How long would it take for him to read the darn thing?

The moments ticked by. The air seemed to be seeping from the room. Licking dry lips, she glanced back. He had put down the pages and was studying her.

"Stop," she said.

"Sorry, do I make you nervous?"

"Great technique, but I'm not one of your suspects."

And the butterflies had nothing to do with the cop, more with the man.

He gave a half smile.

"But you'd have me believe Allen McLennon is a suspect."

"He is. The only one."

Fiona was relieved when Marjorie arrived with the pitifully thin folder. Sam pointed to Fiona and Marjorie handed it to her.

"Let me know if you need something else, Sheriff," the woman said before leaving.

She closed the door.

Fiona opened the folder and began to read. A few minutes later, she leafed through the file.

"No photos, no lab report, nothing about the charges I made against Alan McLennon," she murmured. "That alone should point to sloppy work, if not downright criminal conspiracy."

"One way to look at it. But if you examine other files, you'd find the same kind of reports. And this from the man they elected sheriff for five terms," Sam said.

Fiona tossed it on his desk.

"Well, thanks for letting me see it."

"I don't like the situation any more than you do," Sam said. "If we work together, maybe we can find a way to bring out the truth, no matter what it is."

"No matter what it is? You think it's someone else? That I'm making this up?"

"I prefer to deal in facts."

She thought about it.

"I still like the idea of a full-page newspaper ad," she said.

"If McLennon beat you, you want something to nail him, not just embarrass him," Sam said.

Fiona nodded.

"You're right. There has to be something."

Sam shrugged.

"I haven't heard a word of gossip to support Allen's guilt. What I *have* heard is that one of your schoolmates was the most likely suspect."

Fiona had every moment of that time engraved in her mind. She eyed her report on his desk, hoping Sam would find something in the report that would give him a lead.

"Who?"

"Jack Denton."

She smiled wryly.

"Ironically, he's the reason I'm back, not the reason I left. I've heard many people think he's the one who attacked me. But it was Denton who told me about Margaret's stroke, and that brought me back. I was hoping it'd make a difference."

"What?"

"Her stroke. I had some notion that maybe she'd see things differently, somehow see the truth. But she can't even talk. And her reaction when she saw me was less than welcoming."

Fiona shivered at the memory.

"Would Cassie or Piper have any information?"

"I doubt it. They wouldn't have been quiet when being taken away from the only home we knew. If nothing came out then, they probably knew nothing. We can ask."

She gestured to the folder on the desk.

"This stinks, Sheriff. And anyone with half a brain could see how shoddy the work is. Deliberately covering up for someone, as I see it."

Sam didn't respond.

"I'm telling the others tonight," Fiona said.

"I'll come by."

"Come at seven and I'll reveal all to them." Fiona stood, rubbing her palms on her black pants. "And thanks. Sorry about earlier."

He stood.

"I want justice," he said. "A good policeman does."

After twelve years, Fiona wasn't sure it was possible. Any help she'd hoped for from the past had been shot down by the skimpy report filed at the time.

She still wanted to spend time with Margaret. To clear the air before telling everyone else the sordid tale. Even if she still refused to believe her, Fiona had to try.

The older woman was in bed, eyes closed, when Fiona peered around the door. She must have made some noise because Margaret opened her eyes and half smiled when she saw Fiona.

Wondering if she was dreaming, Fiona stepped inside.

"All right to visit?" she asked.

Margaret nodded, raising her left hand in supplication.

Fiona walked to the bed and sat gingerly on the edge. Margaret looked so small and frail lying there. Her head showed a fresh scar near her temple. Her hair was thin, white, wispy. Fiona swallowed hard.

Now that she was here, she wasn't sure how to say what she wanted. She decided she'd just blurt it out. Good a way as any.

"I'm telling Piper and Cassie the full story tonight," she said.

Margaret didn't move. It seemed as if she held her breath.

"I went to the bank. McLennon's president now. The son of a bitch should be in jail. Instead he has a prestigious job and is doing who knows what. You should have believed me, Margaret. I never meant to interfere with your chance at happiness. But he hurt me badly. And I got no support from the one person I thought I could count on. You. But that doesn't excuse what I did. When you didn't believe me, I lied out of anger at you. I'm sorry. And more sorry that when I told the truth to the sheriff, he wouldn't believe me. No one did. I'm sorry if I got you into trouble. And I'm sorry as can be that Cassie and Piper got shunted away like I did."

"Nnnnoooo," Margaret uttered.

"I wanted to let you know that I'm telling the others. Actually, I already told the new sheriff. I don't think he believes me any more than you did, but he covers it better. Doesn't matter, I know the truth, and I'm going to do my best to expose it to the world. I should have come back sooner."

Margaret nodded, her expression sad.

"I hope he wasn't the love of your life. I heard he dumped you after my accusations. I think you're better off. He's scum. I don't know if he's abusing any other girls. It could be that I was an isolated incident."

Margaret looked distressed again. She shook her head. Her eyes were wide with emotion.

"Anyway, I thought it only fair to warn you. I expect Cassie and Piper will have some questions."

Fiona took a deep breath, looking at the woman who had been the only mother she'd ever really had—until that fateful day.

Piper had shared a lot of fond memories last night, many of which Fiona had forgotten. It had been a good experience, one that made up for the overwhelming, indelible imprint of that last encounter.

Margaret had been strict, but she'd had three wild girls to care for. All had railed against their fate that had put them into foster care, and Margaret had taken the brunt of their anger.

Yet she'd been loving, helpful, supportive. She'd been the one to come to school events, not Fiona's mother. Margaret had stayed up with her when she'd had a miserable bout of flu. Her mother had been in jail that time.

But the facts were as they were. Margaret was not her mother, and when Fiona had needed her most,

Margaret let her down.

The grip on Fiona's hand tightened. If she hadn't known Margaret was recovering from a serious stroke, she'd have thought the woman had been in strength-training, so painful was the hold.

Fiona eased her hand out of Margaret's, patting the back of her hand.

"I said I was sorry earlier. I wanted you to know I meant it. I should never have retaliated like that. I had no idea of the ramifications. I know a lot more about the law now, though, and have to say the investigation Sheriff Halstead did was lousy. I suspect he was in league with McLennon."

Margaret nodded, reaching out again to touch Fiona.

"Bbbaaaa," she tried. A sound almost like a kitten made, but Fiona couldn't understand.

"I'd better be going."

Margaret shook her head frantically.

Fiona looked around the hospital room. The woman was probably going stir-crazy confined here. She could stay a little longer.

Taking a deep breath, she nodded and changed the subject.

"I've done all right for myself, Margaret," she began. "I wanted to make something of my life, not end up like my mother. So I went for an education. It took me a little longer than most to realize the value. I didn't graduate from high school until I was almost twenty, but made up for it in college. I have a degree in criminology. I'm good at my job. Did Cassie or Piper tell you I work for the Los Angeles Police Department? Once I made detective, I opted for Vice, to curtail as much drug traffic as I can. My team and I are good at what we do and have caught a bunch of dealers."

Margaret nodded, her gaze never wavering. She reclaimed Fiona's hand with her left one, as if anchoring Fiona in the room. She said something, but Fiona couldn't understand it.

"Say again?"

Margaret struggled, but the sounds didn't make sense.

"I'm not too good at this," Fiona said.

Margaret squeezed her hand and shook her head.

Fiona studied their linked hands. Her own hand was tanned and strong, Margaret's frail. Would she recover completely as Cassie swore? Or was this the beginning of a gradual decline ending in death?

Fiona looked up at her face again.

"While I'm here, I'm going to do my best to set the record straight for everyone."

Margaret took a deep breath, then nodded.

"I'm sorry things ended the way they did," Fiona said, tears gathering.

Her heart was sore and the regrets spilled out.

Fiona spent an hour with Margaret, telling her about her job in Los Angeles, how she'd ended up there, glossing over some of the experiences she'd had that would shock the gentle Margaret.

She longed to ask her about Piper being her

granddaughter, and about Margaret's own daughter. Fiona knew from Piper that both she and Margaret were happy to have the truth known. Not many people outside the family knew—Matt and Adam and Sam only—but Piper wanted the world to know. Margaret hadn't objected. The question now was how to release the information to cause the least amount of gossip.

Fiona rather thought it should be handled while Margaret was semi-isolated in the hospital, so it would be old news by the time she was out and about again.

But that call was Piper's and Margaret's.

Margaret made some comment, looking at Fiona's hair.

Fiona laughed. She didn't need words to know Margaret didn't like the way she wore it.

"Think of it as part of my uniform," she said.

She yearned to lean over and give the older woman a kiss on the cheek, the way Piper and Cassie had. She wanted to feel connected, a part of the family. But she still wasn't sure of her welcome. Margaret had listened, but said little Fiona could understand. But somehow, Fiona thought, Margaret could have indicated she approved of Fiona's revealing the truth.

When she left Fiona wasn't sure she'd come to visit again. It was too awkward. She'd forfeited her place in the family and wasn't sure she'd ever feel a part of it again.

It was difficult to walk briskly in the heat, but Fiona

made good time in returning to Bradford Hall. She wanted a shower before dinner and was annoyed to find the construction crew still hadn't finished for the day. She tested the water in the hall bathroom, but it was turned off.

"When do I get water?" she yelled.

"We're leaving in half hour," one of the men called back.

Her phone rang and Fiona answered.

"Are you coming over to help us out?" Piper asked.

Fiona suddenly remembered Cassie's edict about helping Piper with planning for the fashion show. "Where are you?"

"I'm at Adam's house or, rather, Sam's—that's where Adam's staying, and we're planning the logistics for the picnic. Your background in crowd control would help."

Fiona shook her head.

"Is that what you think, that cops only do crowd control?"

"I know you arrest bad guys. I don't want to even think about that, it's too dangerous. But you must have some ideas about moving folks along that we haven't thought about."

"I want to take a shower before dinner," Fiona said. "And then after we eat, the sheriff is coming over and I'm going to go over everything I can remember from that day. He said maybe he could do something."

Saying it sounded like more than Sam had really offered. She didn't hold out much hope for his investigation.

She heard Piper draw in her breath in surprise.

"We'll be right there," she said.

"Whoa, I said after dinner."

"So, Cassie can make enough for all of us. And Fiona, once you get out of the shower, do not put on black."

"Sorry, Piper, that's all I have."

"For sure we'll be right there. I have something you can wear."

She hung up before Fiona could protest. She was sure anything Piper had would be unsuitably girlie.

She went upstairs to hurry the construction guys along. If she could be dressed and ready to go before Piper arrived, she had a better shot of holding her own. Piper in a determined mood was formidable.

4

Cassie didn't seem a bit upset when Fiona entered the kitchen in her usual black and told her she thought Piper and Adam would be coming to dinner.

"We've eaten a lot of meals together lately," she said.

Looking at Fiona, she tilted her head slightly.

"Something's different."

"I went back to square things with Margaret."

Fiona took a deep breath.

"And I talked with Sam Witt. He said he'd reopen the investigation. I told him who attacked me."

"And that was?"

"Allen McLennon."

"What?"

Cassie looked at her in astonishment.

"Margaret's boyfriend?"

Fiona nodded.

"I only want to have to go over it all one time, so hold the inquisition, will you? If everyone's here at dinner, I'll answer all your questions then."

"I can't believe it. He's the president of the bank."

Fiona shrugged.

Piper burst into the kitchen from the back door. Seeing Fiona, she rushed over.

"Tell me everything. We've been patient all this time, trying to give you some space, but I can't eat a bite until I know."

"McLennon," Fiona said.

Piper's lower jaw dropped.

Adam entered the room and closed the door. He looked at the three women, his eyes lingering on Piper's stunned expression.

"Did I miss the big revelation?" he asked.

Piper turned.

"It's the banker, Allen McLennon. The scumbag. I can't believe it."

"I want to wait—" Fiona started to say when Matt came in from the front of the house.

"Sheesh, this place is busier than Hollywood and Vine. Okay, I only want to go through the story once," Fiona said. "We have to wait for Sam."

Cassie took charge, organizing everyone into setting the table, helping to prepare the meal, pouring beverages and talking a mile a minute.

Fiona felt shaky. She knew she had an uphill battle to find some proof at this late stage. It could be impossible. Even if she found it, what could she do— expose him, but not prosecute?

Sam arrived as she was ready to begin, seemingly unsurprised to find everyone else there. His glance touched on Fiona, then moved on.

"Here for the exposé?" he asked Adam.

"Think there's a story in it?"

"I think we'll hear what she has to say and then decide what can be done about it."

"Dinner's ready," Cassie called.

Once seated around the table, everyone looked at Fiona.

Fiona took a breath and looked at Sam.

"You should have brought the report I wrote—everyone could have read it."

"Better hearing directly from you," he said.

"Okay," she began. "I was coming home from Gully's Shack. I'd skipped school that day to hang out with Tony Branson. It was late by the time we tried to bluff our way into the bar, and the bouncer spotted us immediately. I knew I was going to get it from Margaret—no way the principal hadn't alerted her I wasn't in school that day. Considering how rebellious I used to be, it's a wonder Margaret put up with me at all. I was clear across town, after nine o'clock at night, and still thinking of ways to sneak in so she wouldn't catch me."

"She was angry that night, I remember," Cassie said softly.

Fiona looked at her and nodded.

"Anyway, Tony tried to get me to put out, and I refused, so he dumped me. I was hitching a ride, trying to cut the time to get home."

"Hitchhiking?" Cassie asked.

"Hey, it was Bradford, where everyone knows everyone else. I didn't figure anything bad could happen. Arrogance of youth or something. Anyway, it was dark and raining. McLennon stopped for me. I hesitated—but only because he was seeing Margaret and I didn't want him telling on me. Still, a ride was a ride, and I was already late and soaked."

She took a sip of her iced tea.

Piper's eyes glinted in warning.

Fiona almost smiled. Piper was so impatient.

"He started out asking me why I was there and what I'd been up to. I blew him off with some dumb answer. Then he turned onto a road I didn't know—it definitely wasn't the way home. I asked him what he was doing. He started in about how pretty I was and how feisty and how he liked me, had ever since he first saw me at Margaret's house. It was creepy. By the time we stopped at this cottage surrounded by trees, I knew I needed to get away. But it was too late. He said he'd noticed me looking at him. I argued with him, trying to get the car door opened. I figured I could run into the woods and he'd never follow me. Wrong. That's exactly what happened."

"You got out of the car?" Piper asked, dinner forgotten.

"Not surprising—Fiona never took orders well," Cassie murmured.

"He followed me, to my surprise. Then tried to kiss me. Do you know how gross I found that? Felt me up. His hands everywhere. He was in his late thirties or early forties at the time, which I thought was really old. Anyway, I fought him off, but he was strong. He pushed me to the ground and tried to keep me there, tearing at my clothes, saying how good it would be. I fought for all I was worth. I scratched him a couple of times, which seemed to enrage him. Then he began to get an advantage and before I could stop him, he beat me bloody."

Everyone watched her. Dinner had been ignored.

"Then what?" Sam asked.

"He got up, pulled me up and slammed me against a tree, knocking me out. When I came to, and I don't know how long it was, he was in the cottage. At least I think he was, because the lights were all on. I didn't wait around to find out."

"You could have been dead for all he knew," Matt commented.

"I was disoriented, didn't know where I was. I followed the road back out to the highway, listening for his car every second. I kept to the side of the road, jumping into the ditch every time a car came from behind me. It was almost dawn by the time I got home. Margaret was up, wouldn't you know? Piper and Cassie were still asleep. I tried to explain but Margaret was furious. She claimed I was making it up, that Allen wouldn't do such a thing. That I was trying to throw a monkey wrench into the situation to confuse the issue. She believed one of the guys from school had beaten me."

"Oh, Fiona, no. She had to believe you," Piper said softly.

Fiona shook her head.

"She refused to believe a word I said. There I was, hurt, bleeding, exhausted, scared, and the one person in the world I thought would believe me didn't."

"So you wanted revenge and blamed her," Sam said.

"That's right. I figured it would pay her back for not believing me. If I could get her in trouble," Fiona sighed. "Anyway, it backfired. The next thing I knew the deputies were there, I was taken to the hospital and fixed up. Then that pig of a sheriff had me come to the office and questioned me. I told him it was Margaret who'd beaten me, and he seemed just as glad to go with that as anything. How stupid could the man be? Margaret didn't have bloody knuckles or scratches from my fighting her. And I was stronger and taller than her."

"So then what happened?" Adam asked.

"When I learned we were going to be taken away, I recanted—told the truth. No one believed me. And McLennon was gone. No one could find him. Convenient, don't you think? Gone, so his hands couldn't be examined or the scratches on his face commented upon."

"Then what?" Sam prodded.

"Then I got sent to Meridian and a new family. I stayed two months and split."

"The official report relates that there were allegations made against Margaret Nunes, nothing proved that I could find. No photos were in the file, either of Fiona or Margaret. It's as if everything was dropped once the three teenagers were sent away," Sam said.

"Odd way to handle things," Adam said.

"I never heard that McLennon and the sheriff were close. But I was a kid back then and had my own problems," Matt said.

He leaned back and gazed off into space for a minute.

Cassie caught his eye. "Do you think Allen McLennon was the A in your sister's diary?" she asked softly.

"I was just wondering the same thing."

When the others looked puzzled, Matt explained he'd found his sisters diary a few weeks ago and that she'd mentioned an A who had gotten her pregnant.

"She referred to it as the incident. In light of what Fiona's telling us, Dolores could have been raped."

"She never named A?" Sam asked.

Matt shook his head.

"Sometime around that time the sheriff moved to a bigger, more upscale house. I think he bought it—land records would tell. I want to know where he got the money," Fiona said

"Would that show some sort of connection, a cover-up?" Cassie asked.

Fiona shook her head.

"I doubt it. McLennon strikes me as too calculating to leave something like that open to investigation. Were he and the sheriff pals before?"

"I doubt it," Adam said. "Usually, in the social

structure of a town, the sheriff doesn't mix with the banker. Anyway, it doesn't matter—you were a child and you told those in authority. Being friends with someone doesn't mean you don't do your duty."

"So why can't Fiona press charges?" Piper asked.

"Statute of limitations has run out, for one thing," Fiona said.

"Plus, it's her word against his," Sam said, holding Fiona's gaze.

"Right, and look at me, compared to the upright pillar of society," she said wryly.

"I told you to stop wearing black," Piper grumbled. "Is that it, Sam? All you can say is sorry, Fiona, but it's too late to make things right? We just let him go free?"

"I still like the idea of placing a full-page ad in the newspaper," Fiona mumbled.

"That would be great," Cassie said.

"Except for libel charges," Adam countered. "We'd need to show proof before you could get away with defaming a man in a public forum."

"How about a civil suit?" Cassie asked. "I have a former fiancé who's an attorney—he could give us some advice, I'm sure."

"I'd still need proof," Fiona said. "Where am I going to get that?"

"You're a cop," Cassie said. "Find it."

"Twelve years later?" Matt asked.

"Hey, Fiona's good," Cassie said.

Sam studied Fiona for a moment.

"She'd have to be very good to find anything, but

she has no jurisdiction in this state. I told her I'd look into it."

"Margaret has to know what happened," Cassie said. " I think she stopped seeing Allen right after that. Maybe it was because she did believe you? Or maybe she discovered something afterward."

"Like what?"

"I don't know, but why else would she break off from Allen? She knew *she* hadn't done it. Once she knew Fiona hadn't been attacked by one of the boys from high school, she had to know it was McLennon."

"And how do you know it wasn't one of the boys at the high school?" Sam asked. "Doesn't appear in the report that anyone was questioned."

The group fell silent for a moment.

Fiona glared at him. He didn't believe her.

She wanted to scream she was telling the truth, but what good would it do?

"Fiona said so," Cassie said, raising her chin.

"I believe her," Piper stated. "We need to talk to Margaret."

Fiona looked at Cassie and Piper, the warmth of their love flooding her. They believed her without question. For one moment she thought tears would flood her eyes. She blinked and looked at Sam. Nothing like a man who didn't believe her to drive away sentimentality.

"I suspect she'd have said something at the time if she had any proof," Sam said. "Her own reputation was on the line. What happened to her after that?"

Matt looked around the table.

"Nothing bad, actually. There was gossip, but so was there about my sister. Then the town busybodies moved on to something new. There was no opposition to my recommendation that she be a house mother for the new pregnant-teen home."

"Which shows no one took the charges seriously. How did social services get them moved so fast and without more investigation?" Adam asked.

"The sheriff again, I bet," Fiona murmured. "Maybe McLennon bribed him with a new house or something."

"Interesting conspiracy/cover-up theory," Adam said with a smile. "Just the kind of conundrum I like."

"We are a week from Independence Day," Cassie said. "Can we get this wrapped up by then so the entire world can know? It's so unfair to Fiona."

"I doubt it," Sam said.

"Especially if we don't want to tip our hand," Fiona said. "I want to see what I can find out before McLennon even knows I'm here."

"Too late for that," Cassie said. "Betsy's been telling everyone, both at the café and on our catering gigs, that the three girls from Bradford Hall are back again. He's bound to have heard it by now."

"Be interesting to see how he reacts when he runs into you," Sam said.

"Force the issue, so to speak?" Fiona asked.

"Maybe."

"So if I see him eating at Ruby's Café, I go up and

ask if he's beaten up any young girls lately?"

"Thought you didn't want to tip your hand."

"Ah." Fiona smiled. "Much better to be subtle and have him squirm."

"You need to go undercover," Piper said with a broad smile.

"What do you mean?"

Fiona didn't trust that expression.

"Look at you. I know you like the edgy look, but honestly, we want people to think you are the sweet, demure, butter-wouldn't-melt-in-your-mouth type. Not someone who would cause trouble or wrongly accuse an upright citizen. Dress like a girl, act demure. Think of it as undercover from your tough-cop role. And make up to people in town. Then when the chips are down, it won't all be one-sided in McLennon's favor."

"You're determined to dress me in pink, aren't you?" Fiona said.

Cassie laughed.

"Why not? Be the survivor who rose out of adversity and has triumphed. Now you've come home for a visit, and oh, dear, run into the very man who hurt you so badly. But you'll get even. And let him figure out how."

"Meantime, you can check things out, dig for facts and use that brilliant street-smart mind your boss raves about," Adam said.

She stared at him.

"How do you know my boss?"

Adam shrugged and glanced at Sam.

"You checked me out!" she accused him.

Her anger rose another notch. The man was insufferable!

"Darn straight I did," Sam said. "After the accusation you made, I couldn't let it go without some kind of authentication. I don't know you, Fiona Hunter, and I do know Allen McLennon. Or thought I did."

"It does change things, doesn't it?" Matt asked.

"I thought he was a sleaze by trying to sell Margaret's land while she was so ill," Cassie added. "Now I really think he's scum."

"Let's go get him," Piper said.

Fiona looked around the table. She was a little surprised that Piper and Cassie stood beside her after her actions that last day had split them up and changed the course of their lives.

Still, they'd all been close when young. But what was more surprising was the fact that Adam and Matt looked equally determined and committed. She felt a shaft of hope for the first time in a dozen years. Maybe they could find something to prove her allegations.

If nothing else, Cassie's plan to rally round Margaret and show their support would lay to rest all speculation about any wrong on Margaret's part.

As much as she hated to admit it, Piper's idea to change her look had merit. She was too good a cop to dismiss the obvious. Fiona needed to gain some credibility in Bradford if she was ever to be believed.

She liked shocking people and was used to standing on her own two feet. But sometimes she knew she had to bend to prevailing sentiment.

And what might work in the barrios of L.A. wouldn't fly in sleepy southern Mississippi.

She had to decide how badly she wanted to bring Allen McLennon down. As she looked around the table, her thoughts jumbled with memories and might-have-beens, she knew she had him to blame for the way things turned out. That and her own anger at Margaret.

"Okay, let's do it."

"Where do we begin?" Cassie asked.

Adam glanced at Sam.

"Let's have a review of all the facts we know, see where there're holes and plug them."

"It'll mean asking people to remember things from twelve years ago," Fiona warned.

"Has there been any breath of scandal about McLennon?" Sam asked Matt. "Was he fixated on Fiona or is he just clever enough to get away with terrorizing other teenagers? Twelve years is a long time and this is a small town. You must have heard something if there was anything to hear."

Matt shook his head.

"At the time, I was still reeling from my sister's death. Once my mother died, I didn't spend as much time in town. I never heard any gossip about McLennon."

"He dated Margaret for a while," Fiona said. "I

thought he stopped dating her because of the scandal surrounding her. Maybe once I had gone, he had no reason to keep coming by. Often predatory men select women with children to court, so they'll have easier access to the children once married."

"No use speculating—we need hard facts," Sam said.

She glanced at Sam and found his gaze on her. He didn't fully believe her, she knew. But at least he seemed willing to keep an open mind.

She knew the task was almost impossible, but at least it gave her some direction. She'd apologized to Margaret, was regaining her friendship with Piper and Cassie. She should have come back sooner, should never have let the banker get away with it for so many years.

"I appreciate everyone's support, but this is something I want to do myself," Fiona said. "Cassie has her hands full establishing her business. Piper is busy with the Independence Day plans and getting ready to marry Adam. I'll ask for help when I need it, but let me focus on this."

She wasn't ungrateful, but she had a burning desire to clear Margaret's name herself. It would go a long way to making up for what she'd done.

After some discussion, the other women reluctantly agreed, only if Fiona kept them apprised. The meal was consumed, cold though it was, and the conversation moved on to the festival.

Fiona was feeling antsy by the time the men made

noises about leaving. She wanted to be by herself to think.

"Walk me out," Sam said.

It didn't sound like an invitation, but an order.

She nodded and they went to the front porch.

The night was quiet and stars filled the sky. The warmth of the air enveloped her, felt good after the coolness inside the house.

"What?" she asked.

Sam leaned against the porch post, gazing out toward the front gardens.

"I don't want trouble in this town," he said.

"I didn't cause this."

"But your trying to prove it now could stir up a lot of problems. If you're not careful, you're the one who'll get burned."

"So you think I should let him get away with it?"

"If you can prove it, what are you going to do? The statute of limitations has—"

"I know, but I can sue him in civil court."

Sam looked at her and saw a tall, slender, determined woman. Her mouth was set, her jaw firm. He had an idea she'd be a formidable adversary. Her boss had given a glowing review, praising the way she thought, the coolness of her reactions. Somehow, Sam thought it likely she was a bit more passionate about this quest than the cases she worked in L.A.

"For what?" he asked, curious.

"For loss of family, loss of reputation. I don't know, I'll find something. Bringing the suit might be enough."

"If you can get a lawyer to take the case. Be sure you want to carry this out, Fiona. Allen McLennon is a powerful man in Bradford."

"But not above the law."

"No. Not above the law."

Looking at her, he could see her striding forth in the name of justice. He'd felt that way once, a long time ago. But that burning flame had dimmed after Patty's death. After he'd worked the dregs of society for so many years in New Orleans, the change of working in Bradford was refreshing. And needed.

While he wasn't the wide-eyed rookie of a few years ago, he liked his job, felt he was making a contribution. It was a good feeling. He hoped it lasted.

Was she telling the truth? Or did Fiona have some other motive in mind? He'd start his own discreet investigation. He didn't want anyone to get away with battery on a child. But something about Fiona made him wary.

"I don't really need your help if you're having second thoughts," Fiona said.

That she picked up on his hesitation surprised him.

"I said I'd look into it."

"I plan to do everything by the book. No sense ruining the investigation by sloppy work," she said.

"I can't imagine you doing sloppy work."

The smile was unexpected. Who would have thought the woman had a weakness for compliments about her work?

"I think some people believe it's possible because of the way I dress," she explained. "I fit in with the scene I work."

"That's not Bradford."

"No, Piper's right, I need to blend in."

"Go undercover in a different direction."

Fiona laughed.

"I guess so. Think I can do it?"

"I suspect you can do anything you set your mind to."

"What a nice thing to say. And I didn't think you liked me."

"I'm not sure I do."

"Honest, to boot. We may never be good friends, Sam Witt, but I expect we can work well together. I appreciate your looking into it."

"Come by in the morning and we'll map out a plan."

Better to know what direction she planned to take than let her go off half cocked. He had his own ideas on who and what to ask, but would be interested in hearing hers.

"I can—"

Sam shook his head.

"I heard what you said earlier, but I'm involved. This is my jurisdiction and I want to make sure we do things by the book."

"Fine. See you at eight."

She turned and went back inside the house.

Sam lingered a little longer, leaning against the

porch support. It was quiet here, the yard dark, the crickets humming their nightly song. There was nothing at home. Adam wouldn't come in until later.

Sam sometimes wished he and Piper would hurry up and get married and find a place of their own. But Sam knew once they were married, they'd be heading for Paris. His friend was only staying until after the Independence Day fair and their wedding. He had a new position to take up in France.

Pushing away, Sam went to the patrol car. He'd drive through town one more time before going home. He wasn't on duty, but he still liked to make sure things were quiet. He was putting down roots in Bradford, starting to feel like he belonged. And he had a protectiveness toward the town that served him well in his position.

Fiona slipped back inside and went upstairs to her room. She heard the murmur of voices in the kitchen, but she wanted the silence of her own room to think.

For the first time in ages, she felt a growing bond with other people beside the ones she worked with. She knew she had to stand on her own, but it was comforting to know Cassie and Piper would stand with her. Not that she would rely on them—that might place too much of a strain on their newly renewed friendship.

Sam confused her. He admitted tonight he wasn't sure he liked her. That hurt a little, but only because everyone wanted people to like them. They could work together. He was a professional and so was she.

The fact he was willing to go out on a limb for a stranger touched her, despite her efforts to remain aloof. He'd known the banker for the two years he'd been in town. He'd met her for the first time a couple of days ago. Yet he was willing to investigate based on her say-so. Amazing.

Not that it meant anything. Would he give it more than a token look? He really didn't believe Allen McLennon had done it. Why was she the only one who could see she had no reason to lie about it at this late date?

Cops often developed a sixth sense about crimes. Maybe Allen had done more than a one-off attack on a teenager twelve years ago. If so, Fiona wanted to find out what else might have transpired.

Bradford hadn't changed much in the intervening years. How many of her friends from high school were still around? She hadn't made lifelong friendships with classmates, preferring Cassie and Piper to others. But there had been one or two she wouldn't mind seeing again. Maybe she could visit and pump them for information at the same time.

Frowning, she rolled over on her side. Was that what her life had become—no friends, only sources?

For the first time in years, Fiona wanted more.

The next morning Fiona was barely awake when Piper knocked on her door and peeped in.

"I wanted to catch you before you got dressed," she

said, pushing the door wide and stepping in.

In her hand were an assortment of clothes.

"You're as tall as I am and slender, so these should fit. At least until you get to a store to buy your own."

"I have clothes," Fiona protested halfheartedly.

She'd agreed to change her image, so she might as well give in gracefully.

"Try these. I wear pastels mostly, because of my blond coloring, but I do have a few other things. These muted colors will look good with your darker hair."

She held out a maroon top and stonewashed blue jeans.

"It'll be hot today, but you can wear the jeans until you get some skirts or shorts."

"I'm surprised you even have them."

Piper smiled and Fiona knew why she was a top model.

"I have a wide assortment of clothes—you never know when something will be needed. Case in point."

"Okay. I'll wear them."

"And let me do your hair."

Fiona sat up and shook her head. "It's short. If I don't mousse it to spike it, it'll just fall as it was cut."

"But we can make it look softer, styled, instead of cut by a barber."

Fiona hid a smile. Trust Piper to be able to recognize the difference.

"Anything else?" she asked.

"Makeup."

"Oh, no, I'm not going that far," Fiona protested.

She was willing to try something different in her new covert role, but she drew the line at some things.

"A little mascara and blush, nothing much. It's too hot to wear a lot. Just wait."

A half hour later Piper turned Fiona to face the mirror.

"Ta-da! You look fabulous."

For a long moment, Fiona stared at herself. The softer hair did seem pretty. The mascara on her lashes made her eyes seem larger and mysterious. The light blush enhanced her own coloring, giving her a healthy look that she liked. Even the maroon top and tight jeans—Fiona wasn't quite as thin as Piper—changed her appearance. None of the cops in her precinct would recognize her.

She smiled, liking the change.

"If I don't look like Miss Mississippi," she drawled.

Piper laughed.

"Not quite, but close. Now, go be nice to the natives and soon you'll have them eating out of your hand—and willing to listen when you say you were attacked."

Fiona's eyes grew hard. The change was slight, but definite. She wasn't here to play dress-up.

She thanked Piper, who then gave her a hug. For a moment Fiona hesitated, then hugged her back.

"Go get 'em," Piper said.

Walking down the stairs, Fiona realized a couple of the workmen had already arrived by the sound of their whistles. She turned and glared at them, but they grinned unabashed.

"Looking good, babe. Want to go out for drinks after I get off?" one asked.

"In your dreams," Piper said, hooking her arm with Fiona's as they turned her toward the stairs. "Ignore them. I do."

"I ought to bust his chops," Fiona grumbled.

But deep inside she was flattered. She didn't think any guy had ever whistled at her before.

When they stepped into the kitchen, it was to the fragrance of fresh-brewed coffee and muffins baking in the oven.

Cassie looked up, then did a double take.

"Wow, Fiona, you clean up real good."

Self-conscious, she shrugged and headed for the java. A hot cup would get her going.

"Today, you really need to come over to Sam's place and help Adam and me plan the booth," Piper said, following Fiona to get herself a cup of coffee.

"I have an area for the models to change, then the long runway where they'll model the clothes. We want to accommodate a large crowd to raise as much money from tickets as we can," Piper said.

"She mostly wants help with traffic flow," Cassie said.

"Then Adam has two New Orleans Saints coming, so we need a place for them to sit and sign autographs and have their pictures taken."

"I thought we could have Margaret attend the fashion show so people can see her. Even if it's in a wheel chair," Cassie said. "If she's up to it."

"When are you telling people you're her granddaughter?" Fiona asked Piper.

"I don't know. Should I put up a banner?"

"No, you should tell a couple of people in town and let them spread the word," Cassie said.

"I hate gossip," Piper said. "And I couldn't control the way it got out if I did that."

"What's to control?" Fiona asked. "She had a kid, her father forced her to give it up, and when that kid had a baby and then died, Margaret came to get you. Seems to me the villain in all this was her old man."

"He was," Cassie agreed. "He did it to save his own reputation."

"Once he died, she could have said something," Fiona said.

"But by then she'd had us for a while. No one knew and it was just easier, I guess."

"You asked all the time about a family," Fiona said. "I used to envy you not knowing who your parents were. You could have had folks like mine."

"I heard your mother died," Cassie said. "I'm sorry."

"She was a junkie. Drugs took over and she wasn't strong enough to fight them."

Fiona spoke with a casual air she hoped camouflaged her hurt that her mother had always preferred drugs to her only child.

"Don't judge her too harshly, Fiona. That addiction is powerful. And she didn't have much else going for her with the man she'd married."

"Yeah."

Fiona leaned against the counter, sipping her coffee.

"She had a kid. She had a responsibility to me. Instead of releasing me for adoption, she kept me dangling and yanked me back and forth. When she was clean I stayed with her. When she wasn't, I was here. Not a lot of stability."

"Maybe she wanted to stay clean and found it just too overwhelming," Cassie suggested gently.

"Water over the dam," Fiona said.

"At least when you have kids, you'll know how not to treat them."

"I'm not having kids. I'm not getting married."

Piper smiled.

"I thought that, too. At least after two marriages I had a reason to swear off. You'll change your mind if you meet the right man."

"You're braver than I, trying it again this time with Adam."

"I'm stepping out in faith that we'll make it work. I love him more than I thought possible. And he loves me. We're not kids. I think it'll last until we die."

"That's how I feel about Matt," Cassie said, a soft smile on her face.

"You always felt like that about him," Fiona said.

"No, actually I think I hated him for a while. He blamed me for his sister's death and refused to listen to me. Maturity helped with both of us. Maybe that's all you need, a time to become a full adult and see things from an adult perspective, not that of a hurt child."

"Sheesh, were you both so philosophical when we were living here before? I don't think so."

Cassie laughed. "Maybe planning a future with another person makes me see life differently. Do what you want, Fiona. You have to make your own self happy. But don't close off the possibility of marriage just because your own mother and father messed up."

"Though you might wish to change your job," Piper said.

"What's wrong with my job?"

"For one thing, you're probably more macho than most men in that kind of job. How many guys do you know carry guns?"

"Almost all of them."

"How many do you date?"

Fiona was quiet for a moment.

"None."

"A nice accountant isn't going to be up to you."

"Good, because I don't want a nice accountant."

"Who do you want?"

"No one."

But the moment she said the words, Sam Witt's face danced in front of her eyes. Cops had lousy records in the marriage stakes, but sometimes like drew like, and they understood each other's jobs as no one else could. He was single and available, and sexy to boot.

Not that he was in the running. It figured, the one time she might indulge in a daydream, the man didn't even like her.

5

Despite her best efforts, Fiona was feeling self-conscious when she entered the sheriff's department. She'd walked to town and greeted several people she passed.

She should have been in the theater, she thought as she headed toward the back of the building and Sam's office. She smiled in all the right spots, playing the role she'd chosen to perfection. There'd be no curtain call, but she hoped the play would end as she wanted.

Marjorie Tamlin looked up without recognition for a moment, then, "Fiona. I almost didn't recognize you."

"Piper can't resist trying to make me over."

"She did a great job. You sure look different from the other day. Better. Did you come to see Sam again?"

"I did. Is he in yet?"

"Oh, yes. He gets here before eight every morning, after he drives through town to keep an eye on things. Such a change from...oh, never mind. I'll tell him you're here."

Marjorie knocked on the closed door and opened it

enough to stick her head inside.

Fiona felt a flutter of butterflies. There was such a thing as taking this acting bit too far. She wasn't a local girl seeing a good-looking guy. She was a professional law-enforcement officer consulting with a colleague. So why the nerves?

Sam came to the door. He stared at her as if he'd never seen her before.

Fiona took a deep breath. He was going to make this difficult. If he said anything—

"I expected you earlier," he said.

"I got waylaid."

Fiona smiled at Marjorie.

"See you later."

Sam stood aside so she could enter the office, then he closed the door.

"You look different."

He leaned against the door and crossed his arms as he surveyed her.

"I've assumed my new persona. I even smiled at folks as I walked down the street and greeted Mrs. Broderick, my fifth-grade teacher."

But Fiona didn't want to talk about that; it had nothing to do with her quest. She went to the desk and looked at the stacks of files and papers.

"Anything new?"

"After one night, I hardly think so."

Sam pushed away from the door and went to sit behind the desk.

"I know you want answers. I do, too. But if nothing

turned up years ago, I doubt it'll fall into our laps now," he said.

"I know."

She leaned against the desk.

"So do I just go question everyone in town who lived here when I did?"

Sam looked appalled.

"No way!"

"I'm yanking your chain. The last thing I want to do is spook the man. There has to be something, though. Wouldn't someone have seen him? It was raining, but still, if we could find someone who saw him turn into that road, or saw his hands the next day, or his cheek. I know he didn't get away unscathed. I fought as hard as I could."

"No one came forward twelve years ago," Sam said. "It wasn't exactly a quiet event at the time."

"If the sheriff thought a high-school kid had done it, why send me away? Why not investigate the high school? No charges were ever filed against Margaret. I wish I'd known that back then. I've carried a ton of guilt around thinking I ruined her life, like I did mine and the other girls."

"I don't think you ruined anyone's life. All of you look like you've ended up just fine."

He opened the thin file and looked at it once more.

"There's nothing here. Sheriff Halstead is dead. The office clerk who was here at the time moved away years ago. I checked with one of the old deputies. He didn't remember much, except the sheriff handled the case himself."

"So I'll wander around town, making nice with everyone, and when I make my move, maybe someone will believe me?"

She wished Sam believed her.

"There's no move for you to make. There has to be a better plan. And thus far, being patient doesn't sound like your style."

"You're right."

She looked at him for a moment.

"You're a good judge of character, Sheriff. What do you think about the banker?"

"Well, he has a superior attitude that grates on my nerves. But that doesn't mean he commits battery."

"Or attempted rape? Want to go with me when I open a checking account?" she asked.

The thought came to her that if she had an account there, she'd have a legitimate reason to go to the bank whenever she wanted. The guard couldn't escort out a customer.

Maybe putting some pressure on the man would make him crack. If nothing else, it would be interesting to see how he took her return.

"You staying long enough to need a local checking account?" Sam asked.

"Probably not. Still, I can open one for however long I'm here."

He rose and reached for his hat.

"I'll go with you, see how things stand. But we're not going to have a confrontation without more evidence, is that clear?"

"Yes, sir."

She didn't need a confrontation, she just was going for recon. Time to make plans after she learned a bit more.

They walked out together. Marjorie raised her eyebrows. Fiona just smiled and waved. She wondered if Marjorie thought there was something personal between her and the sheriff. She glanced at Sam, noting dispassionately his good looks and his height—he was taller than she, and muscular, but not bulging like some of the guys she knew at the gym in L.A.

When they reached the sidewalk, she was struck by the surreal nature of what she was doing, the role-playing. The disengagement from who she really was.

"Marjorie probably thinks there's something between us," she said, wondering what his reaction would be.

"Like what?"

She refused to answer that dumb question. He knew exactly what she meant.

"The town hasn't changed a lot since I was here. I wasn't sure about coming back."

"What happened at the foster home that made you run away? Cassie thought you might come back to Bradford, but no one ever saw you."

"Complications. I decided I'd had enough of foster care, and could deal with life on my own, so I took off."

"For L.A.?"

"Not initially, but as far from Mississippi as I could

get. I was a year in Texas, then moved on to New Mexico. But California beckoned, and now I call that home."

They reached the bank. Pushing in through the glass doors, Fiona took a deep breath and went on alert. Her years of training took hold. She scanned the premises. For a second she wanted to storm over and confront the man who had changed her life so radically. As if sensing the impulse, Sam put his hand on her shoulder and leaned closer.

"New Accounts is over there," he said softly, pointing in a direction opposite of where she was looking.

He took off his hat and held it in front of him.

"Play this cool, Detective," he added.

Fiona consciously relaxed and smiled sweetly at Sam. She drew the line at batting her eyelashes, though she could just hear Piper suggesting it.

"Thank you, Sheriff. I didn't have a checking account when I lived here before and might not have found my way."

Amusement danced in his eyes.

"Glad to help a visitor to our fair city."

"Ugh."

Sam at her side, she walked to the desk with the New Accounts sign, not recognizing the woman seated there.

"Hello, Sheriff Witt, how can I help you?" the woman asked, smiling at Sam. She scarcely looked at Fiona.

"Hey, Sharon. This is a friend of mine who'll be staying in town for a while. She wants to open a local account," he said easily.

"Oh. Have a seat," she said to Fiona, still barely acknowledging her.

The woman's attention was firmly on Sam.

Fiona smiled, feeling as if her face might fall off. She hadn't acted this cheerful since she could remember.

A movement caught her eye and she saw Allen McLennon leave an office and head across the wide lobby to the tellers. She watched him, feeling anger spike through her. That was the man who'd attacked her—and she'd let him get away with it.

She should have come back years ago and made enough of a pest of herself the authorities took some action.

Of course, Sheriff Halstead had been in charge until recently. It probably wouldn't have made a bit of difference.

Once again Sam put his hand on her shoulder. Fiona almost shook it off. Then her common sense took hold. Dragging her gaze away, she concentrated on the woman opposite her. Time enough for McLennon to learn of her presence.

Filling out the paperwork only took a few minutes. When the account officer reviewed it, she raised her eyebrows. "That's Margaret Nunes's address," she said in surprise, looking at Fiona. "Are you living there?"

"Yes. I'm one of her foster children. We've come

home to be with her since her stroke."

"Which one are you?" the woman asked.

"The one who was beaten and then shipped off as if I'd been the one who did wrong," Fiona said with bravado.

The woman stared at Fiona for a long moment, then blinked and looked back at the papers.

"Everything's in order. Your check from your California bank can be deposited. Normally we put a three day hold on checks from out of town."

"Yes, all right," Fiona said, scarcely able to concentrate on the matter; her whole attention was honed on McLennon.

Sam had been standing nearby; now he moved closer. Fiona glanced up, tried to remember her role and smiled.

"Incoming at seven o'clock," he said softly.

She looked over her shoulder and saw Allen McLennon heading their way. She'd already noted he'd left the tellers' area.

Quickly she reached for the interim checks and the paperwork the woman had completed. She wanted them in her purse before he could snatch them away and say she couldn't be a customer of his bank.

"If that's all," Fiona said brightly.

She stuffed the checkbook into her purse and rose. She wasn't going to meet him sitting down.

"I guess we're done here," she said to Sam.

"Sam, good morning. Anything I can help you with?" Allen asked, drawing even with the sheriff before he saw Fiona.

His genial attitude was perfect for a man in his position.

Fiona turned and stared at him, daring him to say something.

For a split second she thought he might give himself away, but no. His eyes flickered briefly in her direction.

"We have a new account," the woman said, rising and smiling at her boss.

"Always glad to have new people come to town," he said.

"I used to live here."

As if he didn't know, Fiona fumed.

"Indeed?"

"Fiona Hunter was one of Margaret Nunes's foster children," Sam said.

"Ah, Margaret had several as I remember. It was a long time ago. Moving back?"

"I'm on an extended visit. I have some...unfinished business," Fiona said.

She wished she dare accuse him in front of everyone in the bank. But hard-earned wisdom prevailed. She needed proof.

Fiona was suddenly conscious of the attention they were drawing from the other customers and employees in the bank. People in small towns were notoriously curious about everyone else's business. She didn't want speculation about hers.

Allen inclined his head slightly and smiled. It did

not reach his eyes.

"Enjoy your visit."

"I plan to see she does—no hardship there," Sam said easily.

Fiona almost laughed at the look on Allen's face. Sam played it as if he were personally interested in her. What would Allen think about that?

"Ready?" Sam asked, his hand reaching out to touch her again.

Honestly, he didn't have to be that solicitous.

"For now," she told the bank president. "I'll be back."

Fiona skipped a couple of steps in glee when they reached the sidewalk.

"That was great!" she said.

She turned and grinned at Sam.

"You saw it, didn't you? He was spooked. I wonder if we'd pushed a bit more he'd have cracked. Maybe he talks a good line, but he might break under the right pressure."

"I didn't see anything but an astute businessman greeting a new client. Leave him alone, Fiona. Don't be trying to force the issue. I'll see to the work necessary to find out the truth. If your story proves out, he could be dangerous. He has a lot more to lose now than he did twelve years ago."

"*If* it proves out? It *will!* You know, twelve years changes everything a lot. I'm not some kid now. I can handle myself."

What would it take for Sam to believe her? She

wanted to punch something she felt so frustrated. If she'd told her lieutenant a story of the same nature, he'd have gone to bat for her in a heartbeat.

Sam nodded.

"I'm sure you can. I just hope you never need to."

They walked toward the sheriff's office. When they drew even with Ruby's Café, Fiona asked offhandedly if he'd like a cup of coffee.

"I'll stay and drink it this time."

There were only a few seats available. The place was humming.

"Want a table or the counter?" Fiona asked, scanning the crowd.

She thought she recognized several people, but wasn't sure. No one waved or attempted to get her attention.

Sam realized his mistake in coming into Ruby's with Fiona when he glanced around and saw the speculative looks. He hadn't dated anyone in the more than two years he'd lived in Bradford. No wonder everyone was staring. It was the first time they'd seen him with a woman in a social situation. Too late to back out.

"Counter."

That seemed less intimate than a table or booth. He'd order his coffee, drink it as fast as he could and leave. No need to fuel gossip.

And if he did start dating, it wouldn't be with Fiona Hunter. He'd talked with Adam a lot since he'd arrived. After he fell in love with Piper and asked her to marry him, he suggested Sam look for a wife.

But to Sam, Patty was his wife. He couldn't imagine starting over with someone else. And what if she died? If he was as in love with her as he was with Patty, he wasn't sure he could stand the loss a second time.

Another strike against any interest in Fiona. She had a dangerous job. If Patty, a schoolteacher, could be killed, what was the likelihood of a cop buying it early? Too high.

Not that he was interested in Fiona.

He waited while the waitress filled their coffee cups. Then, taking a sip, he looked at Fiona. He could feel her energy. She was wired. He'd known people in New Orleans like that, an adrenaline rush keeping them hyper until their shift ended.

In truth Fiona wasn't that bad. She kept that energy leashed. She'd handled the first contact with the suspect well enough—though he'd had his doubts once or twice, fearing she'd flare up and make an accusation. It still all boiled down to her word over Allen's.

Interesting that he now thought he might take her word over that of an upright citizen he'd known for a couple of years. But he needed proof before proceeding.

"How's Margaret?" he asked to break the silence, hoping to find something else to talk about beside McLennon.

They were in too public a location for that.

"Cassie says she's improving, but I thought she

looked terrible. She's so thin and pale and old. Her trying to communicate had me tied up in knots."

"It takes patience."

"Mmm."

"Nice of you three to rally round when she needed you."

"Especially when she didn't rally round when I needed her," Fiona murmured.

He sipped the coffee. There wasn't much he could say to that. He knew from Adam that Cassie and Piper had reconnected in a way that families usually did. Would Fiona join in now or keep herself apart because of her role in breaking them up?

Only time would tell.

"Tell me about this Independence Day celebration," Fiona said. "Are you involved?"

"Our office doubles up on patrols to keep those imbibing from doing any damage to themselves or others. Any excuse for a drink-fest, you know."

"So you won't be manning a booth or something."

"I wouldn't even if I didn't have to work," Sam said. "You?"

"I don't want to, but I think that's what Piper has in mind."

"Tell her no."

Fiona sipped her coffee. Sam watched her. He liked her new look. It was softer, more feminine.

"I owe them a lot," she said slowly, turning her cup on the counter in front of her. "I don't want to say no if I don't have to."

She looked at him defensively.

"It wasn't your fault the three of you got sent away."

"Still, if I hadn't lied—"

"That appears to be the catalyst, but the authorities are the ones who split you all up. I know a few people I want to talk to to see if I can find out why. I know something about the foster care system, and this went against everything I thought I knew. I plan to find out why."

"I want to go with you," she said.

"I can handle it better on my own."

"Not necessarily. How will you know if things were the way they say they were? Besides, I'd like to face them. Maybe let them know how far-reaching their actions were."

"Hey, I thought I'd find you two here," Adam said, sliding onto the stool next to Sam. "Trust cops to be where there's coffee and doughnuts."

He looked at their cups in surprise.

"Did I already miss the doughnuts?"

"Fallacy," Fiona said. "I prefer pizza to doughnuts."

Adam grimaced.

"Not at this hour, I hope."

"Lunch isn't far off," she answered with a grin.

"I know it, and if you don't get over to Sam's place to help Piper, I don't want to be around to pick up the pieces," he said.

Signaling the waitress, he ordered two cups of coffee to go.

"Can't make your own?" Sam asked.

"Not as good as this. Piper dropped me off after scoping out the fairgrounds where the festivities are being held. She wanted to jot down some notes before she forgot, so I told her I'd get the brew. But she hasn't forgotten you said you'd help, Fiona," Adam said.

Sam glanced at Fiona, amused by the way she bit her lip and frowned, then obviously resigned herself to helping Piper.

"I'm ready."

He almost laughed out loud at her tone. But having her occupied would give him free rein to pursue his investigation. He didn't want to broadcast the fact he was looking into a situation everyone in town thought was closed. Having Fiona around would do exactly that.

She finished her coffee and rose.

"Ready as I'll ever be," she said dramatically.

Adam paid for the two coffees he picked up, placing them in the cardboard tray the waitress provided.

"Can you carry these? I need one hand for the cane."

Fiona glanced at Sam and scowled.

"You could offer us a ride in your copmobile."

"Could, but I'm still enjoying my coffee."

He didn't want to get drawn in, didn't want to join the others at his and Adam's place, where they were camped out, making plans. Time to establish some boundaries.

"Don't you be doing anything without me," Fiona warned.

"Whoa, you two an item now?" Adam asked.

"I'm talking about an official police investigation," Fiona said, reaching for the cardboard coffee tray.

"I'll see you later," Sam said, not making any commitments.

He'd handle things in his own way and time. Fiona was a guest in his town, nothing more, despite her past connections and her job in L.A.

After Adam and Fiona left, Sam finished his coffee and fished out a couple of dollars to pay.

"I remember her," the waitress said when she took the sheriff's money.

"Fiona?"

"Sure. She used to eat hamburgers like they were ambrosia. Never gained an ounce that I could tell. Looks even skinnier now."

"What else do you remember?" Sam asked, settling back down.

He'd take any information he would get.

"Not much. Margaret Nunes raised them proper, though they were always complaining how she was too strict. I never did buy into that story Margaret abused those girls. She loved them. It was plain to see."

"Who do you think beat Fiona?"

The woman shrugged, taking the empty cups and dumping them in a container to be taken into the kitchen later.

"She ran with a wild bunch, that girl. Maybe she

crossed one of them. I don't know. Looks mighty fine these days. She here because of Margaret?"

Sam nodded, reaching for his hat. No leads here. But interesting that another citizen of the town didn't think Margaret was guilty. So why *had* the girls been removed from the home?

Fiona walked with Adam along the sidewalk toward Sam's house, keeping pace with his slower gait. He still used a cane. She knew he was anxious to get to work on some new assignment, but had agreed to stay and help Piper with the fair.

Neither had much to say, and she spent her time studying the establishments they passed. Little had changed in the town, but she saw it differently now. No longer as a child, but as an adult. She could understand the appeal to those who lived here. Everyone was friendly. And it certainly was more peaceful than hectic L.A.

She nodded at an elderly man who tipped his hat as he passed.

"I bet you don't find that kind of politeness in L.A.," Adam said.

"Not at all," she agreed. "You're not from here, so why are you staying?"

"I came to visit Sam while I recuperated. Met Piper and that was that."

"The two of you could head off to Paris. I understand that's where you're going."

"She insisted we wait until after the Independence Day celebration to get married. But as soon as the wedding takes place, we're heading for Europe. Piper has to get back to work, and I'm opening a new branch for the news bureau in France."

Fiona had already heard their plans from Piper, but she murmured something appropriate.

"Sam's not married, is he," she said a couple of moments later.

"He's a widower. His wife was killed about three years ago in New Orleans."

"Wow, tough break. No kids?"

"None. He stuck it out in the Big Easy a little longer, then looked for something different. He sure got it here. I think Bradford's big crime spree is some kids shoplifting at the local discount store."

Fiona nodded, turning onto the quieter road where Sam's house was. She was used to glass and concrete and lots of cars. But once she'd lived here, where there were wide lawns, ancient trees and flowers blooming everywhere. Ten years in Los Angles had altered her idea of home, but for a moment she felt a wistful homesickness for the town's pretty neighborhoods.

"Hey, I thought I was going to have to do all this myself," Piper said when they walked into the living room.

She smiled at Adam, who leaned over and kissed her gently.

"I brought coffee, or rather, Fiona brought it. It'll fire you up and keep you going for the rest of the day," he said, taking one of the cups from the container and handing it to her.

"Sit and help," Piper said to Fiona.

Fiona sat on the chair pulled up to the card table and looked at the sketches and lists scattered over the surface.

"What are you doing, planning a second front?" Fiona asked.

"Some of those ideas are no good. I want the people coming to see the fashion show to flow into the tent, watch the show and then flow out, without colliding with the next group. I think we can do three shows, each less than an hour, if we can get the audience in and out fast enough. Models are quick-change artists, after all. And that way the models will have time to enjoy the rest of the fair."

"It'll be different from what most of them are used to," Adam said drily.

"You're expecting that many people to watch a fashion show?" Fiona asked.

"Yes. I'm expecting everyone attending the fair to want to see the big-name models I've lined up."

"Not to mention our own famous Monique," Adam added, calling Piper by her professional name.

Piper smiled at him, love evident in her eyes.

Fiona studied the drawings, glancing around the room a moment later, more interested in seeing where Sam lived than in the lists Piper was working on.

The room was comfortable. The big oversize sofa looked perfect for curling up on to read, or lazing around watching TV in the evening. Sam was a tall man—the furniture suited him.

The television was a large flat screen. The two reclining chairs also looked lived-in and masculine. There were several photos of a pretty young woman. Fiona longed to go study them, but wouldn't want Adam and Piper to know where her curiosity lay.

"Earth to Fiona," Piper said.

Fiona turned and found Adam watching her. She looked quickly at Piper, hoping the man wasn't as astute as he seemed.

"Okay, you want suggestions about foot traffic to flow, I'm your gal. I worked at some of the big bowl games and pro football games. How hard can a little town festival be? Let's see what you've done."

Fiona left Piper and Adam mid afternoon to walk back to town. She wasn't at all certain going to the fair was in her own best interest with everyone staring and whispering. She preferred to blend into the background. Her undercover work made it imperative. If not for Piper's insistence that she had to help for Margaret's sake, she'd opt to fade into the background for this venue, as well. Only, the background here in Bradford included sun dresses and bright colors.

"Like 'Do it for Margaret' was some magic saying, like 'Win one for the Gipper,'" she muttered.

Maybe it was. She'd do anything to make up for the past.

Arriving at the sheriff's office, she went straight through to the back. Marjorie was on the phone but covered the mouthpiece and shook her head.

"He's not here."

"Be back soon?" Fiona asked.

Marjorie shrugged, then said something to the person on the phone.

Fiona debated leaving a note, waiting or trying to catch up with Sam later. The third choice won and she headed back outside. Pausing on the sidewalk, she looked down the street to the bank. Two times in one day might be a bit much, but she sure would like to do something to spook the man into making a mistake.

Though she had no idea what would do that. Sam was right. As it stood, it was Allen McLennon's word against hers. And given her track record in Bradford, he'd win hands down.

The hospital was only a block over. But she couldn't go there again. Not yet. Not without something positive to tell Margaret.

That left her totally at loose ends. Not something she was used to. At home she had her work, and then more work.

"Afternoon," someone said as they passed.

"Afternoon," she responded, smiling.

Did she know how to work undercover or what? The guys at the precinct would bust a gut if they could see her latest role. But if it helped catch McLennon, it'd be worth it.

It still felt awkward, though. She turned and

headed back to Bradford Hall. She thought best with a pen and paper in hand. Maybe she'd list the pros and cons of investigating such an old case, hoping something would occur to her as she tried to plot out her game plan—similar to what she'd been doing with Piper's layout for the fashion show.

She'd sketch what she remembered about the car, the road and the cabin she'd seen through the rain. Anything to help identify the scene. Maybe she could locate the site and find some trace of the crime.

She sighed. She'd never been inside the cabin, so there'd be no long-lost evidence with her DNA or anything dramatic like that. But there had to be something that could prove she was innocent and a guilty man had gone free for more than a decade.

6

Sam arrived home after eight. The house was empty. He fixed himself a sandwich and took a beer from the refrigerator. Heading for the patio at the back of the house, he knew he'd be assured of some privacy there. Sometimes he and Adam sat on the front porch and watched as people drove by. But if someone had a question or just wanted to shoot the breeze, they stopped to talk. If he was in the back, no one would know he was home.

He was tired. He leaned back in the patio chair and propped his feet on the small wrought-iron table. Munching on the sandwich, he wondered where Adam was. The man was gone more than he was here. Not that Sam blamed him. If he had a woman like Piper wanting to marry him, he'd spend every moment with her, too. They were either over at Bradford Hall, or out somewhere, just the two of them.

More often than not Sam ate dinner alone. As he had for most of the past three years, ever since Patty had been killed. He was used to it. Didn't like it much, but unless he ate at Ruby's or someplace like that, he was his own company.

He hadn't started dating again. No one could take Patty's place. He'd loved her from the time they started high school. He felt cheated and angry they hadn't had fifty or more years together.

Being around the lovesick Adam only made things worse. Where once he and Adam had talked football and world events, now the topic of conversation was when Adam could move to Paris and how he'd like Piper's apartment. Or whether they should get a new one together.

Adam and Piper were due to drive to Baton Rouge right after Independence Day so she could meet his parents. The wedding was going to be short and sweet, and the weekend after the Fourth so they could get back to Paris.

Sam wished them happiness. He hoped his longtime friend had the fifty years he and Patty hadn't.

When Adam was gone, Sam would rattle around this old house again. He liked the town. Liked the people. But—

He was lonely.

Patty was gone. Maybe he should move on. The thought seemed disloyal somehow, and he felt a pang of guilt.

Taking a long swallow of beer, he leaned back, resting his head on the high back of the chair. Thirty-two years old and he hadn't a care in the world. Except for being alone.

He thought about Fiona. If he was invited to eat one of Cassie's fabulous meals again, she'd be there.

She had a chip on her shoulder the size of a redwood. He almost smiled, thinking how she'd gotten riled at the bank. For a moment there, he'd thought she'd go after McLennon with her bare hands.

Once he'd thought she'd go after *him*. She was angry that he wouldn't jump right in and go along with her accusation. He wanted proof. Just because he didn't jump on her bandwagon didn't mean he wasn't looking into things.

If her story was true, and for some odd reason he was starting to believe it, she'd shown great willpower by not railing at McLennon at the bank.

How long would she keep that willpower? Or would the frustration of not finding evidence sway her into doing something foolish?

It was up to him to keep that from happening.

He finished his makeshift meal and headed inside to take a shower. He wondered how Fiona was doing as the odd person out in a household of newly engaged people. Probably no worse than he was.

He stood beneath the cool spray for a long time, wondering about Fiona Hunter. She was nothing like Patty. His wife had been sweet and petite and feminine. She'd loved making a home for them in New Orleans and would have made a great mother. He knew her parents and her grandparents, her siblings and friends.

He knew nothing about Fiona Hunter except she was the daughter of a drug addict, lied when she'd been a teenager and was a respected cop in Los

Angeles.

And for some reason, he was growing fascinated with her. She had a real talent for undercover work. She'd looked like a biker babe when she'd roared into town. Today she'd looked like everyone's favorite niece, sweet and demure and Southern-friendly.

He shut off the water. He wasn't going down that road. Just because going to Bradford Hall for a meal meant he'd be paired with the only other unattached person was no reason to start thinking the thoughts he was thinking.

Like wondering if her lips would be soft beneath his. Or if her height would throw him off if he tried to kiss her. Patty had been several inches shorter. And rounder.

Fiona was reed slender, but the sleeveless top she'd worn that morning had showed off her arms. He could see she was in terrific physical shape. Her breasts were small, but on her they were perfect.

"Oh, no," he said, drying off. "I'm not thinking about a woman's breasts."

He felt another pang of guilt.

He quickly dressed in khaki slacks and a cotton pullover. Barefoot, he went back to the living room. Maybe there was something mindless on the tube he could watch until it was time for bed.

Ten minutes into the crime show Sam selected, Adam called.

"You're home. I called earlier but the phone just rang. We're going for ice cream and to discuss the booth for Margaret's fund-raiser. Join us?"

"Who's us?"

"Piper, Cassie, Matt and Fiona. And me. We can swing by your place to pick you up. We're walking. What's with these people? Haven't they ever heard of cars?"

Sam heard the murmur of voices in the background and then Adam's laugh and warning to Piper.

"Yeah, well, we'll see when we reach Paris."

He returned to Sam.

"Or, how about we just meet you there?"

"I'll pass. I've had a long day."

"Hey, old man, you aren't that old. Come on."

"Another time."

When Fiona wasn't there. When it wasn't couples and he didn't feel like he was being set up.

"Your loss. See you when I get home. If you're in bed, I'll tiptoe."

Sam gave him a suggestion about what he could do with his tiptoe and Adam laughed again before hanging up.

Twenty minutes later there was a knock on the door. Sam flipped on the hall light as he went to answer it. Darkness had fallen and he hadn't bothered with lamps.

Fiona stood there, licking an ice cream cone and holding a container with a lid.

"This is for you—praline delight. Adam said it's your favorite flavor."

She held out the container.

Sam took it and she promptly turned and headed back down the steps.

"Hey, where're you going?"

"Home. Do you know how uncomfortable it is to go out for ice cream with two lovesick couples? If you'd come, at least we could have talked about the case. See ya."

"Wait. I'll get a spoon and eat this. Stay and finish your cone."

She looked at him for a long moment, eyes narrowed.

"*You're* not going to be infected with the love bug, are you?"

He chuckled and relaxed. Maybe he'd felt he was being set up, but the woman in question obviously wasn't going along with the plan.

"Not if I can help it. Sit. I'll be right back."

Fiona sat on one of the two rocking chairs on the porch, settling in the cushions and gazing out over the quiet street. Lights were on in the houses across the way. Occasionally a car drove by, but she couldn't see the occupants in the darkness. She felt cocooned in the night, invisible in the darkness of Sam's porch. The house she and the others were sharing was too far back from the road to see other houses or passers by. This was fun.

Sam pushed opened the screen and joined her a moment later, spoon in hand. He sat in the rocking chair next to her and pried off the lid.

"It's probably melted a little," she said. "I had to lick like crazy to keep mine from dripping all over my hands."

"I like it soft."

The words sent a shaft of awareness through her. She blinked and looked away. Where had that come from? She'd been serious when she'd told him she'd been uncomfortable with Cassie and Matt, Piper and Adam. But she was also a bit envious.

Not that she wanted to start anything with Sam Witt or with anyone else. She wasn't going to get dependent on anyone. She'd learned that lesson as a teenager.

She only needed him to work on getting Allen McLennon to admit he'd been the one to attack her. To make sure there were never lingering doubts with anyone about Margaret's innocence.

"So did you find out anything about McLennon?" she asked.

She'd keep the conversation impersonal and focused. Once she finished her cone, she'd head for home.

"I have some feelers out, but nothing concrete yet."

She waited a heartbeat, but he didn't say anything more.

"That's all?" she asked. "What angle are you working on?"

She was impatient for something to happen. Living in Bradford any longer than she had to would drive her crazy.

"I'm working on trying to find out what happened twelve years ago without alerting anyone."

"Why? Why not let people know, spread the word? Maybe someone will come forward."

"And maybe we'll get sued for defamation," he countered easily. "Proof, evidence, remember that from your basic training?"

She fumed. Of course she remembered.

"Nothing happens in a vacuum," she muttered, licking a running drip from the cone.

This ice cream was taking forever to eat.

"Tell me again," he said.

She complied, once more reliving that night, the shock and fear she'd felt.

"Nothing he'd ever said gave you a hint he might behave this way if he ever got you alone?" Sam asked.

"No. I thought he was courting Margaret."

"Cassie and Piper said he never hit on them. And you've got to admit Piper is gorgeous," Sam said. "Then again, maybe you're more his type."

"Not twelve years ago. I was scrawny, skinny and had an attitude."

"So what's changed?"

Fiona sat up at that.

"I'm not scrawny, for one thing."

Sam laughed softly. The sound sent shivers up her back.

"You've got the attitude," he said.

She wished there was more light on the porch. She wanted to see him. Was he teasing, or telling it like it was? She did have an attitude. Did that bother him?

And what did she care if it did?

"Good cops do," she muttered.

She finally finished her ice cream cone. There was nothing holding her to the porch. She wanted to leave before she got some screwy notion that she wanted to change his opinion of her.

She wasn't going to be in town long enough to make friends with Sam Witt. The Independence celebration was in four days, then Piper would be getting married and leaving. As soon as Margaret was well enough to attend, Cassie and Matt planned to marry and find their own home.

"Gotta go," she said, rising abruptly.

"Stay a little longer," Sam said.

She dusted off the seat of her jeans. Not that it needed it.

"I've got things to do."

"Like what?"

She floundered for a moment, then zeroed in on the one thing they had in common.

"Come up with a list of people to question about McLennon."

"Leave it, Fiona. I mean it. I'll do the investigation as I see fit. You'll only muddy the waters," he said in a hard voice.

"It's a free country, last I heard. I can do what I want."

"And if you muck things up, then what? Thought you wanted justice."

"What kind of justice do you think I'm likely to get? McLennon's the president of the town's bank, for heaven's sake. He probably attends church every Sunday and is in the Rotary or Lions Club or some other philanthropic organization spreading goodness and light everywhere."

"But not according to you."

"I've thought about it over the years. Do you think I was the only one?"

Sam shrugged. "Could have been."

"Or he could be hitting on young girls to this day."

He nodded. "Could be. But there's never been a hint of rumor to that effect."

"Who would believe the upstanding bank president would ever do such a thing? You know the stats as well as I do. Criminals do not all have beady, shifty eyes."

Sam rose, putting his empty cup on the railing.

"I'll walk you home," he said. "Just let me get some shoes on."

"I can manage."

"I'm sure you can," he said, heading inside.

For a moment Fiona debated leaving before he returned. She couldn't imagine any harm coming to anyone on the streets of Bradford. Yet something had twelve years ago. It would be nice to stroll through the quiet little town, maybe hear laughter from a window—though most people had air conditioners and shut themselves up in their cool homes.

She walked to the top of the steps and looked

around. The neighborhood was nice. Why had a single man bought a home in a neighborhood like this? Was he planning on another wife and a family?

She'd seen what marriage could do to two people, beginning with her parents, and later several cop friends, whose marriages hit the rocks. She was determined to stay single. It was safer that way. Maybe Piper and Cassie would make a success of marriage and she envied them that. But it wasn't for her.

"Ready?" he asked, stepping back onto the porch.

"I can manage," she said again.

It was almost ten when they turned up the crushed-shell driveway leading to Margaret's home. The lights were on in the house. Cassie's van was in the drive, along with Piper's rental and her own rental.

"Everyone home?" he asked as they walked up the drive.

"Probably. Thanks for the escort. The town seems different somehow from when I lived here, smaller and definitely quieter. There were beer parties by the river when I was in high school. And I know there was a rash of break-ins on Main Street. I suspected Jack Denton was involved even then."

"Jack Denton? I've heard that name. Some say he was the one who beat you."

"Rumors only. No question who did that to me."

"Fiona."

Sam stopped her some distance from the porch.

She looked back at him curiously.

"Don't mess with McLennon. I can find out all

there is to discover myself."

"I hear you."

Sam looked at her intensely and Fiona almost squirmed. She *did* hear him. She still planned to do what she thought best.

Bidding him good-night, she hurried the rest of the way to the house. She paused at the door and saw him turn to leave. Chivalry was alive and well in Bradford, Mississippi. On the other hand, he could have escorted her right to the door.

Like a date?

The thought danced in her mind. If it had been a date, would he have kissed her?

Her heart thudded.

Climbing the stairs, she called Cassie and Piper. No response. They must already be in bed.

In only a few minutes Fiona was, too, with a pad and pencil to continue her brainstorming. She was trying to remember every detail of those last few months before they'd been sent away. Were there other clues that could nail McLennon?

Would Sam really look into the situation? Or was he just trying to keep her from rocking the boat? He had to live in this town when she left. She could imagine how uncomfortable a man with McLennon's influence could make it for an elected official. Sam could lose his job in the next election.

She wanted justice, however. Not only for what happened to her but for what happened to Margaret. She should never have lost her foster license, never been forced to give up her girls. She stared at the yellow writing tablet, willing some names to come.

"Fee?" Piper opened her door and stuck her head in. "Good, you're awake."

She pushed it open all the way and sat on Fiona's bed near the foot.

"Why did you take off like that?"

"I brought Sam some ice cream."

She wasn't going to make a big deal about feeling left out with her two engaged friends. Anyone with half a brain ought to be able to figure that out.

"I've closed up the downstairs," Cassie said, walking into the room.

She pulled the chair near the window over and sat in it, resting her feet on the mattress.

"I'm tired."

"Go to bed," Fiona said, scooting up so she was sitting against the headboard.

"I'm not sleepy, just tired. My feet hurt from being on them so much, a hazard of being a chef."

Cassie toed off her shoes and wiggled her toes.

"What are you doing?" Piper asked, nodding at the tablet. "Making a list of how you can help at the fair?"

"I've helped. I figured out your crowd flow."

"That's preliminary work. What are you going to be doing that day?"

"Nothing."

"Ha!" Cassie said. "I think we need something to make a statement about Margaret."

"A banner?" Fiona asked. "One that says,

'Margaret was innocent, your local banker is the culprit'?"

"Not bad," Piper said. "Not realistic, but not bad."

"I called Stephen today about you," Cassie said.

"Stephen?"

"You remember, fiancé number one," Piper said. "That was last month. Now she's on number two with Matt."

"At least it was only an engagement," Cassie said without heat, smiling lazily at her friend. "I wasn't married twice."

"But this is my first and only engagement," Piper returned smugly. "The marriages were spur-of-the-moment."

"Get back to Stephen," Fiona said.

She could only stand so many details about her friends' love lives.

"He's a lawyer and he said you could sue the man in civil court. For loss of home and punitive damages. But you'd need a strong case."

"I thought you said he lived in Massachusetts. Is he licensed to practice in Mississippi?"

"No, but law is law. At least the basics. Contact a lawyer locally," Cassie said.

"Not until we have more. I know enough basics myself to know I wouldn't stand a chance giving my version against his."

"You need a witness or two," Piper said.

"Well, duh. What do you think I'm trying to do? If I could only find one person, preferably someone of sterling character and reputation, to say they saw me get into his car, or saw the two of us driving in the rain, or something."

"What does Sam think?"

"That there was something fishy about the investigation. But the old sheriff is dead, so no help there."

Cassie scowled. "Can we get back to what we're going to do about Margaret?"

"Okay," Fiona said. "But doesn't the fact that we're doing things to raise money to help with Margaret's medical bill and help start this group home say enough?"

"Well," Piper said, "I'm contributing models and designer clothes. Adam is bringing in a couple of New Orleans Saints football players. Cassie is donating dinners and having a bake sale. Matt is offering a one-room renovation. What can *you* do, Fee?"

"Offer security services?" she replied, feeling guilty she wasn't doing more.

But she had no talents or resources in Mississippi.

"Maybe swear on a stack of Bibles Margaret never laid a hand on me."

"Security sounds good, but I think Fiona's being here says lots about the situation," Cassie said.

"People will ask who did if not Margaret," Piper said.

"I think they'll be more concerned about Margaret being your grandmother," Fiona interjected. "My situation is old news, only important to those of us involved. But this, wow, you'll surprise the entire town."

Piper smiled. "I was thinking of sitting with her at the fashion show. Ringside seats, and introducing her to one and all as my grandmother. What do you think?"

"Cool," Cassie said.

She looked at Fiona.

"Tell me what you think of Sam."

"He seems efficient. I like the things he's doing with the teenagers—cutting back on crime that way."

Cassie exchanged glances with Piper.

"I don't mean as a cop. I meant as a guy."

Fiona was instantly on her guard.

"What do you mean?"

"Well, I think he's hot," Piper said.

"He's good-looking," Fiona conceded warily. "Don't get any ideas about him and me, though."

"But you'll be hanging around here for a while yet, won't you?" Piper asked. "Besides, we've just reconnected."

"You're taking off, Piper, and Cassie and Matt don't need me."

"Stay for our wedding," Cassie said. "Matt and I set a date tonight—the Saturday after Piper's wedding."

"Why don't you marry at the same time?"

"No way," Piper said. "I'm not sharing that special day with anyone, even Cassie."

"Same for me," Cassie said. "I want to be the center of attention once in my life. Can you see anyone looking at me if Piper's also a bride?"

"Piper's getting married a little over a week from now," Fiona said. "But I thought she was leaving right afterward."

"I can stay one more week, since it beats flying home and then back a few days later. I wouldn't miss Cassie's wedding for anything."

"It's going to be a small wedding. Margaret's doctor says we can bring her home for meals and visits until she's fully recovered. So she can attend both weddings, which is what I've been waiting for," Cassie said.

Piper rose and gave Cassie a quick hug.

"That's so cool. I'll have my grandmother at our wedding. Just think, a couple of months ago I had no family at all, hadn't heard from you two in ages, and now I'm getting married, I've found my grandmother and the three of us are back together."

Cassie looked at Fiona with speculation.

"Adam and Sam have been friends for years. Matt has become a friend with them both. Think how cool it would be to have you and Sam pair up."

"Give it a rest, Cassie," Fiona said. "I'm not going to take up with some guy to even the numbers or because he's friends with your main man. I told you, he's off-limits for a number of reasons, not the least of which he doesn't even like me."

Not to mention the flare of anger she felt around him each time he downplayed the investigation.

She wanted someone whole heartedly in her

corner.

"Fiona never takes the easy way out," Piper murmured, her eyes dancing in amusement. "But it would solve a lot of problems."

"No."

Fiona was firm in this.

No way was she going to become personally involved with Sam Witt.

"Spoilsport," Cassie said.

Fiona was glad to see them leave a half hour later. In the old days they'd often gathered in one bedroom or another after some event to discuss the evening. Usually it was when Piper went on a date. Fiona had missed those gabfests when she'd been moved. Now it looked as if they were stepping right back into them as if they'd never parted.

Still, it was after midnight and she was tired.

And skittish about their bringing up Sam Witt. From what they'd said earlier, he didn't date. Wouldn't the man in question have some say in a new relationship? Ha. No worries in that direction.

Ignoring the attraction to him, she felt, was the best policy. Fiona switched off her light and tried to go to sleep. She had other things to think about. Being tempted by a sexy cop who didn't like her wasn't in the cards.

7

The next morning Fiona looked up Halstead in the telephone directory. There was a listing on Morning Glory Court. She wasn't sure where that was, but would find it. Her hope was that this was Sheriff Halstead's widow and that she knew something about her husband's cases years ago. At least hers.

Fiona dressed in her undercover role, looking as fresh as a daisy, as Margaret used to say, with a light-colored top borrowed from Piper. She put on some makeup, feeling oddly at home with the feminine rituals she normally ignored. She even sprayed herself with perfume. Wow. The things women did to attract a member of the opposite sex.

She smiled. Wouldn't her fellow cops at the precinct howl with laughter if they could see her?

She drove the red convertible, top down, of course. It took her a little while, but she found Morning Glory Court. It was in an older section of town. The lots were large with mature trees, and the homes were big without being lavish. Fiona was skeptical that a sheriff's salary could cover the cost of one of these houses. She knew real estate prices were lower in

Mississippi than in L.A., but so were salaries.

Maybe there was something to that conspiracy theory voiced at dinner the other night.

She parked at the curb and walked up the path to the small porch and front door. There was a knocker. She tapped on the door.

A few moments later a woman of about seventy opened the door.

"Yes?" she said.

Fiona had never seen her before.

"Mrs. Halstead?" she asked.

"That's right. What can I do for you?"

"Are you the widow of Sheriff Halstead?" Fiona clarified.

The woman nodded.

"I knew your husband a long time ago."

She smiled.

"How nice. Do come in. Jerry died a few years ago. I still miss him. But he wouldn't listen to me about his diet. Doctor told him he was heading for a heart attack, and sure enough that's what killed him. Did you work with him?"

She looked at Fiona closely.

"You don't look old enough. Would you like some iced tea or lemonade? It'll be hot today."

The house was cool and inviting. Fiona stepped into the living room and glanced around. The furnishings were comfortable and pretty, yet nothing looked especially high end.

"Actually, I didn't work with your husband. He

investigated a crime in which I was the victim."

"Oh, dear," she said, tilting her head in concern. "I'm so sorry. Did he catch the crook?"

"Not that I ever heard. I thought he might have discussed the case with you."

"Oh, no, dear. He never brought his work home with him. He wanted to keep his work life and home life separate, he always said."

Fiona bit her lip, glancing around again.

"How about a journal or something? Did he keep anything in which he might have put down his thoughts about the crimes he was investigating?"

"No."

Mrs. Halstead smiled sadly.

"Jerry wasn't real interested in writing. He never even wrote his mother when she was alive. We'd phone, or I'd be the one to write to her."

Dead end. Fiona guessed she'd learn nothing from the former sheriff's widow.

"Nice place you have," she said politely as she rose to her feet. No sense in staying any longer.

"I love it and I never thought we'd be able to afford something this big. We used to live over near the hospital. But now that it's only me, I'm not sure I want to stay. It's hard to keep up. A smaller place would suit me, I think. But Jerry was so proud when he told me we were buying this place, I haven't had the heart to leave it yet."

"When was that?" Fiona asked as they both moved to the door.

"Let me see, about twelve years ago, I guess it would be. Right before school let out. Not that we had any children, but I remember the kids always used to cross our yard when going home from elementary school. It used to annoy me no end. Now I miss seeing them."

"Well, thank you for your time," Fiona said, turning to open the door. "It was a long shot, but I had hoped maybe he'd said something."

But it looked as though there was a connection between the sheriff's getting a bigger house and McLennon's attack. The time was the same.

Somehow McLennon had made the mortgage affordable to the sheriff, and for what reason other than a cover-up?

"I'm sorry the crime was never solved," Mrs. Halstead said as she walked onto the porch with Fiona.

"So am I, but that may change."

Fiona almost ran back to the car. She jumped in and headed for town. Next stop, city hall. She was going to find those records of the house sale to see what they revealed, then show Sam.

Forty-five minutes later Fiona entered the sheriff's department. She glanced at her watch. It was just after noon. Marjorie's desk was empty. She was probably at lunch. Fiona knocked on the half-closed door to Sam's office, but there was no response. His office was empty.

Rats! Just when she had something, he was out.

She went back to the front. The woman at the

switchboard looked up. "May I help you?"

"I'm looking for the sheriff."

"Turn around," she said with a grin.

Sam walked through the door, hat in hand. He looked surprised to see Fiona.

"What's up?"

"I have something," she said, almost dancing with excitement.

He nodded at the switchboard operator and headed for the back.

"Something as in–?"

"As in I think the sheriff and the banker were involved in a cover-up. Did you know that just weeks after I was sent away, the sheriff and his wife bought a house in a very nice neighborhood they should never have been able to afford? Totally out of the blue."

"So?"

"The house was a foreclosure by the bank, and it was sold at a loss compared to appraised value."

Sam ushered her into his office and closed the door. He tossed the hat onto a rack.

"I told you to stay away from this case, Fiona. How do you know this?"

"I went to see Sheriff Halstead's widow. She told me part of the story. The rest is a matter of public record."

"What part of 'Keep out of this investigation' do you not understand?" he asked, eyes narrowed in anger.

She flared up.

"Hey, this is important to me. To you it's one of many, and a cold case at that. I don't have a lot of time before I'm heading back to L.A. You're moving too slow."

"I'm moving just right, and you stay out of my way," he countered.

"I'm not doing anything I don't have a right to. If I do decide to sue the bastard in court, I need evidence. And I need more than what I have to win a case. Once I hire a lawyer, it'll be a matter of public record, anyway, and the entire town will know about it."

"Nothing's provable yet," Sam warned.

"It's been twelve years."

"I've only known about it for less than two months," he said. "And you're right, it's not a high priority. But I am working on it. And yes, I already have copies of the paperwork regarding the house. It does look suspicious, but in and of itself, it's not enough."

Fiona stared at him.

"You *are* doing something."

"I told you I would. But I'm not discussing a case with the victim."

"How about with another cop?"

"Which way are you going to play it, victim or cop? I don't want to jeopardize any case I can build by crossing the line."

"I hate your logic," she said, turning to glare out the window.

The view from the back wasn't much to look at, but

at least it gave her a moment to sort things out. So he'd been investigating and had already come up with the information she'd found.

"Okay, you're right," she admitted.

She knew the drill.

"The case will stand better if you find evidence on your own, with no help from me."

"I'll do my best for you," he said, stepping closer. "I despise men who prey on kids. If he slipped up anywhere, I'll find it."

"It's not just for me," she said.

"No?"

"It's also for Margaret. I want her to know I wasn't lying when I said it was Allen. I lied when I told the sheriff she'd done it, but that was because she hadn't believed me. I wanted her to listen, to know I tried to tell her the truth and she wouldn't believe me."

Sam put his hands on Fiona's shoulders, easing some of her tension. She stared out the window, remembering how she'd railed against Margaret for not believing her. She'd felt so stunned, so betrayed.

"She knows," Sam said.

Fiona shook her head.

"No, she thought it was Denton or one of his friends. She was dating Allen and thought he could do no wrong. She never believed me. It showed me once and for all that I was on my own. Sometimes I thought—"

She stopped abruptly. She was not sharing all this with Sam Witt.

"Hey, once we get proof, you can show Margaret," he said, turning her to face him.

She looked up into his eyes, warm and dark. For a moment she felt she could move mountains if he had faith in her.

"You're saying that to placate me. I'll be gone soon and that'll be that."

"Actually, I'll follow any clue to find the truth."

Fiona stared at him, hope blossoming. "Really?"

So what if he didn't believe her yet? If he really pursued it, wouldn't the truth be revealed sooner or later?

"Really," Sam said.

Unexpected to both of them, he lowered his head and kissed her.

Fiona was surprised at the feel of his warm lips against hers. It was a short kiss. Before she could even think to respond, he'd pulled back, pushing lightly against her shoulders and stepping away.

She snapped her eyes to his and stared.

"What was that about?" she asked, taking the offensive lest she reach out to pull him back.

Sam rubbed the nape of his neck and turned away.

"Heck if I know. You looked so—"

He stopped abruptly.

Fiona's curiosity flared. "So what?"

He turned.

"Let's forget it, all right? An aberration on my part. I apologize, if that's what you want. It won't happen again."

Darn, Fiona wanted to say.

Had she sent off vibes that indicated she hadn't liked it? Granted, a kiss had no place in police investigations, but he'd told her to butt out, so she wasn't really involved.

Turning, she looked out the window again, wishing there was more to see besides the half-empty parking lot and a few old cars.

"I feel so useless," she said moments later. "I came to make amends and Margaret can't even talk with me. I feel guilty as can be around Piper and Cassie. They're trying to make the best of things, but I think they wish I wasn't here."

"You're dead wrong there. They've been looking for you since they first returned. All they talked about before you showed up was finding you, having all of you home again."

"Home."

What was home? Where they had to take you in? Where they cared for you no matter what? Where they believed you and trusted you?

She had no home.

"I thought you three were working on the fair together," Sam said.

Fiona shrugged.

"Piper has the modeling set up. Cassie's doing the food. I'm on the sidelines."

"Your being here means a lot to them."

She turned back to him, frowning.

"Stop being so Mr. Goody Two-shoes. I want to do

something, but what? We're trying to prove to the world that Margaret was good to us, that we're united behind her."

"There must be something you can do to make you feel you're contributing. I thought you were helping Piper."

"We finished the logistics of the fashion show, and we wanted our presence to send a message."

"So find something you can do."

"Face painting, I guess," Fiona said a moment later.

"What?"

Sam looked surprised.

Fiona scowled at him.

"I'm good at it, actually."

"Like makeup?"

"No, like drawing rainbows on kids' faces, or butterflies and Spider-Man and things like that."

He stared at her.

"You know how to draw on faces?"

"Haven't you seen them at fairs and all?"

"Yes, but I'm trying to get around my image of you at a fair painting pictures on little kids' faces. Do you wear biker gear and spiked hair?"

She laughed. "I've been a cop for a number of years. We have events, too, you know. And I'm good at it. I have a whole box of paint and stuff at home."

"Why?"

"Why what?" she asked.

"Why do you do it?"

She was quiet for a moment, then shrugged.

"My deep dark secret. And if you tell a soul, I'll deny it."

"My lips are sealed."

She looked at his lips for a moment, wishing they were on hers. Even thinking about the kiss had her blood warming. She looked away, sorry she'd said anything. Now she had to explain.

"I've always loved little children. They're so sweet and so innocent. The first time I was asked to help out at a police booth, I didn't have a clue what to do. A wife of another officer offered to teach me face painting. Do you ever talk to children, especially small ones? Not mouthy teenagers, but when they're still wide-eyed and everything is miraculous?"

Sam studied her for a moment, shaking his head slowly.

"Still hard to believe."

"Yeah, well, that's about the only time I'm around innocence. The rest of the time I'm on the hunt for drug pushers. I like that small breath of magic."

"Send for your paints," Sam said. "We have three days until the fair. Have someone ship them to you overnight."

"Okay."

A spurt of excitement shot through her. She could get her paints, have a table near Piper's booth, or where Cassie was selling baked goods, and paint designs on children's faces. How benign was that? And she'd do a big sign saying all proceeds went to

Margaret's medical fund. That showed support. Maybe the parents would stop and chat while she worked. She could push the idea that Cassie, Piper and she were all wronged and get public sentiment on their side.

The more she thought about it, the more she liked the idea.

Fiona left the sheriff's office and headed for home. She'd call her partner and get him to ship the box of paints to her. Her head was spinning with ideas. Spying a law office across the street from the courthouse, she stopped and stared at it. Impulsively crossing the street a moment later, Fiona entered the building.

The receptionist was a stranger. Just as well. Fiona wasn't sure she wanted to proceed at this point.

"May I help you?" the woman asked.

"I'd like to discuss a civil suit with an attorney," Fiona said, wondering if she should have gotten a referral or something.

What if they gave her to some junior lawyer who didn't know anything yet?

"Have a seat and I'll see if Mr. Johnstone is free. He's one of the partners."

Partner sounded okay.

Fiona sat and tried to think of how to present the case without giving anything away at this point. She just wanted some indication of what she could expect.

Ten minutes later she sat opposite a man in his late

thirties, desk neat, but with piles of briefs and folders on the credenza behind him.

He had a yellow pad on the desk, and after greeting her, he said, "I hope you don't mind if I jot some notes as we talk."

"Actually, I'm not sure at this point how far I want to take this," Fiona said honestly.

"Tell me what this is about for starters," he suggested, leaning back in his chair.

"My name obviously meant nothing to you," she began.

He shook his head. "Should it?"

"Do you know Margaret Nunes?"

"Yes."

"I was one of her foster daughters. The one who got beaten and was sent away to another home. Nothing like punishing the victim."

"I'm not familiar with the case."

"There was no case. It happened twelve years ago. Apparently the sheriff didn't follow up on anything and nothing ever happened, except Margaret's foster care license was revoked, and her granddaughter and the two other foster children who lived with her were sent elsewhere in the state, and not allowed to contact one another."

"Most irregular. Are you sure of your facts?" he asked, making a note on the pad.

"Yes. I was one of the girls."

"Not Sheriff Witt, I take it. He's too new."

"Sheriff Halstead. He was hand in glove with the

man who beat me and attempted to rape me."

Foster's eyebrows shot upward. "Rape?"

"Attempted. Statute of limitations has run out, so I have no criminal recourse. But I wondered if I could sue in civil court."

"The sheriff is dead, died a number of years ago."

"The man who beat me is not."

"And who is that?"

Fiona hesitated. "This is in confidence, right?"

He nodded.

She took a deep breath. "Allen McLennon."

Foster stared at her dumbfounded. He carefully placed the pencil down and leaned back again. "You have proof?"

She shook her head.

"How long ago did this happen?"

"Twelve years."

He didn't say anything for a moment, then slowly shook his head.

"I would advise against bringing a suit without concrete proof."

"That's it? You'd advise against it?"

"How old are you?"

"Twenty-eight. What does that have to do with anything?"

"I believe if you had returned at age twenty-one and tried to right a wrong, you might have had a chance. Why did you wait so long? Why come forth now?"

Fiona rose.

"Thank you for your time. There were reasons to stay away, and reasons to return to Bradford at this point. I hate to see the bastard walking around like king of the world when I know what he really is. The only question I have is, is he still going after teenage girls?"

She turned and quickly left. Why had she bothered? Nothing good would come of it. McLennon had won twelve years ago, and he was still winning.

It was more important to focus on Margaret and get the town behind her. What was the full extent of the damage she'd caused back then? Fiona wondered. Maybe Cassie's friend Betsy could ask her mother. She'd lived in Bradford her entire life.

Sam stared at the report one of the deputies had written about a domestic-violence call the previous night, but he didn't see a word. He was still kicking himself for kissing Fiona. She'd looked lost, alone and deep-down disappointed. He'd wanted to comfort her.

Not that he'd tell her that. She'd probably knock him upside the head if she found a hint of pity in his manner.

But it wasn't pity, not exactly.

So exactly what was it?

It didn't matter. Once he'd touched his lips to hers, all thought of comfort fled. He'd felt a jolt of desire that almost overwhelmed him. He couldn't believe he hadn't thought of Patty at all for the past several moments.

He'd kissed another woman.

And liked it.

Fiona Hunter, of all women. Nothing like Patty.

Maybe not dating since his wife's death had been a mistake. Especially if he got a hard-on for a hard-nosed cop with an attitude that didn't quit.

There was nothing in it for him. He wasn't looking for a relationship. Besides, she lived in L.A.

He picked up the paper, as if changing the angle would help him concentrate. Instead, his thoughts kept returning to the kiss. Throwing the sheet down, he rose, got his hat and headed for the door. A quick walk through town, a cup of coffee at Ruby's and he'd return to normal.

No more thinking about Fiona Hunter.

"When will you be back?" Marjorie asked as he headed out.

"No telling," he said.

The walk through town in the hot morning sun had an effect, all right. It made him hot and edgy. He spoke when spoken to, but made no effort to charm everyone he encountered.

He went right to the counter at Ruby's and slipped onto a stool.

"Glad you could join me," Adam said from his right.

Sam looked at his friend.

"I didn't see you."

"You didn't see anything. What's up?"

"Nothing."

He nodded at the waitress and she brought him a cup of coffee.

"Anything to go with that, Sheriff?" she asked.

"Piece of apple pie, if you've got it," he said.

"Coming up. Anything more for you, Adam?" she asked.

"I'm fine."

He waited for her to leave, then looked at Sam.

"Trust my finely honed instincts. Something's got you tied in a knot. Crime wave in town?"

"Try a frustrating brunette who dresses like biker trash and butts in where she's not wanted," Sam replied.

"Aha. So our Miss I'm-an-L.A.-cop has you all wound up. What did she do now—order you-know-who's arrest?"

"Almost as bad. She interrogated Mrs. Halstead."

"And that's bad because–?"

"She can't tamper with witnesses. She's the victim in this case, not the investigating officer."

"What tampering?"

Sam sighed, smiled at the waitress when she delivered his pie and took a big bite. She'd heated it just the way he liked it.

"She didn't tamper with anything, but it's the principle. She uncovered something that may or may not tie in."

"Could she have altered the facts, anyway?" Adam asked.

Sam shook his head.

"I'd already found the info. It's the principle of the thing."

"Then I don't see a problem."

"I kissed her."

Adam's mouth fell open. He stared at his longtime friend.

"As in mouth to mouth?"

"Oh, yes."

"You don't seem very happy about it."

"I'm not."

Adam nodded, frowning, as if trying to understand.

"Then why do it?"

Sam wasn't about to admit he couldn't help himself.

"I don't know. She's not my type."

"Patty was your wife—was she a type? Women are individuals. You could well fall in love with someone totally different from Patty. I didn't know you were looking again."

"I'm not. I don't date. I still love Patty."

"Huh."

Adam sipped his own coffee and stared off into space for a moment.

"Patty's been dead for three long years, Sam," he said. "Maybe it's time to move on. Probably kissing Fiona was just hormones."

"That's a woman's cop-out. Not a man's."

"So go with your feminine side."

Adam grinned.

Sam gave him a look.

"You know what you can do with your feminine side."

Adam laughed. "There had to be a reason you kissed her, and what better excuse than lust, which comes from hormones. Anyway, what I'm trying to say is cut yourself some slack. You're young. Time to find a mate. Patty wouldn't have wanted you to grieve forever."

"Patty wouldn't have wanted to die young."

"No, but she did. You didn't. Move on."

Adam spoke softly, conscious of others in the café.

"She looked so needy," Sam said slowly.

Adam shook his head.

"Fiona Hunter? Man, she eats sharks for breakfast."

"She wants you to think so. I believe she's had a tough row to hoe her whole life. Anyway, it was an impulse. One I don't plan to repeat."

"No good, huh?" Adam said.

Sam didn't respond. It had been too brief to rate. The only thing he knew for sure was it left him wanting more.

Not that he planned to admit that to anyone.

"Cassie's trying out a new recipe tonight," Adam said. "Want to come to dinner?"

Sam looked at him suspiciously.

"Why?"

"'Cause I'm going to be there with Piper, and you'll

have to eat alone again if you don't come."

"What time?"

"Six-thirty. It's some chicken dish, and then a coconut cream pie for dessert. I'm going to miss her cooking when we leave for Paris."

"Piper doesn't cook?"

"Apparently not. I'm sure we'll muddle by, but I want to enjoy Cassie's meals as long as I can."

"I'll be there."

Sam didn't question his decision. For the first time since his wife's death, he looked forward to a social event.

Piper wandered into Fiona's room around five-thirty.

"What's up?" she asked, tossing a couple of dresses on the bed.

"Not much. What are those?"

"Some clothes I thought you might wear in your new undercover role."

Piper looked at the black jeans and black tank top Fiona wore.

"What happened to the softer image? Getting town folks on your side."

"Waste of time. I saw a lawyer today and he said as much. No criminal charges, no civil suit, nada. I'm back to being me."

Piper sat on the bed.

"Bummer. Nothing to be done?"

Fiona shook her head. She tried to concentrate on

the magazine she was holding, but Piper's silence caused her to look up.

Her friend looked at her suspiciously.

"Not like you to back down," she said.

"I'm not going to bang my head against a brick wall."

"What are you going to do? Just slink back to L.A.?"

"I'm not slinking anywhere. I'll stay for the blasted fair and then head out. Actually, I thought of something I could do at the fair."

She explained her idea to Piper, who thought it was wonderful.

"Imagine you with children. Who'd have thought?"

"Hey," Fiona said, scowling, "I like kids. I never said I didn't."

"I know, but seeing you dressed like that, one naturally thinks that children would be the furthest thing from your mind. It's so cool. Can you paint something on my face, too?"

"Sure, it's extra, though."

"Why?"

"You can afford it, and all the proceeds go to Margaret's medical fund."

Piper pursed her lips a moment.

"Fine. I think this event will work, don't you? The models coming have volunteered their time, and two have already sent a donation. Adam says his friends with the New Orleans Saints plan on donating, as well as signing autographs and getting their pictures taken with people. Margaret's coming for an hour or so. Cassie got the doctor to sign off on the idea. Which leads me back to the dresses. You can't wear clothes like you have on or you'll scare the kids. Try on the dresses and see what you think. I love the blue one, but the yellow might be more your color."

Fiona grudgingly gave in and changed into the blue sun dress. It was fitted at the bodice and had a straight skirt that fell to just above her knees. She simpered as she crossed the floor, mocking the modeling techniques she'd seen.

Piper laughed at her antics.

"I never have to fear competition from you. I don't like it on you. Try the yellow."

Fiona complied, getting into the swing of things. It was much more suited to her, with spaghetti straps that showed off her shoulders and arms and a flared skirt that swayed when she moved, caressing her bare legs. Once again she felt that kick of femininity.

"Ooh, looking good. Let's see what else we can do," Piper said, jumping up and going to the dresser. "Don't you have any makeup?"

"Just that mascara."

"I'll be right back."

Piper left the room on a run. Fiona went to the small mirror and tried to see as much of herself as she could. She and Piper were both slender, though Piper was an inch or two taller. The dress fit as if she'd bought it for herself. Yes, it would be more suitable for the fair than wearing black.

"Here, sit and let me do something with your hair,"

Piper said the instant she was back.

She went into full dress mode, and in less than half an hour she'd styled Fiona's hair, put on a minimum of makeup and declared Fiona fit to be seen in public.

Piper tilted her head to study her work.

"You'll have the guys lined up at your door."

Fiona looked into the mirror. Her eyes looked large and mysterious, her hair soft and almost sweet. She looked pretty.

"Dinner in fifteen," Cassie called up the stairs. "I could use some help down here."

"We're ready," Piper said, tucking her arm into Fiona's and moving them toward the door.

"I don't need to wear this to dinner," Fiona said. "It'll do for the fair, though."

"Why change? Let's get downstairs now to make sure we get all the food we want."

"Who else is coming?" Fiona asked as they walked down the hall.

"Now, you just guess," Piper said.

"Matt and Adam. Dumb question."

"Hey, be glad I'm sharing time with you. I could spend it all with Adam."

"You will soon enough."

"Soon, maybe, but not soon enough. You'll have to come visit us in Paris."

"Next vacation," Fiona said as they walked down the stairs.

"How soon will that be?"

Fiona grinned.

"Who knows?"

Entering the kitchen, they were both stopped by the heat. Steam rose from two pans on the stove. The oven was on. Cassie was taking biscuits out of it. The fragrance of baking chicken and biscuits filled the room.

"Oh, man, it's hot in here."

"Do you think?" Cassie asked. "I thought it too hot to eat outside, so it'll be the dining room. Can you two set the table?"

"It's Piper's turn," Fiona said quickly.

"What?"

"That last night we were all here with Margaret, it was your turn to set the table and you didn't," Fiona said.

Both women stared at her.

"You've remembered that all these years?" Cassie asked at last.

"Sure. I remember everything."

"Amazing."

Piper went to get the silverware.

"But I can still help," Fiona said, reaching up in the cupboard for iced tea glasses.

"Six for dinner," Cassie said.

Fiona turned. "Who else?"

"Adam asked Sam."

Fiona blinked, looking at Cassie, who was stirring the white sauce on the stove. She looked at Piper, but she was already on the way to the dining room.

Sam was coming to dinner? And here she was, dressed fit to kill.

Conspiracy all around.

8

She stormed into the dining room.

"This is a setup," she said, placing the glasses on the table and glaring at Piper.

"Whatever are you talking about?"

Piper carefully set each place, her eyes on the silverware.

"You got me all dolled up for Sam."

Piper did look up at that, her eyes wide.

"For Sam? There's something going on between you and Sam?"

"No."

"Cassie, come in here," Piper called.

Fiona groaned, sorry she'd opened her mouth. Now they'd want to know every detail. Well, she was determined not to give an inch.

"What?"

"Did you know there's something going on between Fiona and Sam and she didn't tell us?" Piper said.

"Shut up," Fiona grumbled.

"Fiona and Sam?" Cassie looked between them. "You're kidding. Is that why she's all dolled up tonight?"

Piper laughed.

"Apparently."

"I'm going to kill you," Fiona said.

"Then the sheriff would have to lock you up," Piper teased. "Maybe kiss you while he does it."

Cassie looked at them, a smile starting.

"Mmm. Kisses from the sheriff."

"Only one," Fiona snapped, annoyed.

Obviously Sam had told someone. Probably Adam.

"And if anyone says a word during dinner I will personally make your life miserable."

Fiona turned to head for the stairs, but Piper caught her arm.

"Oh, no, you don't. I didn't spend all that time and energy to have you show up in your motorcycle mode. Finish setting the table and you can fill us both in on what's going on."

"Nothing's going on."

"Darn," Cassie said.

"It was one lousy kiss," Fiona growled as she slammed down the glasses at the tip of each knife.

Both her foster sisters stared at her.

"Lousy as in not any good?" Cassie asked. "Seems to me Sam could do better than that."

"He hasn't looked at anyone since his wife died, Adam told me," Piper added.

"Is that how you know about the kiss, from Adam? Did Sam *tell* Adam?"

Fiona wasn't sure how she felt, but she would never

have said a word. What kind of game was the sheriff playing?

"Hey, Adam's an investigative reporter, and he has sources and ways of finding out things," Piper said, amusement dancing in her eyes.

"I can't stay for dinner," Fiona said.

"Of course you can," Cassie said. "Talk to the man. He's nice. I think he's a bit lonely. He's still sort of new in town and hasn't made a lot of friends. Matt likes him."

As if that put the definitive stamp of approval on anything, Fiona thought.

"Give me a break. The man's been here more than two years, been in office almost that long and knows half the town, if not more. If he doesn't have friends, it's because he doesn't want them," Fiona argued.

But her heart wasn't in it. She was intrigued by the man. And what could it hurt to have a mild flirtation while she visited? And mild was probably all it'd be. She was years out of practice.

"He's still mourning his wife, I think," Cassie said slowly.

"Then he has no time or interest in me."

Or maybe that was exactly why he had kissed her—he knew she'd be moving on and so would have no expectations. If it had been years since his wife died, he might just want to get laid. She squirmed with the thought that maybe that was all there was to their kiss—a prelude.

"And do you want him to?" Cassie asked.

Fiona bit her lip. Did she want him to have an interest in her? She'd told herself no. She believed it—sort of.

"Maybe just the tiniest bit," she confessed.

"It's not like we expect you to marry the guy," Piper said, "but why not hang out with him while you're here? Give you both someone to be with. Adam wants Sam to do things with us, but he won't as odd man out. This way all of us can do things together and it won't be awkward."

"Until you two play kissy-face," Fiona said.

"Okay, we won't while you two are around," Cassie said.

"We won't?" Piper protested.

"If that's what it takes."

"If what is what it takes?" Matt asked, entering the dining room from the front of the house.

"Whatever works, love. How was your day?" Cassie asked, coming around the table to kiss him.

Fiona watched, wishing secretly that the kiss Sam had given her was more like what Matt was giving Cassie. Her toes almost curled, but she couldn't look away. There was as much joy and delight in the kiss as there was lust. What would it be like to be part of a couple that was so deeply committed and in love?

She glanced at Piper.

"So much for no kissy-face."

"Oops."

Cassie pulled away.

"We're embarrassing Fiona," she said.

"Hey, don't stop on my account. It's better than an R-rated movie."

Matt grinned at her.

"Much better live and in person," he said, reaching for Cassie again.

But she evaded his hands.

"Dinner's almost ready. You can help bring things in."

She motioned with her head toward the kitchen and Matt followed.

"Oh, that was subtle," Fiona said with a small smile.

"Well, at least it isn't in front of you," Piper said, looking over the table to see if anything was missing.

"Not me, me and Sam. Did he tell Adam?"

"Sort of. He's not sure what's going on. I think he believed he'd mourn Patty his whole life and now finds he's attracted to you."

"Come on, Piper, we're worlds apart."

"Both cops, both want justice—I see a lot of similarities."

"What was his wife like?"

"I haven't a clue. Adam doesn't talk about her much. He knew her, of course—he and Sam have been friends since they were in grade school together in Baton Rouge. He liked her and said it was a tragedy she died like that."

"How?"

"Young, for one thing. It was a drunk driver, what else? Seems so prevalent these days. It was during

Mardi Gras, lots of drinking and carousing."

"Hard to deal with, whatever the cause," Fiona said.

Fiona heard a car in the driveway and tensed. She felt foolish, like she was on some stupid blind date or something. Trying to quell the nerves, she went into the kitchen to see about getting the pitcher of iced tea. Filling the glasses would give her something to do when Adam and Sam arrived. Anything to avoid that awkward first few minutes. Once they began to eat, she expected things to settle down.

She was surprised at the instant awareness that hit when Sam entered the room. She looked up, and then dropped her gaze back to the pitcher, as if pouring tea was as important and delicate as brain surgery.

He looked super. For one thing, he'd changed into khaki slacks and a pale sports shirt, opened at the throat.

"Hello, Fiona," Adam said, coming in right behind Sam.

"Hi."

She reached the last glass. Now what?

"Evening, Fiona."

Sam's sexy low voice sounded right by her left ear. She looked up and into his dark eyes.

"Hi."

That breathy voice was not hers. She never sounded like that.

"Let me take this," he said, reaching for the almost empty pitcher. "Cassie will want to fill it up and get it cooling."

He disappeared into the kitchen.

"Looking good, Fiona," Adam said easily, leaning over to give Piper a quick kiss.

Piper whispered something in his ear and he looked at her in astonishment.

"Not really?"

"Yes, really."

Adam looked at Fiona and she knew Piper had told him no kisses in front of her and Sam. Sheesh, he'd think she was some Victorian prude. Unless Piper told him the reason, in which case, Fiona would be even more embarrassed.

Once everyone was seated and began to eat Cassie's chicken, Fiona began to relax. The conversation was general, and no one was paying special attention to her. She looked across the table at Sam, who was talking with Matt about the local sewer system. Life seemed back to normal.

What was a brief touching of lips among colleagues?

Of course, if her own partner had ever kissed her, she'd probably have decked him.

Sam was different.

"You need to go see Margaret again. You haven't seen her that much since you've been here and she wants to see you," Piper said.

Conversation stopped and everyone looked at Fiona.

"How do you know that? She can't talk. Besides,

I've been there a couple of times."

"She *can* communicate. She's really getting good at it. You just have to know how to interpret things. She's slowly getting her speech ability back. She can say some words now, only they're not the ones she's trying to say. I can't think of anything more frustrating. Hope I never get a stroke. Anyway, you'll need a lot of patience, but she can usually get her meaning across."

"Things like strokes run in families, don't they?" Fiona asked.

Piper beamed.

"You're right. So maybe I'm in trouble, but I don't care. It's all worth it to have family. Go visit her, Fiona."

Fiona shrugged.

"I have nothing more to say to her. I apologized for my lies. Told her about my life in L.A. What else is there?"

"Tell her you missed her, that you love her and are glad to be here again. And tell her what you're doing."

"About what?"

"Anything and everything."

Tension spiked again. She didn't need this. Her glance flicked to Sam, then away from his knowing gaze.

"We can walk over after dinner if you like," he said. "She should see you all dressed up. I expect you were in black when you went before."

"Safe guess," Piper said. "That's all she wears."

"This is not black and I'm wearing it," Fiona

protested.

Piper started to open her mouth, then closed it and shrugged, glancing pointedly at Sam.

Fiona frowned and tried to get control of her wayward senses. She seemed attuned to Sam. It was only the suggestions placed in her mind by her so-called friends. She needed some distance to get things back into perspective.

"I'm sure Margaret would like to see you again, too, Sam," Adam said.

Fiona didn't respond. Time enough later to make her position on not visiting Margaret clear. No need upsetting anyone at dinner. But she didn't want to go.

By the time dinner was eaten and the dishes washed, the others had decided to walk to town for ice cream.

"You did that the other night," Fiona said, unsure she wanted to be paired with Sam parading through town.

"I could eat ice cream every night," Adam said.

"Comes from being in those arid countries so much," Piper said, patting his shoulder. "Paris has lots of things you can indulge in."

He grinned at her.

"Mostly it has you," he said.

Fiona wasn't sure she could stand this lovey-dovey stuff much longer.

"Okay, let's go if we're going."

"Impatience isn't good in a cop," Sam said, coming next to her. "Ever done stakeouts?"

"Only twice—about drove me up the wall," she said, stepping away.

He moved closer again.

"I like my space," she said softly.

"I like your space, too," he said, stepping even closer.

She could feel the heat radiating from his body.

Turning, she pushed open the back door and started out. Before long all six were paired on the sidewalk heading into the main part of Bradford.

Piper walked on Adam's left, leaving the right side for his cane. Matt slung his arm around Cassie's shoulders, pulling her close. Her arm was around his waist. Fiona remembered they used to walk around high school like that when they'd all lived in town.

"What's the problem with seeing Margaret?" Sam asked quietly.

They were the last couple, and he slowed his pace slightly, letting the distance grow between them and Adam and Piper.

"It's awkward," she said, not wanting to go into details.

"The woman loved all you girls when you lived with her. Cassie told me how much she'd done for each of you, making dresses, keeping your rooms like shrines. She had to expect you'd come back."

"I should have returned long ago."

"Maybe, but the point is, you're here now. Don't waste time in regrets. She's getting better, but who knows when another stroke might hit, with different results?"

Fiona walked a few steps as the words penetrated. Life was fleeting. She wished so many times over the years she could have turned back the clock to before that fateful day. She would have done everything differently.

Sam took her hand, threading his fingers through hers. She was shocked at the contact.

"Come on, Fiona, I'll go with you."

She tugged slightly, but his grip only tightened.

"What is it you want, Sam?" she asked, looking at the two couples ahead of them.

"Just to be friends. Colleagues."

"To set the record straight, I don't hold hands with my colleagues in L.A."

"Good," he said, squeezing her hand gently, then relaxed his grip slightly. "I don't want to be one of many."

When the others reached the ice cream parlor, they turned to wait for Fiona and Sam.

"We'll catch y'all later," Sam said. "We're going to see Margaret."

"Maybe she'd like some ice cream," Fiona said, stalling.

"Good idea. What's her favorite kind?"

"Vanilla," Fiona said.

Piper and Cassie looked at each other and then at Fiona. "You remembered," Piper said.

"Sure, and Cassie's is pralines and cream and yours is chocolate."

"And yours is peach," Cassie said with a beaming smile.

"I hate it when they start reminiscing," Matt said easily. "Here I am at a loss what Adam's and Sam's favorite flavors are."

"Oh, you," Cassie said, giving him a slight push. "Who cares. Come on and let's sample whatever they have. This is one dessert I don't fix."

With a small cup of vanilla ice cream in hand, Fiona entered the hospital ward a little later, Sam at her side. She felt as nervous as when she'd made her first bust, hoping she'd do things right, uncertain about the entire scenario.

Margaret was in bed, sitting up and watching television. There was another woman in the bed next to her, crocheting as she also watched.

"Hi," Fiona said.

Margaret looked, her eyes brightening. "H-h-h-ah-ah-ah," she tried.

"You're looking good," Sam said, pulling a chair near the bed for Fiona. "Gave us quite a scare, you know."

Margaret smiled her lopsided smile and nodded. Patting the bed awkwardly, she looked at Fiona.

"We brought you some ice cream. You can have it, can't you?" Fiona held out the carton.

"Sure she can, she's not on a restricted diet like me," the woman in the next bed said. "Just push the call button and tell the nurse you need a spoon."

"We brought one," Fiona said, holding up the plastic spoon wrapped in a napkin.

Margaret took the spoon in her left hand. Sam popped the lid off the carton and held it while she scraped ice cream onto the spoon.

"Mmm," she said, savoring the taste.

"Fiona remembered your favorite was vanilla," Sam said.

Margaret tried to say something, but the words came out garbled.

"Can say a word or two if she takes her time," her roommate said. "I'm sure she'll be talking as normal as the rest of us in no time, right, Margaret?"

Margaret nodded her head, her eyes on Fiona.

"Pr-pr-pr..."

"Pretty?" Sam guessed.

Margaret nodded.

"She is pretty. Should dress like a girl more often, wouldn't you say?

Fiona ignored him.

"I'm undercover," she said to Margaret.

"Undercover? Are you a cop?" the roommate asked.

"She's teasing Margaret. I'm Sheriff Witt, I don't believe we've met," he said.

"I'm Harriet Moore. I live outside town and haven't had a need for the sheriff. Glad to meet you."

"This is Fiona Hunter. Fiona, meet Harriet."

Sam gave her shoulder a gentle nudge.

"How do you do?" Fiona said with mock politeness.

"Pleasure. You kin to Margaret? Her granddaughters are in here all the time. Don't think I've seen you before."

Fiona was startled to hear Harriet call both Piper and Cassie Margaret's granddaughters. It fit with Piper. Did Cassie know? She'd probably be happy enough with the designation.

Fiona wished she could feel she deserved to be included as kin.

"Just a friend visiting."

Margaret shook her head. She dropped the spoon in the cup and reached out to grasp Fiona's hand. "Mohmoh."

"More?" Sam said.

She nodded emphatically.

Fiona turned her hand over and held tightly to Margaret's, feeling the ice around her heart begin to melt slightly.

"Thank you, Margaret."

"Shall we take a walk?" Sam asked.

Both women looked at him.

"I see a wheelchair in the corner. Isn't it for Margaret?"

"It is," Harriet confirmed. "Go on, dear. I'd go in a second if a handsome young man like that asked me."

She grinned at Sam and Fiona, then resumed her crocheting, keeping an eye on the television screen.

Once away from the room, Sam relinquished the chair to Fiona.

"Take her to the solarium. My guess is it will be pretty empty at this time of day. You two can have some privacy. I'll be waiting in the lobby."

Fiona looked surprised, but took the handles. Sam waited until she'd pushed Margaret down the hall, watching Fiona until he couldn't see her anymore. She looked so different tonight, he'd almost forgotten his own name.

Why the change? For a split second when he'd first seen her in the dining room pouring tea, he'd thought she was someone else. Her eyes tonight seemed glowing, mysterious. Her hair was soft enough to entice a man's hand. The dress emphasized her slender, toned body. Curves in all the right places. His palm had itched all night to caress the creamy skin of her shoulders. Maybe he'd get the chance on the walk home.

Maybe he could invite her back to his home.

And what? Adam was staying there. And did he think Fiona's new look was due to anything other than Fiona's idea of working undercover to reestablish a good reputation in Bradford, pending whatever legal action they came up with against McLennon?

He took the elevator to the lobby and found an empty seat near the doors. He could see everyone going in or out and had a clear view of the elevators.

He hoped Fiona would use the time with Margaret to mend fences. He could see the hunger in her for acceptance, though she'd erected such high walls around herself most others wouldn't have a clue.

Did Cassie or Piper?

Was it only a game to her, pretend to be a sweet Southern gal, get the truth accepted and then move on? She'd made no pretense to anything but being a cop on a mission. And never hinted she had any liking for Bradford.

Sam wondered if he'd like L.A. He'd never been to California, though he and Patty had traveled a bit around the East Coast. After her death, he'd grown weary of living and working in New Orleans. The crime was never-ending. The slower pace of this little town suited him, which constantly surprised him.

"Sheriff?"

Sam looked up. He'd been lost in thought and hadn't seen his deputy come.

Sam rose. "Evening, Michael. Did you need me?"

"No, I didn't know you were here. My great aunt Alice is here. She had her hip replaced and is here until she can go home," the deputy said.

Sam nodded. Standard procedure.

"I didn't expect to see you here," Michael said.

"I'm waiting for a friend."

"Oh."

Just then Fiona came out of the elevator and spotted Sam. She walked over, studying the deputy.

"All set?" Sam asked.

"Sure. She's back in bed and tired out. Thanks for waiting."

"Of course."

The deputy looked at Fiona, and then at Sam, a

smile popping out.

"I haven't met your girl yet, Sheriff," he said.

Fiona looked startled, her eyes widening.

Before she could say anything, Sam spoke.

"Fiona Hunter, Michael Deview, one of my best deputies. Fiona's visiting from Los Angeles."

"Nice to meet you."

Fiona murmured the same.

Michael nodded and went to the elevators.

Fiona looked at Sam.

"Your girl?"

"Good a cover as any, don't you think?"

"Is that what everyone in town thinks, that I'm your girl?"

"I have no idea what everyone in town thinks. But I heard from Marjorie that there's rampant speculation in the department at least about my seeing you."

"Because you usually don't date."

"Usually not. And you've been to the station several times already," he said. "Ready to go?"

Fiona nodded and started for the door.

"This is ridiculous."

"What is?" Sam asked easily as they headed out into the night.

Fiona looked around, but no one was paying them any attention.

"We need to be searching for proof of McLennon's crime, not making nice for the townspeople."

The sidewalk was deserted as they walked toward the center of town. The crickets hummed. Stars dotted the sky, dimly seen through the ambient light from the streets.

"I said I'd handle it," Sam said.

He was coming to realize how impatient Fiona was.

"So what have you done so far?" she challenged.

"Talked to George Wilson, for one thing," he said.

"Who's George Wilson?"

Sam stopped near the square. The playground was empty this late. The gazebo shone with the spotlight the town had erected a couple of years ago, right after he moved to Bradford.

The benches were in darkness. All the better for kids when they wanted to make out. Too early for that.

"Come on and sit down. I'll fill you in and hope to curb some of your impatience."

"Jeez, do me a favor."

"I am."

They sat on the bench nearest the sidewalk.

"George Wilson was, until a year ago, a loan officer in the bank. He helped me when I applied for a mortgage for my house. I was new to town, had started in the job and was a renter in New Orleans, so didn't know my way around mortgages. He walked me through every step, and then cut a few corners, because it's a small-town bank and George doesn't want people caught up in red tape."

"How nice for you."

"He was there for more than thirty years, working his way up from teller to senior loan officer."

"Nice for him. The point?"

"He remembers Sheriff Halstead's mortgage."

9

Fiona sat up at that. "And?"

"And he said it was strange how the entire thing came about, and the outcome," Sam said.

"How strange?"

"The sheriff had too many debts to qualify for the size of the mortgage he got on the house, even though the bank sold it at a loss."

"Sold it at a loss?"

"You knew they sold it at below appraised value. What you didn't see was Halstead got it approved at ten thousand less and the bank absorbed the difference. And approved a marginally qualified mortgagee."

"They can do that?"

"When the vice president signs off on it," Sam said.

"McLennon was the vice president then."

"You got it."

Fiona leaned back on the bench, gazing off into nothing. Sam could almost see the wheels turning in her mind.

"When was this?" she asked.

"The week after you and the others were sent to

different homes," Sam said.

"And George remembered it all these years later but didn't think it odd at the time?"

"He thought it was very odd. That's why he remembers it."

"Why didn't he say something then?"

"To whom and why? No one had any idea there was any connection between McLennon and you. People thought either Margaret had done it or one of your boyfriends."

"I didn't have boyfriends," Fiona said.

"No?"

"I hung out with some boys, but none of them were, you know, a *real* boyfriend, if that's what you think. Mostly we talked about getting out of Bradford, or how to steal from the local five-and-dime."

"You stole from the five-and-dime?" he asked.

"Naw. Margaret would have skinned me alive. But I listened to their talk. And offered some quiet persuasion against it."

"How?"

"Every way they thought of, I found a glitch that could get them caught. If they wanted out of Bradford, they sure didn't want to go to juvie. As far as I know, it worked."

"Teen cop in disguise," Sam said, almost laughing at the irony.

Everyone thought Fiona was the wild one, and instead she had done her best to deter juvenile crime sprees.

"It was sort of fun, challenging, if you know what I mean."

"That led you to police work?"

"Maybe. Now what?"

"I'm not sure. Knowing there was a connection adds another layer, but it's not enough to do anything with."

"I know. I wish the sheriff had left a note, you know, the Open-If-Something-Happens-to-Me kind, with all the facts neatly laid out."

"Ever see one of those?"

"No."

"I think they're only in TV and movies. Can you remember where the cottage was he took you to?"

"Yeah, I think so. I could find it if I cruised the road long enough. It wasn't a place I'd ever seen before and I was whisked out of town so fast, I was never sure where it was. But if it's still there, I probably could find it. I drew a sketch of it the other day. I was never inside. Any blood that dropped would have long been washed away by rain."

"I wasn't thinking of that, just curious. Could be there are neighbors who saw or heard something that night."

"No lights anywhere. I know, I was desperate when I got away and looking for any place I could get to. Besides, no one came forth at the time. Who do you expect to pop up as a possible witness at this late date?"

"I don't expect anything, just want to see it."

"I need to get back to the house," Fiona said, rising.

They walked in silence for several blocks.

"No special boyfriend?" Sam asked.

"No."

Sam began to calculate the odds.

"Someone waiting for you in L.A.?"

"No. What is this—twenty questions? I don't ask you personal questions."

"Feel free," he offered.

A nagging suspicion took hold.

"I don't have any."

He was disappointed and surprised he'd feel that way. She had no reason to want to know anything personal about him. To her he was just the sheriff looking into an old case.

"Maybe one," Fiona said a moment later.

"And that is?"

He braced himself. Adam had asked him why he wasn't dating. Did he have an answer to the question?

"How can you stand living here after New Orleans?"

"That came out of left field," he said.

"Why? It's a fair question."

"I asked about your love life and you ask about living here versus living there?"

"I wanted to leave so badly when I was a kid," she explained. "I couldn't imagine why all the people who lived here stayed—at least, not the adults who had the opportunity to get out."

"So tell me what L.A. has that Bradford doesn't."

"Excitement, for one. Things to do, places to go."

"Like?"

Fiona walked almost half a block before answering.

"I work a lot," she said.

"You must date, go to all those places, do things."

"I go to the beach on my off time."

"With?"

"Friends."

"You could go to the pool here, if you wanted to fry your skin."

"I don't go to sunbathe. I swim and enjoy the surf."

"I've found since I moved here that I can do all I want here in Bradford. I can drive into New Orleans if I choose—it's only a little over an hour and a half away. I thought by moving away from the city, I'd be bored out of my mind. But I like knowing my neighbors. Like feeling what I'm doing makes a difference."

"Everyone knows your business," she said. "Look at that deputy."

"Everyone looks out for one another," he said. "You and Piper and Cassie came home to look out for Margaret."

"I came to make things right, if I can."

"How did your visit go tonight?"

"I still feel guilty about what happened."

"I'm thinking you weren't totally to blame. Think about it, Fiona. The investigation was shoddy. The cover-up swift and complete. And nothing else ever came of it. You were a double victim, first of the crime, then of someone's manipulations. Yeah, we all agree you should never have lied about Margaret, but there were adults in charge. They were supposed to investigate and discover the truth."

"And the sheriff got a new house," Fiona said bitterly. "If I had come back when I was eighteen, maybe I could have changed things."

"Or maybe not. Don't forget, the sheriff had even more reason to keep a lid on things if he'd actually taken a bribe to do it."

They reached the house and walked slowly up the crushed-shell driveway. Fiona was reluctant to have the evening end. She told herself it was because Sam made such sense and she wanted to continue discussing the case with him.

There was also a small hope he'd kiss her before he left.

"Hey, we wondered when you two would show up," Piper called from the front porch.

Fiona's heart sank. There was no way she'd let Sam kiss her in front of an audience. If there was speculation now, what would happen if someone *saw* them embrace?

"I spent longer with Margaret than I thought I would," she said.

"I'll take off," Sam said.

Fiona stopped and looked at him, wishing that they were alone on the front porch.

"Thanks for everything."

"Let me know if you think you can locate that cottage. I'd like to see it."

"Will do."

Sam turned and headed back. Fiona watched a moment, then realized what she was doing and quickly headed to the house. Piper and Adam sat on the old swing on the porch, lazily moving it back and forth.

"Did Margaret like the ice cream?" Piper asked.

"She sure did. Sam left us alone for a while. I still find it frustrating to try to communicate with her. And she gets so frustrated."

"You're too impatient. She and I do fine. But I have all the time in the world, so don't mind if it takes her a long time to get her thoughts together."

"And she's your newly discovered grandmother. You'd probably be just as happy to sit in silence all day."

"Pretty much," Piper agreed.

"See ya," Fiona said, and went into the house.

The place smelled of paint and sawdust. Cassie refused to let Matt's men get started on renovating the kitchen as long as she was living in the house. So the work continued on the second level. Soon they'd move to the third floor and then have nothing left to do except the kitchen.

Fiona got ready for bed and slipped between the sheets. Flicking off the bedside light, she lay in the dark thinking about things, like what her life might have been like if she hadn't skipped school that day and ended up on the other side of town. Or if she'd refused to get in the car with Allen McLennon. Or if she'd never accused Margaret. So many wrong steps along the path, any of which would have caused problems.

Still, she'd been sixteen years old, not an adult. She had done nothing to invoke Allen's attack. She didn't remember even once seeing the man after she'd escaped his clutches. Shouldn't he at least have been brought in for questioning, given her accusations?

No wonder he'd rewarded the sheriff. A hint of scandal would have been deadly in his job. It still was. Even a visit to the sheriff's office would have fueled speculation.

Now it appeared no one, except Margaret, had any idea whom she'd accused.

She heard Piper come upstairs and go into the room she was sharing with Cassie. There were soft murmurs. Cassie must already be in for the night.

Fiona smiled. It felt like the old days. All three of Margaret's girls were home and safe.

The day before the Independence Day fair was hectic. The fairgrounds, beyond the high school football field, were used for 4-H and other activities during the year, but on the Fourth of July a carnival was set up. The carnies were already bolting skeletons of steel together for the Ferris wheel and other rides. Huge cables snaked across the grass, bringing electricity to the booths and rides that needed them.

The tent for the fashion show had been erected the day before. Fiona and Piper were unfolding dozens of chairs and lining them up. Three of Matt's crew were assembling the platform runway and speaker's area. The heat and humidity made Fiona wish she could forget the entire thing and go find a cool spot to lie down in.

"Suzanne DeBois arrives tonight," Piper said, mentioning one of the models volunteering for the fund raiser. "The others will be here during the day. I hope the accommodations at the motel will suit."

She slammed open another folding chair.

"I'm tired of this. Oh, for a cold drink. The bottled water is getting warm in this heat."

"I could go get us something," Fiona offered.

She wanted the break, but also wanted to see the other booths. She had a small one for the face painting nearby. She'd received her paints yesterday, along with a packet of balloons she could use to make characters for children. Toy dogs, clowns, angels. She'd offer that as long as her supply lasted.

Piper looked over the empty expanse that was left.

"We're halfway done. Let's keep going and get it over with."

"Okay."

Fiona opened another chair, aligning it with the one beside it.

"I haven't seen Sam since the other night when he came to dinner," Piper said, starting on the row behind Fiona.

"I expect he's busy," Fiona replied, opening another chair.

She wore jeans and a sleeveless top and wished she'd worn a dress like Piper. Dresses, she'd discovered, were cooler.

"Adam said Sam responded to an accident on the interstate yesterday. It was a multi car pileup. Guess it took all the sheriff's department and some patrol guys from the other county. Gruesome. Don't know how you cops do it."

"It's not easy. But we get used to it, I guess. In my area, vice—in high schools—I don't see a lot of dead bodies."

"You're coming to dinner, right? Cassie and Betsy will have everything at the Elk's Club at seven. All the models will be in by then, except Suzanne. And those New Orleans Saints Adam's so high on."

Fiona smiled. Piper had never been into sports.

"I have to if I want to eat. Nice of Cassie and Betsy to cater the meal."

"It's the least we can do for everyone volunteering their time and letting us trade in on their reputations."

Fiona nodded, feeling a small knot of apprehension. Tomorrow she'd be on public display, on her own, painting faces and making balloon animals. Cassie would be busy with her booth, and Piper would be running things here. They'd discussed it last night. Piper was worried about the news of Margaret being her grandmother causing unkind gossip. But Cassie was certain that the three girls from Bradford Hall making a solid show of support for Margaret would be stronger, more interesting news than Piper's blood relationship to Margaret.

Fiona wasn't so sure. She had a feeling there'd be a lot of speculation and gossip about each of them. If anyone asked about the fateful day, they'd decided to tell the truth: Fiona had been attacked and the sheriff had not done his job in apprehending the culprit.

After Fiona's consultation with the lawyer, they'd agreed not to tell anyone else who the culprit had been, pending getting enough information to bring the case to court.

"Where is Adam?" Fiona asked.

"Meeting his friends from the Saints. They're all staying at Sam's. Adam and Michael Thomas were friends in high school. Sam, too, I guess, since they are all from Baton Rouge."

"Have you met Adam's parents yet?"

"No. Odd, isn't it? I'm getting married in a few days and will meet them just before the wedding. His sister and her family, as well."

"Not so odd. You aren't marrying them, just him."

"I'm not sure it works that way. I want a large family, and being an aunt and all is part of it. I can't wait to meet Alice and her kids. I hope they like me."

"What's not to like?"

"My past, for one thing."

"It's the present and future that count," Fiona said.

She opened another chair, turned it around and sat on it.

"What are you doing?"

"Taking a break before I melt. It's never this hot in

L.A."

"Five minutes only," Piper said, sitting in the chair behind Fiona.

"Then I'm going for a cold drink."

She ran her fingers through her hair, lifting it to get some air on her neck.

"Do you ever wonder about staying here?" Fiona asked, half turning so she could see her friend.

"We plan to buy a place to retire to here."

Fiona sighed.

"We wanted out so badly when we lived here. Bradford seems so different now."

Piper let her hair drop and nodded.

"Because *we're* different. We've seen the world out there and it's great. But this little spot is okay itself. I realized that when I learned Cassie's planning to stay. She likes it. Likes the neighborliness, having roots. I want a place to call home. To come back to. I love Paris, but don't see myself living there when I'm old."

"What about kids?"

"What about them?"

"Planning on having any?"

Piper was silent for a moment.

"I want to. But it'll play havoc with my career. Unless I can get some special deal for maternity clothes. But a model's career doesn't last that long, anyway. I think children with Adam would very much ease the loss of my job. Don't you want kids?"

"I don't plan to marry," Fiona said.

"You say that now, but if you meet the right man,

you'll change your mind."

"With my history? Look at my parents. My father tried to kill my mother. She was an addict. Not a good family to be from. What if I turn out like one or the other, or pass on bad genes to children?"

Piper laughed.

"You are *nothing* like your parents. Margaret made sure of that when she raised us all. And I think that was environmental circumstance, not genetics. You think little babies are born programmed to become drug addicts?"

"Only if their mothers are hooked when they're pregnant."

"Yours wasn't, not then, and you turned out fine."

Fiona tried to smile. She didn't feel fine. She felt messed up and confused and uncertain.

"Goofing off on the job?" Cassie called, entering the tent with a large basket.

"Guilty," Fiona called back.

"We're taking a break and talking about babies," Piper said as Cassie approached.

"Ooh, I want in on that conversation." Cassie sat by Piper and set the basket on the ground. "I've brought refreshments."

"I hope there's something cold and wet in there," Fiona said, leaning over the back of her chair for a better look.

"Lemonade, icy cold with lots of ice cubes to keep it that way," Cassie said, taking out a large jar. She unscrewed the wide top and poured it into the cups

Piper had pulled from the basket.

"Heaven," said Fiona after she'd taken a swallow.

"Now, what's this about babies?" Cassie persisted.

"Fiona asked if I wanted any. I do. Don't you?"

"I'll have a dozen if I can. Wonder if Matt would like that many. We're both alone in the world, except for you two and Margaret. I want a large family."

"Me, too," Piper said. "Though maybe not immediately. I'll have to give up modeling once I have a baby. I want to be there full time for my kids. Fiona says she doesn't even want to get married."

Cassie nodded. "So have a kid without a husband, Fiona. But I think it would be more fun with."

Fiona frowned.

"I don't see myself as a mother, either."

"Wait until you fall in love. Then you'll want lots of little girls and boys running around looking like you and your mate."

"That is so not likely to happen," Fiona said.

Without warning Sam's image danced before her eyes.

Cassie exchanged looks with Piper.

"What?" Fiona asked, immediately suspicious.

"Nothing," they chorused.

"Forget Sam, if that's what you're thinking. We are involved in an investigation, that's all," Fiona said quickly.

"Right," Piper said.

"Okay, if you say so," Cassie said.

"He hasn't even called or stopped by since the other night," Fiona said, instantly regretting revealing her frustration.

First no kiss good-night, then no follow-up call. Fiona didn't date much, but she knew enough about dating practices to know if a man was interested, he followed up.

Not that she *wanted* him interested, did she?

"He's been busy," Piper said.

"He's invited to dinner tonight, so maybe you'll see him there."

"Great, put me in a room full of super models and then hope any guy in the room looks my way."

Piper laughed.

"You'll be surprised to see some of these gals without their makeup. You could be a model if you had a different attitude."

"What's wrong with my attitude?"

"Nothing, if your goal is to scare everyone. A model needs to look alluring, sultry, provocative, not like she's ready to wipe the floor with you."

"Yeah, that's me, sultry and alluring."

"Hey, y'all, let's not get into name calling," Cassie said. "If Sam's there tonight, I bet he never even looks at the other women in the room."

"Maybe," Piper said. "But he could be running scared. He's mourned his wife for a long time now and any attraction he feels for Fiona probably threatens the status quo. Guys don't like that."

"No worries. I'll stay as far away from him as I can." Fiona drained her glass and put it back in the basket. She rose and began to unfold chairs again.

Fiona made sure her own booth was set up the way she wanted it before she left. Her paints and balloons were at the house. She wouldn't risk leaving them overnight even in Bradford. But the table and chairs were fine; the sign Betsy had drafted for her was perfect. And the awning would keep the sun off.

She headed for home, feeling grimy and grouchy. For two cents she'd stop at Ruby's, get takeout and skip dinner. She didn't need to meet people she'd never see again.

Although...she wouldn't mind meeting Michael Hansen and Devine Ozigbo of the Saints. Especially if she had her picture taken with them. That would give her some major bragging rights back at the precinct.

A shower improved her mood, but not enough to keep her from dressing in black. Comfort clothes, she thought as she pulled on the tight black jeans and black tank top and looked at herself in the mirror. She was tempted to spike her hair just to shock the natives. But that would be stupid. Instead, she lightly brushed her eyelashes with mascara and smudged some eyeshadow on her lids. Hot red lipstick completed her makeup.

Piper and Cassie had gone to the Elk's Club to set up and meet their respective fiancés earlier, so Fiona walked there on her own. If this kept up, she thought, waving to one of the neighbors as she walked down the sidewalk, she'd turn in her rental car. It mostly sat in the driveway.

The Elk's Club was swinging when she entered. Lots of people seemed to be talking and laughing and mingling. She spotted Piper in the center of a group of women, gesturing and laughing. Scanning the room, Fiona saw Sam in a group that appeared to include the two players from the Saints. Suddenly he looked over and caught her gaze.

Fiona's heart fluttered. Resolutely, she looked away. Moving in the opposite direction, she headed for the bar. She didn't drink much, but some wine would be nice around now. As soon as dinner was over, she was out of here

"Back in biker attire, I see," Sam said, joining her in the short line for drinks.

"Are bikers the only people who wear black in Mississippi?" she asked, staring at the back of the man in front of her.

"Old widow ladies do. You don't fit either category. Is the attitude back to match?"

"Give me a break about attitude. I'm who I am, okay?"

"And who is that?"

She looked at him. Big mistake. He was standing so close she could feel his breath brush her cheek. His eyes were focused on her with an intensity that was upsetting. She took a deep breath.

"An L.A. cop dedicated to ridding the earth of scum."

He gave a half smile.

"Tonight you're a guest in Bradford, Mississippi. Let me show you around."

He touched her lightly at the small of her back, urging her forward. She saw that the man ahead of her had received his drink and she was next up. But her mind went blank. Sam's touch was doing strange things to her thought processes.

"Weren't you talking with those football players Adam called?" she asked once she gave her order for a glass of white wine.

"Yes. Want to meet them?"

"I sure do. My partner loves football. Of course, he's not a Saints fan, but still, it'd be pretty cool to tell him I met those guys."

"Ouch."

"Huh?"

"Aren't you going to brag about meeting me?" Sam teased.

She looked to him. Suddenly the thought of leaving Bradford and Sam and everyone else struck her with a poignancy she hadn't expected. She didn't respond.

Sam was still in uniform, and when he and Fiona joined the football players Michael Thomas teased him mercilessly about always being on the job, never knowing how to let loose.

Finding out Fiona was also a law enforcement officer, Michael began a new round of teasing, but

Fiona enjoyed it. She was used to being around men, liked the discussions of sports and world events.

Plus, she didn't feel the need to worry about how she looked.

A few minutes before dinner was to be served, there was a commotion at the door. Fiona looked over and saw Piper proudly wheeling Margaret in, Adam beside her. She pushed the chair to the head of the room, near one of the round tables already set for dinner.

Everyone began to clap and Fiona felt tears prick her eyes. A lot of these people didn't even know Margaret but had rallied to help.

Cassie looked around, saw Fiona and beckoned. Fiona shook her head, but Sam took her glass and pushed her toward the front.

"Go on, they want all three girls with Margaret at dinner."

"I don't think—" she started, but he took her arm and gently led her toward the front.

"Just do it, don't think," he said.

In no time Cassie, Piper and Fiona were seated with Margaret at the table. Matt next to Cassie, and Adam next to Piper. Fiona looked at Sam, but he was already moving back toward his friends. Sitting next to Margaret, she ignored her disappointment at Sam's leaving, and smiled at her foster mother.

"Surprised?" she asked.

Margaret nodded, her smile lopsided but bright.

"Betsy and I hired two high school girls to help

serve," Cassie said, "so I could sit with you and enjoy the meal. I've checked everything and I think we're good to go."

She glanced toward the kitchen.

"Relax, honey, and enjoy the dinner with Margaret," Matt said. "They'll take care of everything."

Fiona glanced around and spotted Sam at a table to the left. Devine Ozigbo was sitting with him—and two of the most beautiful women she'd ever seen.

10

Cassie had prepared jambalaya, tasty rolls and a big salad for each table. The food was easy for Margaret to eat and regional enough to appeal to those who had flown in for the Independence Day fair.

Despite her reservations, Fiona enjoyed the meal. She relaxed and tried to make Margaret the center of attention. Cassie and Piper easily joined in. It was almost like the family meals in the old days, when Matt had sometimes joined them.

"Tomorrow, Margaret will sit with you for a while," Cassie told Fiona. "We told her you'd be doing face painting and she wanted to watch."

"Sure. I'll even paint your face if you like, Margaret."

Her foster mother gave her an odd look.

"Just joking. You can watch the attendees at the fair, as well. I have a spot that has a clear view of the carnival."

"Fi-fi-fi-fiiii..." Margaret tried to say something, but it was unintelligible.

"Fireworks," Piper said. "Yes, we'll all stay for them. If you get tired before, we can arrange for you to have a nap, and then be fresh to see the fireworks. Remember how we all crowded together on that old blanket so we could lie back and watch? I don't know where that blanket is, but I have another one that'll be perfect."

"You'll need two—we've expanded our family," Cassie said with a smile at Matt and Adam.

"Okay, two it'll be. And I want everyone to be there." Piper looked at Fiona. "No sneaking off to be with some guy."

Fiona made a face at her.

"I only did that one time. What a bust that turned out to be. He wanted to hit the local store while everyone was at the fireworks."

"And did he?" Cassie asked.

Fiona shook her head.

"For some reason, his car wouldn't start."

Adam looked at her.

"Know anything about cars, Fiona?" he asked.

She smiled. "Enough."

"Sam told me about your early law enforcement days," he said.

"Sam has a big mouth," Fiona said.

She wasn't sure how she felt about him talking about her to Adam. Nice that he was interested enough, but some of what they had said was private. How much did he share? He'd told him about their kiss.

Their only kiss. Was she making more of it than was warranted? Probably.

"What early law enforcement days?" Cassie asked.

"Tell you later," Fiona said. "So what's for dessert? It would be hard to top this meal, Cassie. It's fantastic. And one of Margaret's favorites."

"Ice cream and pralines. Easy, fast and regional."

By the time Margaret was ready to return to the hospital, Fiona was ready to leave, too. "I'll take her," she offered.

"She came in my car," Matt said, holding out his keys.

Sam's hand grabbed them, then he tossed them back at Matt.

"I'll take Margaret back. I have to check a few things at the fairgrounds before calling it a day. I can give Fiona a lift, as well."

Fiona was torn. Stay with Margaret or tell Sam she could manage on her own? Margaret won.

"Fine, but I can walk from the hospital," she said in defiance.

Sam shrugged and bent to speak to Margaret. Soon they were in the Crown Vic and heading through town. Fiona sat in the backseat with Margaret. Sam had stashed the wheelchair in the trunk, which was huge.

Margaret seemed very tired, resting her head on the backseat, eyes closed.

"It wasn't too much, was it?" Fiona asked her softly.

Margaret opened her eyes and shook her head. "Tiiii…"

"Tired?" Fiona guessed. "You'll be back in bed in

no time. Maybe you should give tomorrow a miss."

Margaret shook her head. "No!"

"Okay, okay, it was only a suggestion. I see the stroke didn't damage any of your determination. I remember how you'd say we were going to church on Sunday and that was that. So we all did, every week, no matter what excuses or tricks we tried to come up with. You were a force to be reckoned with—still are. Matt tells me he's just waiting for you to get better to run that home for unwed teenagers for him."

Margaret looked at Fiona. She wished she knew what was going on in her mind. Her lack of ability to clearly communicate must drive her up the wall.

"We're here," Sam said, pulling in near the entrance.

"Can you stop here?" Fiona asked.

"Perks of being sheriff," he said easily.

A nurse came out and quickly had Margaret in her wheelchair and headed inside. Fiona and Sam were not needed.

"Still want to walk home? I can drop you off before making rounds."

"Let me ride with you," she said on impulse.

She was feeling wired after the evening and not ready to go back to the empty house.

"Fine by me. Hop in front. I'm not a chauffeur."

"And riding in the back reminds me of being a suspect."

"You ride in the back often?"

Fiona grinned as she slid into the front seat.

"If I did more than once, it was more than I wanted."

"Non answer."

"Yep."

They drove around town, neither speaking. Occasionally Sam directed his spotlight at a dark place, but never discovered anything out of the ordinary.

After a while Fiona grew restless with the silence.

"Do you see your parents often?" she asked.

"What brought that up?" he asked.

"I merely wondered. Margaret was more of a mother to me than my own. Yet I hadn't seen her in more than a decade. I wondered if normal families got together more often."

"I see them most holidays. My wife, Patty, loved to celebrate the big ones, like Christmas and the Fourth. Sometimes her folks and mine would come to our place, other times we'd go to Baton Rouge."

"You must miss her."

"We started going together in high school. I went into the service, got out, went to college, and all through that, she waited, writing me every day. Then we got married. I couldn't imagine being married to anyone else."

Fiona gazed out the windshield, hearing nothing in his tone she didn't expect.

"Where's she buried?"

"In Baton Rouge. Near her grandparents."

His voice was neutral, without expression.

"Did they catch the drunk driver?"

"Oh, yeah. He's serving ten years for manslaughter."

"Should have been more," she said.

"I agree, but I wasn't the jury. Seems a short time to compensate for a life. Patty was only twenty-seven when she died."

Younger than Fiona was now. Yet in that time, Patty had loved a man enough to marry him, made a home in New Orleans and loved to celebrate holidays.

"It's getting late," Sam said, turning up the hill that led to Margaret's home.

He pulled into the driveway. The house had some lights on, including the porch light. Cassie's van was in the driveway.

"Guess the others are home already," she said when Sam stopped.

He got out and walked her to the front door.

"Thanks for the ride along. You should come to L.A. sometime. I'll get one of the patrol cops to give you a tour. It's a bit different."

She was babbling, suddenly a bundle of nerves.

"Ever think of leaving?" he asked. "Finding a safer place to work?"

She shook her head.

"No. Good night."

When she reached for the front door, Sam stopped her. His hands on her shoulders, he pulled her closer.

"People change as they grow, Fiona. Sometimes the memories of the past are distorted. Sometimes we need to look at the present with different eyes."

With those cryptic words, he held her head between his palms and kissed her. His lips were warm and demanding. Fiona gave as good as she got, reveling in the sensations that swept through her. Her heart pounded and she felt amazingly alive. Her hands gripped his wrists, holding on lest she be swept away on the tide of passion that heated her blood.

"Good night," Sam said, pulling back and releasing her.

He turned and walked back to the car. In seconds, he was gone.

Fiona entered the house, annoyed with herself for giving in so easily. So the guy was a terrific kisser. She'd been kissed before.

Not like that, a voice inside whispered.

Not that it changed anything, she argued.

Cassie came to the top of the stairs.

"We're both up here, Fiona. Turn off the lights when you come up and join us."

When Fiona walked into the shared bedroom, Piper and Cassie were sitting on their respective twin beds. Fiona went to sit at the foot of Cassie's.

"What's up?"

"Rehashing tonight, what else?" Piper said. "Why are you so much later getting home than we were when you left ages before we did?"

"I went on patrol with Sam."

"And did what?"

"Patrolled. Drove around town."

"Boring, I bet," Cassie said. "Nothing bad happens here."

Fiona didn't say anything. Something bad had happened twelve years ago.

"What did you think of the people at dinner?"

"Nice of them to come. I couldn't believe some were here," Cassie said when Fiona remained silent.

Piper looked at her.

"And you?"

"I didn't talk to any of them."

"Why not?"

Fiona shrugged.

"I think Margaret enjoyed it, but she was tired when we left."

"I could see that," Piper said. "I thought about canceling tomorrow, but she seems to want to go. You'll have to keep an eye on her and make sure you let someone know if she should get back to rest. I hope it won't be long before she can come back here."

"Someone else should watch her," Fiona said.

"Why?" Cassie asked, sitting yoga fashion on her bed.

"I can't see why she'd want to be with me. Not after what happened."

"That's it!" Piper said, jumping up.

She went to Fiona, stopping just in front of her and spreading her arms wide, then closing them into a circle. She stepped back, almost staggering. Fiona watched her, puzzled. What was she doing?

Piper moved back another step and then turned,

acting as if she were carrying a huge stone pillar. She lurched to the doorway, thrusting the invisible thing out into the hallway and shutting the door. Then she turned and gazed at Fiona in triumph.

"I will not have that guilt around you or me again. It's gone. I forgive you. Cassie forgives you. Margaret forgives you. Forgive yourself, Fiona. It happened, life changed but went on. Now we're back together. I've missed you two so much I couldn't stand it sometimes. I want that closeness we once had—and I'm tired of your perpetual penitent behavior because of one lousy teenager act. You are excused. Show me the wild child I knew twelve years ago!"

Cassie clapped.

"Bravo. I echo your sentiments." She smiled at Fiona. "I love you, girl. We need to rejoice we are together, not mourn what can't be changed."

Fiona looked at her two best friends in the world. Could she let go of the past? Was it as easy and as hard as forgiving herself?

It couldn't be.

"Maybe you two forgive me, but how about Margaret? You don't really know her feelings."

"I can guess. You should have seen how delighted she was when you visited. And how she looks for you when one of us visit and you're not with us. She loves you, Fiona. We all do, hard as it is to understand why," Piper added teasingly.

"I'm not good with mushy stuff. You're not getting all mushy, are you?"

Despite herself, Fiona felt a weight lift. She saw genuine affection shining in the faces of both women. Piper held up a finger with a small scar. Cassie rose and placed her own scarred fingertip against Piper's. Fiona smiled. She was home again. Rising, she placed her finger against the two of her sisters of the heart.

"Sisters forever," they intoned in unison as they had one day so long ago.

Fiona surveyed the booth she'd been assigned. The canopy sheltered it from the direct rays of the sun, but the temperature was already rising. It would be stifling by mid afternoon. She hoped for some breeze.

She wore another of Piper's endless sun dresses. She'd done her hair softer and put on eye makeup. Not that she was dressing up for anyone—it was still part of her undercover trappings. She wanted everyone to think she was some sweet young thing. And according to Cassie and Piper, she looked the part.

The fair officially opened at ten. It must have been 10:02 when the first child raced to the booth. A little girl of about six, with white-blond hair tied back in two ponytails at the side, each bouncing as she ran.

"I wanted to be first," she said breathlessly as she stopped at the opening, a dollar bill clutched in her fist. "I saw the sign. My mom told me what face painting is. I want to be a cat."

Fiona pointed to the chair near the table. "Have a seat. One cat coming up."

The little girl held out her dollar, which Fiona took and put in the large pickle jar she planned to use for the donations. In seconds she began drawing the whiskers for a cat on the girl's smooth cheeks.

"Where's your mom?" Fiona asked as she worked.

"She's coming. She has to push the stroller with Jenny. It's not easy on grass, you know," she confided. "But she said I could come ahead."

Fiona worked swiftly and competently, finishing just as a young woman pushing a baby stroller stopped by the booth.

"Oh, Carrie, you look darling. Wait while I take a picture."

The woman brought her phone and stepped into the booth.

"Hi, I'm Suzy Bryant."

"Fiona Hunter."

Suzy snapped the photo and smiled. "Do you do babies, too?"

Fiona glanced at the toddler sitting placidly in her stroller.

"What would she like?"

Suzy looked at the sketches of different designs and characters Fiona had as suggestions, ones she was capable of doing.

"I like the butterfly one. What does a two-year-old know?"

Fiona moved to kneel beside the stroller. When she tried to paint the little girl's cheek, she pulled away, watching the brush with wide eyes.

"She needs a distraction," Fiona said.

The child's mother reached in for a floppy dolly and held it out. Jenny reached for it. Fiona began to paint, going as fast as she could, knowing her time with a toddler was very limited. Soon a small butterfly adorned the child's cheek.

"So cute," Suzy said. "Do you do moms, too?"

Another family was coming down the wide walkway, heading for the carnival. The rides had just started.

"Sure, which do you want?"

"I want the unicorn. What fun this is! I love face painting but have never seen it here before."

By the time Fiona finished with Suzy, a short line had formed, with children excited at the prospect of colorful designs on their cheeks. Fiona hadn't even had time to do the balloons.

"Come back after lunch and I'll make some balloon dogs," she told the children over and over.

The morning flew by. Fiona had a steady line of customers. She painted dragons and flowers, rainbows and Spider-Man, flags and fireworks. The money in the jar grew as people donated various amounts to help Margaret Nunes.

Former classmates stopped by. Some to exclaim about seeing her again, others to reminisce. It was surprising to discover almost all the men and women from her class were married. One woman was divorced. None had left Bradford for any length of time.

It turned out to be more fun than Fiona expected to talk with people she'd known so long ago. And the memories altered somewhat her view of their childhood.

The circumstances of her departure had been front and center in her mind for so long, she'd forgotten the other aspects of growing up in Bradford.

She'd enjoyed most of her childhood, she realized, feeling safe and secure in Margaret's home, no longer having to deal with her drug-addict mother. Even when Fiona was sent to live with her mother on her good times, she knew she could depend on Margaret and find a refuge there if she needed it.

Until that last day.

Late morning brought a lull. Fiona debated closing the booth for fifteen minutes to give herself a break when an elderly woman approached with two young children.

"Can I have my face painted, Grandma Sarah?" the older child, a girl, asked.

"Me, too," the little boy said, looking at the choices. "I want Sponge Bob."

"That's babyish," the girl said. "I want the rainbow and unicorn."

"I'm not a baby!"

"Are, too!"

"Hush, the both of you," their grandmother said. "You both may get the design of your choice, but only if there is no more bickering. Do I make myself clear?"

"Yes, Grandma," the girl said promptly.

The little boy nodded, and Fiona had to hide a smile. She always liked the time she spent with children, finding them enchanting.

"I'm Sarah Atwood," the woman said, smiling at Fiona. "Two faces ready for paint."

"Have a seat," Fiona said to the little girl. She began to paint as Sarah walked around to the donation jar. She read the notation, then looked at Fiona.

"You're one of Margaret's girls, aren't you? I heard you all were doing different things to raise money to help with her medical expenses. I think that's wonderful."

"I'm Fiona Hunter," Fiona said, concentrating on the unicorn. It was one of the more difficult designs. She was gratified word was spreading about the fundraising. Each time someone mentioned it, however, she held her breath, wondering what else would be said.

Several of her high school friends had asked for the true story about her departure. She'd told them she'd been attacked and taken away. She didn't go into details, which left several of them more curious than they'd started.

"I knew Margaret back when she was dating Allen McLennon," Mrs. Atwood said.

Fiona paused, glancing up. "Oh?"

"I worked for Allen. I was his secretary for years. Retired about six years ago. I really like being retired—gives me so much time for my garden. And these two."

She smiled fondly at her grandchildren.

Fiona resumed painting, wondering how to question the woman about what she remembered from twelve years ago. An opportunity like this didn't come along to be ignored. Sarah must have known something of what was going on back then.

"I knew Mr. McLennon, too—he was over at the house a lot," Fiona said. "I haven't found out yet why he and Margaret stopped seeing each other."

"All Margaret's doing. I think it was because he didn't stand by her when the accusations—"

She stopped abruptly, as if realizing who she was talking to.

"As I understand it," Fiona said, "the sheriff didn't fully investigate the situation. He didn't believe me and refused to follow up on anything I said, claiming I was making it up to cause trouble."

She kept her tone neutral. She wanted to throw down the paints and interrogate the woman, but knew any show of intense interest would raise speculation and try the woman's loyalty.

"There were rumors flying around town at the time. Some folks said Margaret beat her foster children, but that was nonsense. I've known Margaret Nunes all my life. She would never strike a child, as I told Allen more than once."

"He believed the rumors?" Fiona asked, concentrating now on the rainbow that would arch over the delicate figure of the unicorn. She'd always wondered how he'd explained things.

"He was out of town when the attack took place,

called away unexpectedly. By the time he returned, speculation and accusations had died down a little. He tried to see Margaret, but she wanted nothing to do with him. Unfair of her, I always thought. He hadn't known he would be called away like that."

"Called away where?" Fiona asked, putting down her brush and studying her work.

She wanted to look right at Sarah, but was afraid to show her intense interest for fear of her shutting down.

"Now, where was it he went? Mobile, I think it was. Goodness, that was a long time ago. I don't really remember the details, only that he wasn't there for her when she needed him and she never forgave him for it."

"Does sound a bit extreme," Fiona murmured. "There you go, young lady, all set."

She offered the hand mirror and the little girl beamed at the drawing.

"Thank you," she said.

"You're welcome. Next," she addressed the little boy.

"Were Mr. McLennon and Sheriff Halstead friends?" she asked Sarah when she began to outline Sponge Bob on the cheek of the little boy.

"Oh, my, no. Why would you ask that?"

"Just wondered. If they had been, maybe the sheriff would have talked about the situation with him."

"No, they were scarcely acquainted, as far as I know."

"Yet when McLennon was vice president, he made a very advantageous deal on a mortgage for the sheriff," Fiona couldn't help saying.

Sarah looked puzzled.

"He did? How do you know that?"

"Mrs. Halstead told me," Fiona said.

She'd better watch what she said, or Sarah would get defensive on behalf of her former boss.

"I don't remember," she said. "Not that I would necessarily. Mortgages were handled in the loans department."

"Probably helping out from civic duty," Fiona murmured, almost choking on her words.

She wanted to tell Sarah about her precious boss. Find out if there were other incidents or had hers been the only one?

She finished with the little boy's design and held up the mirror.

"There you go, young man. How do you like it?"

The child grinned at his reflection.

"Cool," he said, hopping down from the chair.

"Thank you," Sarah said. "Tell Margaret I send my best."

She moved away and stuffed several dollars into the donation jar.

Fiona smiled back.

"Thanks for the donation. It's wonderful how many people are supporting Margaret."

"Most of us have known her for many years, dear. Come along, you two, time for lunch."

Fiona watched the trio walk toward the hot dog stand, feeling a bit hungry herself. She looked for something to write "Back in fifteen minutes" on just as Adam approached, bag in hand.

"Hey, Cassie sent me with lunch."

He held up the bag.

"Her booth is swamped. How're you doing?"

"Been busy all morning. This is the first lull, and it looks like another family is approaching."

"Sorry, folks," Adam said, standing in the archway. "Closed temporarily while our painter eats lunch."

"Thanks," Fiona said when he turned back and moved the chairs to the archway, backs to the outside.

"That's as close to a barricade I can get. Eat up. Need anything else?"

"No."

She opened the bag and smiled. A typical Fourth of July lunch from Cassie—cold fried chicken, a small container of potato salad, buttered rolls and a slice of pecan pie for dessert. "Nothing like PBJ sandwiches," Fiona murmured.

"Not from our Cassie."

Adam sat on one of the chairs and leaned his cane against the one next to it.

"Have you eaten?" Fiona asked, offering a drumstick.

"Yes. I finished about five minutes, then I have to plunge into the fray—the tent where Piper and her friends are going crazy. I hope everything ends up running smoothly, because Piper in a temper is not a pretty sight."

Fiona laughed and began to eat.

"Frantic and yelling and almost throwing things, then she'll be as sweet as sugar. You wonder if you have a Jekyll and Hyde on your hands."

"I like the sweet-as-sugar part," he murmured.

A familiar figure walked down the wide thoroughfare, wife at his side. It was Peter Johnstone, the lawyer Fiona had consulted. She nodded in greeting. He paused a moment, spoke quietly to the woman at his side and then stepped over to Fiona's booth.

"I'm at lunch," she said.

He glanced at the face-painting apparatus and shook his head.

"I'm not here for that. I had a call from Stephen Cabot in Massachusetts. Apparently your foster sister Cassie insisted he do something to help. About all he could do was tell me that if you told me something, I could take it to the bank. If you'd like to discuss the situation with me again, I'd be most interested."

"Oh?"

Hooray for Cassie's old boyfriend.

"I have a bit more information. Maybe I could stop in one day this week?"

"Call the office and make an appointment as early as you want. I'll tell Irene to expect your call."

He nodded to Adam and rejoined his wife.

"What was that about?"

"He's the lawyer I saw about bringing a civil suit.

Guess he changed his mind after talking with Cassie's former fiancé."

"Things are getting interesting. Does Sam know you've consulted a lawyer?"

"I told him," she said, not wishing to discuss the sheriff.

He confused her. One moment acting like a stranger, then the next kissing her socks off. If she wore them in this heat.

"Good luck. Gotta go." Adam rose, took the cane and limped around the chair.

Fiona watched him, her attention suddenly snagged by Allen McLennon. The man was at the side of the booth beyond the large tent Piper was using. He was talking to a young girl who didn't look happy to be there.

11

Without thought, Fiona rose and quickly headed in that direction. The girl looked at her in panic and hurried away. McLennon glared when he saw Fiona.

"What do you want?" he asked.

"I was wondering what you were doing with that girl," Fiona said, stopping close enough to talk, yet out of reach.

"I was merely talking with her, not that it's any of your business."

"When I see a sixty-something man threatening a teenager, I make it my business," she said.

"I'm hardly sixty. And I wasn't threatening her."

"Looked like it to me."

"Go back to wherever it is you live now," Allen said. "You're not wanted in Bradford."

With that, he turned and headed off in the opposite direction.

"Problem?" Matt asked.

Fiona swung around. "Where did you come from?"

"From Cassie's booth to yours and on to Piper's. I'm checking to make sure everything is okay. Then

I'm off to get Margaret. You ready for her?"

"Yes."

"What's up with McLennon?"

"He was talking with some teenage girl. It struck me as wrong."

Matt was silent for a moment.

"Really wrong or colored by your experience? I mean, the guy was right here in the midst of the fair. There are too many people around for him to try anything."

"Intimidation can take place anywhere," Fiona said stubbornly.

She headed back to her booth.

Sam stood near the entrance of the wide corridor that bisected the fair. To the left was a series of booths, including the large tent in which Piper was holding her fashion show. Across from it was the booth Fiona used for her face painting. He'd made the rounds of the fair twice already, seeing lots of happy children with brightly painted faces. She must be doing a booming business, he thought.

But what else was she doing he wondered. He'd seen her talking with Allen McLennon, and then Matt. Peter Johnstone had stopped by her booth earlier and spoken a few words. Fiona was a popular woman this afternoon.

Might as well add himself to the mix, he thought, walking toward her.

He was struck at the anticipation he felt. Fiona was not a beautiful woman like Piper. Pretty enough in a tomboyish way. Her hair was shorter than he liked, and dark. Patty's had been light, worn long. He'd loved tangling his fingers in it. With Fiona, it would be like stroking a sleek cat.

He'd thought a lot about what Adam had said. And it was true. Patty had loved life. She'd want him to embrace all the adventure it held.

He wasn't sure he was ready.

Fiona's intensity amazed him sometimes. She appeared totally oblivious to him as a man, only using him to further her own ends. Yet that very intensity drew him back again and again.

Justice was an overriding concern of hers, one they shared. He liked to have the scales balanced. If McLennon had attacked her as she stated, he wanted to see justice done.

If nothing else, Fiona's, Piper's and Cassie's return had to tip the scales of public opinion in Margaret's favor. They were adults. They had been away from Bradford for more than a decade. To return to help indicated a strong loyalty, if not more.

Fiona spotted him before he reached her.

She said something to Matt and then hurried to meet him. Sam slowed, his anticipation building.

"Hey," she said when she reached him.

"Hey yourself. What's up? Saw you talking with McLennon."

"He was hitting on some girl."

Sam went on alert. "Are you sure?"

"I'm sure. Matt thinks I'm projecting. Anyway, I wanted to tell you something I learned today."

She glanced around and frowned.

"There must be a hundred people within earshot."

"And this is confidential?" he asked.

"For the time being. Come on."

She turned and headed away from the booths and crowd. Soon they were on the fringe of the parking lot. It was full of cars, hardly any people in sight.

"I met Sarah Atwood," she said.

"Who?"

"She was McLennon's secretary twelve years ago. She retired a few years back. Today she brought her grandchildren to have their faces painted and got to talking."

"And?"

"She said an odd thing. McLennon wasn't here when the scandal broke. He'd been called out of town unexpectedly. Sarah thought Margaret broke up with him because he hadn't stood by her. I wondered how people could ignore the scratches, and now I know. He left until they healed."

Sam looked thoughtful. "Could be."

"And the lawyer I saw, Mr. Johnstone? He said he wanted to see me again. Things are looking up, and not a moment too soon, if you ask me. I think McLennon was bothering that girl. She sure didn't look happy. She reminded me of me."

"What do you mean?"

"Thin, tall, dark hair. Kinda like I looked back then. I wonder if that's the type he likes."

"Or maybe it's the daughter of a friend and he merely spoke to her."

"Matt thought I was overreacting. Adam would have followed up, I bet."

Sam planned to follow up on every aspect, but he saw no reason to tell Fiona at this point. No sense getting her hopes up. So far he only had circumstantial evidence, not enough to convince a district attorney something was worth pursuing.

"I've seen a dozen or more face paintings as I've walked around," he said, trying to change the subject. The last thing he needed was Fiona to go off half cocked.

She smiled. Once again he felt that kick of awareness. Had he been too long without a woman, or was Fiona starting to get to him?

"Business is booming. I think I've raised more than two hundred dollars already. And with the information from McLennon's secretary, I count this a great day. Find that girl and maybe we'll have a current investigation, not one that's twelve years old."

"Know who she is?"

"No, and she ran off when I approached them. But if I see her again, I'll know her."

"If you do, let me know. I'll handle things."

"Right."

He looked at her, not liking the way she agreed so fast.

Fiona turned and headed back toward her booth.

"Where are you going?" Sam asked.

"Margaret will be arriving soon. Matt left to get her. I need to be there."

"Have supper with me tonight," Sam said.

She stopped and looked at him suspiciously.

"Why?"

"I want to see you," he said bluntly.

"Why?" she repeated.

"Heck, why does a man want to see a woman?"

She blinked. Then stepped closer, tilting back her head to stare into his eyes.

"We live thousands of miles apart. I have a lot of baggage from my past and you have the ghost of your wife hanging around. What part of this is a happy relationship in the making?"

He leaned over and brushed her lips with his.

"That part," he said, standing back up.

He needlessly readjusted his hat, gave her a two-finger salute and walked away. Let her think about that for a while. He knew he'd think of little else all afternoon.

For the first time, his thoughts didn't turn to Patty. He thought only of Fiona.

Sam couldn't ignore the first signs of life in his body since Patty's death. He wanted that heat that seared to the soul. He wanted a connectedness that came from knowing someone intimately. He still longed for a home and family. And he wasn't getting any younger. A good cop knew when to push and when to hold back.

It was time to push this lady a bit and see what happened.

Fiona watched Sam walk away, stunned at his kiss in broad daylight—where anyone from town could see. And half the town, if not more, was at the fairgrounds.

She started to follow him to challenge him, call him to account. Or was it to have another taste?

Instead, she stomped back to her booth. She had other things to do than worry about some sexy sheriff in a small town. She was Los Angeles-bound as soon as— She wasn't sure precisely when, but soon.

Fiona slipped back into the booth. Several children were lined up at the entrance.

"Who's next?" she asked brightly, refusing to think about her return to L.A. She had weeks left for vacation, if she chose to extend her stay beyond the original plans. Not that she would. Except, she did want to see Piper and Cassie married. There was so much to think about.

A bit of commotion nearby made Fiona look up. Matt was wheeling Margaret along. People were greeting her. Piper came out of her tent and rushed to Margaret's side.

"Hi, Margaret, we're starting earlier than planned to get in an extra show. We've sold a gazillion tickets. Come for the first one. We saved you the place of honor. After the show, you can visit Fiona's booth and

Cassie's," she said, giving Margaret a warm hug. She waved at Fiona.

Fiona waved back and smiled at Margaret. She looked rested after last night. Fiona hoped today wouldn't be too much. She wanted nothing to cause a setback to Margaret's recovery.

By late afternoon, Fiona was growing tired. Margaret had sat with her for half an hour, watching her paint cheek after small cheek, or full-face painting for cats and Batman and other favorites.

Some of her paint supply was getting low. At other events she'd worked, she hadn't had such a steady stream of customers. Some of the parents who had brought their young children were former schoolmates.

Several times Fiona wondered how things would have been if she'd not been sent away. Would she have ended up married with children already? She didn't think so. But there was no denying some of these children were adorable.

Cassie came in and plopped down on one of the chairs just as Fiona finished up a little girl's ideal rainbow.

"I'm so tired I want to crawl into bed and sleep until morning, and it's not even dark and the fireworks are still ahead," Cassie said, stretching out her legs and wiggling her toes.

Fiona nodded.

"I think I've gotten carpal tunnel syndrome in one afternoon. I've never painted so many faces before."

She glanced at the full pickle jar. It had been emptied twice already and was again full to the top with dollar bills.

"But we're raking in the bucks. This should go a long way toward helping pay Margaret's bills. And our support has to be working, don't you think? I've spoken to dozens of former classmates, all who had various theories I shot down. But I did say the police were reopening the investigation and I had to keep quiet until they were through. I wonder if it'll get back to McLennon?"

"With what the gossip in this town is like, you better believe it," Cassie said. "I hope he sweats buckets. Did Piper tell you she introduced Margaret as her grandmother when the fashion show first started? There were a lot of comments about that, I heard. But by the end of the show, everyone was so enchanted with the work the models did, the gossip was at a minimum. I'm sure it'll pick up over the next few days."

"And then die down. How did the football players go over?"

"They were mobbed. Not only by the boys in the crowd, but the men and women, as well. And I never saw so many phone trained on two people before. Selfies to the left, videos to the right. It was a madhouse."

Fiona leaned back and relaxed.

"Nice of them to come for a stranger."

"For all of them to come," Cassie agreed. "Still, I'm

so tired I don't know if I can stay for the fireworks. I've been on my feet since before seven."

"So cops aren't the only ones to stay on their feet at work."

"If I'd known that when becoming a chef, I might have changed my mind. No, I wouldn't. I love it. But you know? Catering is proving more fun than I expected."

"And lucrative. I understand you and Betsy are hiring," Fiona said.

"Yes, but high school girls mostly, to help out with serving and cleanup for large events. And I don't have those kinds of events regularly enough to hire full staff—at least not yet."

"You are happy here, right?" Fiona asked.

"I'm happier than I ever thought I'd be."

Fiona felt a pang of envy. She herself was okay with her life, but not ecstatic about it the way Cassie and Piper seemed to be. Maybe having someone in your life to do things with *was* important. A mate. A lover. A husband.

Fiona rose and began to pack up her paints.

"I'm calling it a day," she said, glancing around. No one waited, and before the next prospective customer could show up, she wanted to be packed and gone.

"What are you going to do about the fireworks?" Cassie said.

Fiona glanced at her watch.

"It's almost six. I'm going to go home and change and then come back, I guess."

"Don't you want to go to the carnival?"

She glanced at the clanging rides, heard the squeals and laughter of those on them and shook her head.

"My idea of a good time right now is to lie down and put my feet up."

Cassie rose.

"Me, too. If I can find Matt, I'll let him know I'm heading home with you. We can come back around nine and still get good seats for the display."

They started for Bradford Hall a few minutes later. As they passed a group of teens, Fiona spotted the girl she'd seen earlier with McLennon.

"Cassie, do you know that girl in the blue top, the one with the dark hair?"

Cassie looked at the group. "Sure, that's Janine Flowers. Betsy and I have hired her a couple of times to help out. She's a good worker. Her family's in bad straits right now, Betsy said, so we're glad to help out when we have the work."

"What's her relationship with McLennon?"

Cassie looked at her in astonishment.

"None that I know of, why?"

"I saw them earlier. Matt thinks I'm seeing things that aren't there, but the entire scene looked odd to me."

"Well, she's with friends now," Cassie said.

Fiona took a quick shower when she got home, changing to her familiar black. Good for undercover work in L.A., she thought as an idea glimmered—and maybe here, too. She checked her watch. She might have time. And if not, she didn't care that much if she missed the pyrotechnic display. She'd seen fireworks before.

"I'm going out," she called to Cassie as she left.

Piper and Adam were tied up with their friends. She didn't have a clue where Matt was. And Sam was working. Margaret had been taken back to the hospital after the fashion show, tired but happy.

Fiona climbed into her rental car, for the first time wishing it was more inconspicuous. She drove through town and headed out toward the highway and Gully's Shack. She and her companion of that fateful night had tried fake IDs to get some beer, to no avail. And then when she wouldn't put out, Tony got really angry and dumped her on the side of the road—in the rain, no less.

She cruised the once-familiar thoroughfare leading out of Bradford. The disreputable beer joint was exactly where she remembered. She pulled into the parking lot and sat for a moment trying to see any glamour in the structure. Maybe at night with the neon flashing it didn't look so seedy. What had she been thinking back then?

Almost as if it were yesterday, she could remember every detail. Slowly she reversed out and headed back toward town. There was where she and Tony had pulled over for some kissing. And where he'd gotten so angry when she called a halt at kisses only.

The turnout was now overgrown, but clearly

visible. She stopped for a few minutes, trying to recall the sequence of events. She remembered being angry at first that Tony had dumped her and that it was raining. Then she realized how far she'd have to walk. She'd debated returning to the Shack, but decided that wouldn't be smart. Walking home seemed the only solution.

Fiona checked for traffic. The road was deserted. Slowly she began driving, watching the side, trying to remember where it was Allen McLennon had found her. There. She stopped and looked. It was different from the way it looked twelve years ago, but still recognizable. She'd gotten into his car and he'd sped off. She increased her speed slightly, watching for the turn. The old road was still there.

She turned into it, immediately enveloped in the old oaks that dripped Spanish moss, the thick undergrowth sometimes brushing the side of her car. Was this the same road?

She'd asked him where they were going, and he'd said it was a shortcut home. Fiona drove slowly, studying both sides of the road. There was a driveway to the left, but they had turned right. She continued past the left-side driveway until–there, on the right, another driveway, two parallel strips with grass growing in the middle. She turned in and a moment later saw the cottage.

It looked different in the daylight, without the rain. It was merely a small cottage in an overgrown yard. Not the horror place of her memory.

She sat for a long time staring at the structure. Then, taking a deep breath for fortitude, Fiona climbed out of the car and went to the door. She knocked, but there was no answer. She hadn't expected one. She glanced around. The silence was comforting. She'd hear if another car drove up, or if someone came through the brush.

Peeking into a window, she could see the place was in good condition. Still used?

She walked around the cottage, not knowing what she hoped to find. Nothing offered up any clues.

Climbing back into the car, she threw it in gear and headed out. At the highway, she turned for Bradford. A moment later a familiar sheriff's car slid in behind her, lights flashing.

She checked the speed, well below the limit. Thinking must have caused her to dawdle. She pulled to the shoulder and got out. She wasn't waiting meekly in the car.

"Didn't expect to find you out here," Sam said.

He was in full official mode, hat included, ticket book in hand.

She shrugged.

"What are you doing here? I thought you were patrolling the fair."

"Got a call at the Shack, drunk and disorderly. Guy was gone by the time I got there. Thought at first your slow driving was a drunk being extra careful."

"First you stop me for speeding, now for going too slowly. Do you have certain ranges in which drivers have to stay?"

Sam looked around.

"What are you doing here?"

"I found the cottage where McLennon took me. I think he's after another teen, so I thought if I found it, I could maybe stake it out in case history repeats itself."

"I've told you to back off," Sam said.

"I heard you say that. Thank you, Officer, for your advice."

"Which you don't plan to take."

Fiona looked at him. "Would you?"

"That's different."

"Why?"

"Let's just say, this is my jurisdiction, not yours."

"As a citizen, I'm free to drive where I want."

"Don't mess with me, Fiona. I want you out of this. A man's innocent until proved guilty."

She debated the feasibility of arguing with him, but decided it wouldn't get her anywhere. She'd do what she wanted, but not blare it to the world.

"And an officer can investigate where there is probable cause," she said. "I have more than probable cause. I know what he did."

Sam looked as if he wanted to argue, but didn't. He touched the edge of his hat and headed back to the patrol car. Fiona wished he'd said something more. She felt exhilarated arguing with him. Or just plain being around him.

Not a good sign.

She made it back to the fair in plenty of time to find Cassie and Piper. They'd found two old blankets and spread them on the grass. Adam was lounging along the edge of one, Piper sitting near him. Cassie was on the other, searching the crowd. She waved when she spotted Fiona and motioned her over.

"I was worried you wouldn't get here in time," she said when Fiona joined them.

"I didn't want to miss the fireworks," Fiona said, sitting on the blanket. "Where's Matt?"

"He'll be along."

"How did the day go?" Fiona asked Piper, and got a glowing report of the fashion show, the money raised and the wild stories she'd heard about Margaret being her grandmother.

Piper smiled in satisfaction.

"Talk about raising awareness. First there were dozens of questions about my parentage, then about how awful Margaret's father had been, and then how everyone loved Margaret and wasn't it great her girls were back—as if we'd gone off on our own and were now returning. I set a few people straight."

"What'd you say?"

"That the former sheriff had separated us, and wasn't that suspicious."

Fiona laughed. "Good for you, Piper."

Matt came through the crowd, a small cooler in his hands. "I brought refreshments," he said, placing it near the blanket and sitting between Fiona and Cassie.

It was almost fully dark, and the crowd had grown

to fill the grassy area. Children ran around, playing with glow-in-the-dark balls and rings. A dog or two barked, part of the family fun. The heat of the day had waned and it was almost comfortable in the twilight.

The scene brought back a lot of memories. Fiona saw herself as a little girl, so fascinated with the colors that lit up the night sky. Then as a pre-adolescent, talking with Cassie and Piper and other friends. The last Independence Day fair she'd attended, she'd been too old to sit with Margaret and the others. She'd wanted to be on her own with the wild friends she had from high school.

Too bad children didn't realize at the time how fleeting childhood was. She'd give a lot to go back to that little girl who was so enchanted by the fireworks.

The town put on a good show. The display lasted well over half an hour and was accompanied continually by the oohing and aahing of the crowd. When the last frantic burst of color faded, the distant rumble of cars starting in the parking lot could be heard.

"Glad we're walking," Piper said as she rose. "That parking lot will be gridlock for a while."

"It seemed different," Cassie said. "I guess because it was the first fair for me as an adult."

"It'd be different with kids," Matt said, leaning over to kiss her softly. "We'll have to bring ours here as soon as they start arriving."

Once again Fiona felt left out. She'd made her mind up long ago to remain single, unencumbered in life.

She didn't want the disappointment of depending on someone who'd let her down again.

But every so often she'd see a couple so complete in themselves that envy reared up. Not enough to change her mind, but sometimes enough to make her think, what if.

Tonight her what-if centered on Sam Witt. What if she'd met him at another time and place? What if he stopped mourning his wife? Or if Fiona could cut loose a bit and see where things would lead? Would he ever want more than kisses?

12

When the fireworks concluded, parents began to gather their children and herd them toward the waiting cars in the parking lot. Some began a short walk home. The rest, teenagers and adults, made their way to the large dance pavilion near the carnival grounds.

Soon the band hired for the evening began to play. A few brave souls started dancing and before long the space was full of happy couples. Cassie and Matt joined in. Adam and Piper found seats on one of the benches that surrounded the pavilion. Fiona sat beside Piper, watching the dancers.

"Feel free to dance if someone asks you," Adam said to Piper. "Just because I can't manage it right now doesn't mean you have to sit out all night."

"I'd rather sit out with you than dance with anyone else," she said simply.

He reached out and took her hand, raised it to his lips for a brief caress, then rested their linked hands on his leg. Fiona could see the bond between the two of them. And it only heightened her sense of aloneness.

The band played old favorites, and requests when asked. Some were fast and furious, some slow and dreamy. Everyone seemed to enjoy the variety.

Fiona was about to get up and head for home when Sam appeared off to one side of the pavilion. He seemed to study the dancers for a moment, then looked around the perimeter. Spotting Fiona, Piper and Adam, he headed for them.

"Still keeping Bradford safe for its citizens, I see," Adam said lazily when Sam reached them.

He sat beside Fiona.

"Not much going on now. We're keeping an eye on the places serving alcoholic beverages to make sure someone doesn't want to over celebrate the Fourth. And I have two men at either end of town watching the roads. So far, it's been quiet."

The music changed to a slow ballad. Sam took a deep breath and put his hat on the bench beside him. Then he looked at Fiona and asked her to dance.

Piper nudged her and Fiona nodded, her heart pounding. She'd make a fool of herself, she knew it. She hadn't danced since high school. Hoping it was something that one never forgot, she rose and let Sam lead her onto the dance floor.

When he took both her hands and pulled her gently into his arms, her breath caught. She shimmered with nerves and anticipation. They fit as if they'd been made for each other. His hand was warm in the middle of her back, the hand holding hers strong and masculine. She felt a flutter of excitement when he tucked their hands in close to their bodies and pulled her even closer. She could feel every solid muscle, every motion of his legs as they moved around the crowded floor. Twice someone bumped into them, squeezing them even closer together.

"Are you enjoying yourself?" he asked.

"Yes," she said simply.

This moment was truly one to savor. For the first time since she could remember, Fiona gave herself up to the moment, relaxed and happy. As they moved to the rhythm of the song, she closed her eyes, her forehead against Sam's cheek. She felt feminine and light and almost cherished. For a little while, she let herself drift on the fantasy, but Fiona was too pragmatic to maintain that for long. Still enjoying the sensations that lapped through her, she opened her eyes and noticed the other dancers.

Reality jarred when she saw Allen McLennon dancing with someone across the floor.

"Who's McLennon with?" she asked.

"Where?"

Sam raised his head and looked around.

"At three o'clock," she said.

He deftly turned her in the dance pattern so he could see Allen.

"That's Milly Carmichael, the mayor's wife," Sam said.

Fiona almost groaned. Another notch for McLennon and another obstacle to overcome if she was to bring out the truth. He seemed to have the entire town on his side.

"They're in the same bridge club," Sam added.

"Which means they run in the same social circle. No one would ever suspect such a fine upstanding guy of doing anything so nefarious."

Sam snorted. "Nefarious? Not a strong enough word for such a nasty crime."

Hope blossomed in her chest. Maybe he was starting to believe her.

Sam's radio kicked in, static, then one of the deputies. Sam led her off the floor and into the darkness of the fairgrounds.

"Go ahead, Mark."

Sam's left hand had captured Fiona's and she stood beside him, watching the dancers, listening to the familiar cop-speak.

"I'll be there in about ten minutes," Sam ended. He clicked off the radio and looked at her.

"Sorry about that."

"Thanks for coming by. Go. I know tonight's a bad night to ignore any potential problem. Need help?"

He squeezed her hand gently.

"No. You're here on vacation, so enjoy. Come on, I'll take you back to Piper and Adam."

He retrieved his hat, spoke briefly to Adam and left.

Fiona resumed her seat on the bench. In only a moment a man she vaguely recognized came over.

"Fiona? I'm Bob Nelson, remember me from high school? Care to dance?"

She remembered Bobby Nelson. He was one of the wild boys, a high school football player whose outstanding ability kept him on the team despite the trouble he was constantly in. Remembering her role, she smiled and rose.

"Why, thank you, Bob, I'd be delighted. What have you been doing since we left school?"

The evening turned out to be fun and several other men from her high school days asked her to dance. Two were married, but after speaking with their wives, Fiona danced with them, urged on by one and all.

Throughout the evening she kept an eye on Allen McLennon, noting who he danced with, wondering what people would say if they knew the truth. Around eleven-thirty, McLennon left, double-checking his watch, walking out as if he had an important appointment. It raised all Fiona's red flags.

She finished the dance, thanked her partner and headed for the sidelines. Adam and Piper were standing and talking with another couple. Fiona joined them, waited for a break in the conversation, and said she was leaving for home.

"We are, too," Piper said. "I'm tired, and we still have a million things to do over the next few days."

Fiona waited until the house was quiet before sneaking downstairs. She was going to stake out the cottage where McLennon had taken her. She didn't like the feeling she'd had when she'd seen him with the teenager earlier. Nor the way he'd left the dance. If something was going down, she wanted to be there.

In the morning, she'd see if she could find out from the assessor's office to whom the property belonged. But in case there was any activity there tonight, she didn't plan to miss it.

The wooden floors of the old house creaked as she walked on them. She hoped the sound wouldn't wake Cassie or Piper. She opened the back door and then the screen door slowly to make sure they didn't squeak. Closing the screen behind her, she took one step and was grabbed from behind, a hand slapped over her mouth.

Fiona fought, but her captor held her too tightly for her to escape.

"Fiona?" Sam whispered.

She went still, almost limp. Her heart raced, adrenaline pumping through her. When he eased his hold, she twisted around to glare at him.

"What the hell are you doing?" she whispered, conscious of the two women inside asleep.

She was almost mad enough not to care if she woke them.

"I stopped by to see if you were up," he said. "Then I saw movement in the dark and waited. What are you doing?"

The moonlight wasn't bright, but she could tell he was no longer wearing his uniform. He was in dark clothes the same as she. Had his shift ended? It was after midnight. A little late to be calling, but she might've still been up, and she was, actually. Only, not dressed for callers.

"I'm going for a walk."

"Okay. We can walk together. Since the house is dark, I assume the others are asleep?"

"Yes. I didn't want to wake them, so I didn't turn on lights. I wanted to be alone."

"Tough. Come on, let's explore the neighborhood in the dark."

Fiona dug in her heels and glared at him.

"All right, I was going to the cottage. What if he drags another girl there? You didn't see him with that teenager today. Nor did you see him leave tonight. It sure looked like he was a man with places to go."

"I said I'd handle things. Why can't you let me?

"Why can't you let me help?"

"We'll go together, then," Sam said a couple of seconds later. "But only to observe. I need more proof than seeing a man use a cottage."

He grabbed her arm again and walked to the patrol car.

"Oh, this'll keep us undercover," Fiona said. "Every person in the county knows the sheriff's car."

"And you think they don't know that rented convertible of yours by now? Relax. I have it figured out. We'll pull into that first driveway on the left, park out of sight."

"How do you know about that?" she asked as she got into the car and quietly closed the door. A glance at the house revealed they hadn't woken anybody.

When he was behind the wheel, he looked at her.

"I went back where I saw you come out this afternoon. Explored both places, but knew from the fresh footprints around the one place which one you'd been interested in."

"You followed me?"

"No, I backtracked. Saw the two cottages. The place on the left looks as if it hasn't been used in a long time. Can't say that about the one you examined."

Fiona didn't know whether to be angry he'd followed her or relieved he seemed to be taking the investigation seriously.

"It did look more recently used, didn't it?"

Fiona settled back in the seat and tried to figure out how she felt about having Sam with her. She so wanted others to believe her. Maybe working as a partner with the sheriff would lead to new discoveries. She usually worked with a partner, after all. But she was not attracted to her partner at home. Sam was a different matter.

It was after midnight. If they hadn't been so tired from working the fair, Piper and Cassie would still have been up. The faint glow of lights from the carnival showed there were revelers in town still enjoying the celebration. It was possible McLennon might use the cottage tonight. If not, she'd try to find Janine Flowers tomorrow and ask her some questions.

A short time later Sam swung the patrol car into the narrow road off the highway. It was a fool's errand, he knew. If McLennon was at the cottage on the right, he'd probably hear the car and see the lights through the trees. Still, he couldn't let Fiona go by herself.

He pulled deep into the left-hand driveway curve, stopped and cut the lights. The darkness closed in.

"Ready?" he asked.

She clicked on a small flashlight.

"As ever," she said, reaching up to flick off his interior light so there'd be no telltale glow when they opened the door. He had to admit she was a pro.

The crickets would provide cover for sounds, he thought as they started back to the narrow road. They could clomp along in gravel and not be heard five feet away. The moist night air didn't stir. The moss-draped trees looked ghostly.

They walked in silence. Sam remembered other stakeouts he'd done in New Orleans. He and his partner had thought alike, communicated only with hand gestures. How often had Fiona done this? Was she often in danger?

He watched as she flicked on the pencil-thin light from time to time. The road was fairly straight and there was enough difference between the darkness and shadows beneath the trees to keep walking in the center. When they reached the second driveway, things would change.

"You're sure this is the place?" he asked softly.

"I'm sure. It was pouring rain, but I remember. I can show you where I took off into the woods. I wandered around for hours, afraid he'd find me or I'd get so lost I'd never find my way home."

The open area where the cottage sat came into view. They slowed, keeping quiet, using the light only when necessary. The house was dark. There was no car in sight.

Finding a spot near the side of the house behind a huge old oak tree, they sat on the ground, leaning against the tree. Now they waited.

"Different from L.A.," she murmured.

"Different from New Orleans," he replied.

"I hope we find something," she said a few minutes later. "I so want him caught and brought to justice."

Sam, too, wanted justice. Especially for this woman beside him. It hurt to think of the pain she had suffered so long ago.

Sam settled in, knowing the chances of anyone showing up were minimal. If the unlikely happened, however, he wanted to be there.

Fiona wasn't at all restless, seeming content to sit in stillness and silence.

The crickets hummed. A car could be heard on the highway.

"It's pretty quiet," he said at last. Might as well take advantage of the downtime by talking.

"If you don't count the crickets."

He heard her get to her feet, could see her silhouette.

"What are you doing?"

"Just checking the house."

"Allen McLennon won't be traipsing through the woods to get there. If he comes, it'll be in his car."

She settled back down.

"I hate stakeouts," she said. "They're so boring."

He asked if she'd done many.

"A couple when I was doing some other drug work, but now I'm undercover. I work high-risk high schools. Stop the kids from getting hooked early."

"So no stakeouts, but a lot of stress maintaining your cover."

"Not any more than here in Bradford," she murmured.

"How so?"

"I've never smiled and greeted so many people in my life. I feel like Suzy Sunshine."

He laughed softly.

"No one would mistake you for a ray of sunshine. You're back to black, I see."

"I like black."

"You look pretty in colors."

Darn, he hadn't meant to say that.

She was silent for a moment.

"What was your wife like?" she asked.

Sam hadn't expected that.

"As in looks, personality, marriage partner, what?"

"Start with looks and move on to the rest," she said. "Why?"

"So I can get a picture of her. And get to know you better. You two went to school together, didn't you?"

"With Adam and Michael," he said, mentioning one of the New Orleans Saints football players who'd come to the fair.

"In Baton Rouge."

"Piper fill you in?"

"As it applies to her. She's a bit nervous, I think, about meeting Adam's family."

"Why? They'll be happy to see him settle down."

"Maybe. Anyway, tell me about your wife."

"Patty wasn't as tall as you and was more rounded, I guess I'd say."

"Filled out more, huh?" she asked.

"She worried about her weight, though I could never understand why. I thought she was perfect."

Fiona stifled a groan. Perfect, great. Just her opposite.

"What color was her hair?"

"Light brown—it had golden highlights when she was in the sun. She wore it long, below her shoulders."

He fell silent. Probably remembering the feel and texture of Patty's hair. Missing her all over again because she was asking inane questions about her.

"What did she do?"

"Taught school, first grade. She loved that age group—eager to learn, not smart-alecky."

"She should have come to L.A. They're born with attitudes."

"She wanted to go to California for a vacation one year. We never made it."

Fiona thought about that. She had no long-range plans, but how sad to make them and not be able to carry them out.

"Would I have liked her?" she asked, suddenly

wondering.

"Maybe, or maybe you would have found her too soft, too womanly."

That stung. Didn't he think of her as womanly?

Probably not. To other cops, she was one of the guys. She fostered that image, so why be annoyed when he picked up on it?

"You miss her," she said.

"Of course. We planned to spend our lives together. Who knew hers would be so short? It's hard to go on without her. I wish I'd done things differently, made changes. She'd have loved Bradford, the friendly neighbors, the slower pace of life. She'd have done well in the schools here, I think."

Fiona didn't want to hear any more. She could hear the pain in his voice. He missed her still. Piper said his wife had died three years ago.

"Do you think you'll ever get married again?" she asked.

"I don't plan on it. I loved Patty completely. What would be left for someone else?"

Nothing, she guessed.

The silence stretched out until Fiona thought she'd go crazy. She wanted to get up and walk around, check inside the house. See if she could find something to let Sam know she was on the right track. She knew he didn't fully accept her story. No one had believed her before, so why should this near stranger believe her now?

"What do you do in your free time in Los Angeles?"

he asked a few moments later.

"There's not much free time."

"Do you surf?"

"Sometimes. It looks effortless when pros do it. It's hard to balance, however, and I never have time to practice as much as I need. Mostly I work, or catch up on sleep on my off time."

"No hobbies? What do you do with friends?"

She thought about how isolated she was.

"I have very few friends who I hang out with, but mostly I visit the local cop bar, or stay to myself. Working undercover, I don't want to blur the lines between my normal life and the one I'm portraying."

"Sounds lonely. You said you had no one special, right?"

"Right."

"Why not? You can't work all the time."

"Maybe I'm not womanly enough."

"I bet you're woman enough," he said, pulling her closer.

Fiona's senses ramped up as he did so. She craved Sam's touch, she realized. She ached with loneliness sometimes, but was too fearful of being hurt to get close to anyone. And this man couldn't be a candidate. He still loved his dead wife. He'd put down roots in a town that had turned on Fiona. He still doubted her story.

He didn't make any moves on her, much to Fiona's disappointment. He just leaned against the wide trunk, easing her back against him to make it more comfortable.

The minutes ticked by, the only sound the crickets.

Fiona became more and more aware of Sam as time crawled by. His breathing matched hers. Despite the heat of the night, his warmth was welcomed. She watched the house, wishing a car would drive up, a light would switch on. Something to make this stakeout worthwhile.

Sam's scent infiltrated her senses. Even at the end of a long day he smelled good. She wished she could close her eyes and lean against him, absorbing every bit of him to hold on to in the years to come.

A truck sounded on the highway, then silence.

"Nothing's going down tonight," Sam said, checking his watch.

"What time is it?"

"It's after two."

She sat up and away from him. Had she dozed off?

"The night's not over," she said.

"But the watch is," Sam said, rising. "No one's coming."

Fiona didn't want to give up, but he was right. Something would have happened by now if it was going to. But it was her best hope, and she hated to see it fade.

"Come on, I'll take you home."

Fiona rose, dusted off the damp earth that clung to her jeans and followed Sam back to the car. A cloud covering had moved in while they'd watched, and the night was darker than before. She was glad for the small flashlight she carried.

They reached his car without incident, however, and without seeing any sign of Allen McLennon. Fiona was disappointed in more ways than one.

"A total bust," she complained, sliding into the passenger seat.

"Things change in twelve years, Fiona. Even if Allen tried something back then, nothing says he would do anything today."

"*If* he tried something? He did. And from the way he was pressuring that teenager today, he hasn't changed."

"Pressuring? You said he was talking to her. She could be the daughter of a friend of Allen's or something."

"Or someone he's pressuring. It looked like it to me."

Sam started the car and reversed out of the driveway to the narrow road, then turned, and headed for the highway.

Fiona vowed to go there again. She knew Sam didn't believe her. It was amazing he'd agreed to the stakeout to begin with. Tomorrow night. And the next if need be. She was sure there was something going on. If she had to find out on her own, so be it.

By the time Sam turned into the driveway of Margaret's old house, Fiona was wide awake and full of ideas. First thing tomorrow she'd see if she could track down the girl. Talk to her, both as a woman and a cop. Maybe she'd get lucky.

If the girl didn't feel comfortable telling her parents or the local law, though, she probably wouldn't talk to a stranger from out of town. It was still worth a try.

Sam stopped in front of the darkened house, the front porch light the only illumination.

"What now?" he asked.

"Now?"

She looked at him in surprise.

"What do you mean? I'm going in and to bed. I thought you'd do the same."

Sam turned to face her, resting his arm on the steering wheel.

"Tomorrow?"

"I guess I'll see what Cassie and Piper want to do. Piper's wedding is coming up next weekend. I expect there're lots of things to see to. And she's taking off to meet Adam's parents, so all the work will fall to me and Cassie."

Sam leaned closer, as if trying to see her better.

"You're not giving up this stakeout, are you?"

Slowly Fiona shook her head.

"I can find my way there on my own. I don't expect you to give up your nights on what may prove to be a wild-goose chase."

"I want to find the truth, too," Sam said.

He reached over and drew her close—as close as the paraphernalia in the center of the bench seat would allow. His mouth found hers in the dark and he kissed her.

Fiona steeled herself not to respond. She was not going to be swayed by some guy who thought she was making things up. But it was hard. His lips were coaxing, warm and firm. His touch had her blood singing through her veins. She longed to wrap her arms around his neck and hold on as long as the night lasted.

But then she broke the contact and pulled back.

"Nice try, Sheriff, but I'm still going."

"I'll go with you."

"I don't need help."

"Do you have a gun?"

"No, I left mine at the precinct until I get back. Do you think he's dangerous?"

"If Allen is the one who beat you bloody, what do you think?"

"I've learned a few things since then," Fiona said confidently.

She was good at what she did. Opening the door, she slid out.

"Thanks for tonight," she said.

Sam was out just as fast, catching up with her on the walk and accompanying her to the porch.

"Don't go unless I'm with you, Fiona," he warned.

"Or?"

"Or I'll bust you so fast your head will spun."

She laughed, taunting him, she knew, but she liked living dangerously.

"On what grounds, Sheriff?"

"Trespassing, if nothing else."

"It wasn't posted."

She hadn't seen any signs, but she hadn't been looking, either. Still, it was a bogus charge, and he had to know it.

"Then I'll find a charge."

He faced her on the porch, his gaze steady.

She looked up and glared at him.

"Sounds like you learned from your predecessor, Sheriff. I know the law—I won't break it."

He sucked in a breath.

"Don't tar me with that same brush. I'm not going to railroad you. If you have justifiable reason, I'm in. If not, you're pushing your luck."

"I know what happened."

"There's still nothing to substantiate your story," he said again, patiently, almost wearily. "And there's reason for you and the others to have a grudge against Allen. Think about it dispassionately, Fiona. Would you follow a case like this if it were in L.A.? The only records I have are of you being a troublemaker when you lived here before. Nothing has been said or done for the past twelve years, and out of the blue you show up and accuse one of the town's leading citizens right after he tried to foreclose on Margaret's property."

Fiona stared at him, feeling more alone than ever. She knew it didn't play well. If Margaret hadn't had her stroke, Fiona would have left it alone the rest of her life.

And missed out on resuming Cassie and Piper's friendship. The few days she'd been back showed her how much she wanted to restore and cling to that old friendship. To be a part of that loving family again. To have a place to belong.

Sam put his knuckles beneath her chin, raising her head.

"I want to *prove* what happened," he said. "Give me a chance here."

"Do what you have to do," she said.

"Sounds like an invitation."

With that, he took her head between his warm palms and kissed her again.

This time Fiona didn't hold back. She craved his touch the way a man in the desert craved water. His mouth moved over hers, opening her lips. The shock of desire surprised her, then it flooded through her, feeling right. She could almost imagine a different ending to things. He pulled her into an embrace, his arms molding her body to his hard contours. She felt his own desire grow and her heart raced. This was more than she expected.

And more than she wanted. She couldn't deal with such an attraction when she was trying to get another part of her life straightened out. This was a dead-end situation. She needed to keep her wits about her.

But for another moment she reveled in the feel of Sam's tongue against hers, the strength of his muscles as he held her, the burning heat of desire.

Old memories and fears flared. She squashed them ruthlessly. This was Sam. He'd never hurt her.

The night air seemed to hold its breath. Time was

suspended. In another life she might have invited him in to her room. But Fiona didn't do one-night stands.

And she didn't take risks with her heart.

She eased back, felt a certain satisfaction in hearing Sam's hard breathing. She was almost gasping for breath herself. For a second, she wanted to plunge back in, but sanity took hold.

"I've got to go," she said.

She opened the screen door and tried the knob. It was unlocked. Some things never changed in Bradford.

"Call me in the morning," Sam said.

"Good night, Sheriff," she replied, closing the door.

She was going to follow through with her own investigation. If Sam found out, he'd have a fit, but so what? Only Cassie and Piper believed her. She had to prove it to the rest of the world on her own.

13

Despite her mixed feelings about Sam, Fiona called him early the next morning.

"What's up?" Sam asked.

"I thought I'd find out from the county records who owns that property."

"Fiona."

"I know, stay out of it. But it's a matter of public record. What can it hurt to find out who owns it?"

"Allen McLennon's aunt owns the property. I checked it out as soon as I saw you coming from that road yesterday. She got it from her folks way back when. No one uses it since everyone lives in Bradford. Sometimes she rents it out, but lately it's been vacant."

"Oh."

More evidence that Sam was investigating. The thought warmed her.

"I worked yesterday, so I can take some comp time. Want to spend the day with me?" he asked.

She leaned against the wall near the living room, hearing the workers on the second floor.

"Doing what?"

"Whatever you like."

"Even going into New Orleans? I'd like to see the place again, and get something for two weddings that are coming up fast."

"How are plans for both events going?"

"Betsy is doing invitations, which are being hand-delivered today and tomorrow for both couples. Piper and Adam leave this afternoon for Baton Rouge and won't be back until Friday. Did you know he hasn't even told his parents about Piper? Talk about a shock when they show up."

"They'll love her. And be glad he's settling down. His sister has been married for years."

"Cassie and Betsy are handling the reception, and everything else seems pretty set. I thought weddings took months of planning and cost staggering amounts."

"Lavish church weddings do," Sam said. "But they're getting married at the chapel, with just close friends and family. It can be as complex or as simple as they wish."

"What was yours like?" she asked.

Why did she keep harping on his marriage? To remind herself he was off-limits?

"Lavish church wedding. We had half of Baton Rouge, I think. Patty had the most exquisite dress."

He stopped.

"And?"

"And it was the longest day of my life. I was glad when it was over."

Fiona thought about it. If she ever thought about

getting married, which she never did, she'd go for simple, quiet and small. But then, she didn't have a lot of friends she'd want to share the event with.

Thinking over the last couple of days, she wondered if that were still true.

She'd seen several friends from high school at the fair and dance afterward. A couple had even made tentative plans to get together with her to catch up. She planned to see what former friends were doing now and to glean any tidbit of information she might be able to in order to build a case against Allen McLennon. There had to be something out there, and if there was, she'd find it.

"I'll pick you up at ten," he said. "We'll head for the Big Easy for lunch, then you can shop."

"I don't take long—I'm not into shopping like a lot of people are. I already know what I want to get for each of them. Pick me up at the convalescent hospital—I'm going to visit Margaret."

Fiona arrived shortly after Margaret returned from physical therapy. There was a young woman in her room talking to her.

"Am I interrupting?"

"Oh, hello. You must be one of Margaret's girls. Come in. I'm Sheila Compton, speech therapist. We normally meet around now, but I have a conflict today and was arranging another time with Margaret. I come to my patients, so even when she moves back home, we'll continue."

Fiona nodded, smiling at Margaret.

"Then we have time to visit a little while. Sam's taking me into New Orleans later to buy presents for Cassie and Piper. Can I get you anything?"

Margaret shook her head, patting the bed with her left hand.

Fiona sat gingerly on the edge and looked at Sheila.

"She *is* getting better, isn't she?"

"Indeed she is. Before many more months, she'll be talking just like before."

Fiona's heart sank. She didn't have many more months in Bradford. She was heading back to L.A.

There was nothing to say she couldn't come back for a visit. Maybe at Thanksgiving or Christmas. Normally Fiona worked those holidays, but this year, she just might ask for the time off.

For the first time since she left Bradford, she wished she didn't live so far away.

After Sheila left, Fiona regaled Margaret with the parts of the fair she'd missed, ending with the dancing and how much she herself had danced.

"I was quite the belle of the ball," she said.

"And as pretty as Cinderella on a good day," Sam said from the doorway. "How are you doing, Miss Margaret?"

She smiled and nodded. "Ffffffffiii."

"Fine, are you? Well, you look almost as pretty as Fiona did last night. I hear you're going home soon and can start to resume activities as you see fit."

"Wedddd," she said.

"First up Piper and Adam's, then Cassie and Matt's. And you'll see them both."

Sam sounded confident.

She nodded, looking pleased.

"Ready to go?" Sam asked Fiona.

Fiona nodded.

"See you tomorrow," she told Margaret, giving her a hug.

The traffic on the highway was light and Sam made good time getting into New Orleans. Fiona had been surprised to see the sedan when he picked her up. She expected him to drive a pickup truck or SUV. Still, it was several years old and probably from the days he and his wife shared it. It was comfortable, and when he put soft jazz in the CD player, she settled back to enjoy the ride.

"What first?" he said as they approached the city.

"Let's park in the French Quarter and wander around for a bit. We have tons of Spanish architecture in California, but little of the fancy French influence the Quarter's famous for."

"So you missed Bradford?" Sam asked as he deftly handled the midweek traffic. Before long, he'd squeezed into a parking space near Adamson Square.

"If you'd asked me that two weeks ago, I'd have given you an emphatic no," Fiona said, slipping out of the car and taking in a breath of air—hot, sultry, smelling of oil and water and age. Nothing like it in the world.

"Now?" Sam asked, feeding the meter and joining her on the sidewalk. As one, they turned and headed for Adamson Square.

"I was thinking earlier that I wished I lived closer to Bradford. I have lots of vacation time saved up. I can make several trips a year if I want."

"Not like *living* here, though."

"Oh!" Fiona said as she saw Adamson Square. She smiled. "I remember the first time Margaret brought us here. I was so awed by the horse and rider," she said, referring to the sculpture that dominated the square in front of the old Catholic church.

"We walked around the park, then she took us for beignets and hot chocolate at the Café du Monde. I think we were around seven."

"We can still indulge in beignets as long as you don't spoil your appetite. There's a place that serves the best gumbo in the state on Royal Street, if it's still there."

"A favorite of yours and your wife's?" she asked as they headed for the famous outdoor café.

"I found it after Patty was killed. She would have loved it. I'm betting you will, too."

"I'm nothing like your wife was," Fiona said quickly.

Sam slowed his pace and looked at her.

"That's right. But does that mean anything she liked you can't? Or vice versa? If she hated something, you'll automatically love it? If it bothers you for me to talk about her, I won't."

"It doesn't bother me. And you should talk about her. The saddest thing is when someone dies and no one speaks of them. It's as if they were never there. People need to remember those who were here and are no longer."

They reached the Café du Monde and Fiona was glad to change the subject.

They ate dessert first by having the sugary French doughnuts before going for hearty gumbo.

Fiona bought her presents and Sam stowed them in the trunk of the car. They wandered the Quarter, window-shopping. When they returned to Adamson Square, the fortune tellers were out in full force, artists were painting the famous scene and horse-drawn carriages lined up to carry tourists around in old-fashioned style. Nothing had changed in the old section of the Big Easy since she'd last been. Probably nothing ever would. It was nice to find some stability in the old town.

"Want your fortune told, dear?" an elderly woman asked, shuffling tarot cards.

"No, thanks," Fiona said.

"Afraid to know the future?" Sam murmured as they walked by.

"No, afraid to count too much on hogwash. I don't mind having everything unfold as it happens."

"I'll offer half price," the woman called after them.

Fiona turned and shook her head, smiling at the rapidity with which the woman tried to cajole another into having her fortune told.

It was late afternoon when they started back for Bradford. Fiona was pleasantly tired. They'd walked miles through the riverside part of New Orleans. She'd eaten more than she should have, laughed more than she'd expected to. All in all the day had been wonderful. Sam was easy to talk to, commanded attention wherever they went, yet didn't seem to notice.

As they were driving back, Fiona checked her watch.

"Piper has met Adam's parents by now. How do you think it went?"

"I think they'll be charmed with her. The most important thing to both of them is Adam's happiness. Of course, the prospect of more grandchildren will also be up there."

"I can't picture Piper as a mother."

"You don't think she'll be a good one?"

"I guess she'll spoil her kids to death. She missed having a family so much growing up, she'll make it up by being the perfect mother—and loving it. Still, I think of her and Cassie as my friends from when we were teenagers, not grown, competent women with lives so different from what we thought we'd have. And children never figured into our talk of the future."

"You were still kids yourselves when you dreamed of being grown-up," Sam said. "I doubt lots of teens think about having children when they grow up. They're too busy flirting with all the guys."

"I guess Cassie and Matt will have a family, too,"

she said.

She'd be relegated to the role of favorite aunt, coming in from the West Coast for holidays, enjoying her best friends' children, then leaving to return to the solitary existence she'd built for herself.

She sighed.

"What's that for?" Sam asked.

"Just thinking about things. I hope Adam's parents love Piper and include her in the family right away. It would mean so much to her."

"Trust Adam, he'll make sure they treat her right."

"In case you haven't noticed, I'm not big on trust," she said.

"It's that chip on your shoulder. Gets in the way, I expect."

Fiona laughed, leaning her head back and closing her eyes. She felt safe and relaxed. She'd nap the rest of the way. Their outing last night had lasted far later than she'd expected.

And she planned to stake out the cottage again tonight and every night as long as she was here, in the chance of finding Allen McLennon with another victim.

"With Piper gone, Cassie and Matt have a chance for dinner alone if you're not there."

"So?"

"So have dinner with me," Sam said. "We'll barbecue or something."

"If you're talking barbecue, let's go to that place out on Route 108. I haven't eaten there since I got back, and it's the best in the state."

"Done."

Sam wasn't sure why he'd extended the invitation to dinner. They'd spent the day together. Nothing said they had to stay in each other's company. Yet he was reluctant to end the day. Fiona's enjoyment of New Orleans had been sincere. She wasn't one to dissemble. If she liked something, everyone knew it.

She was focused and honest and didn't care a whit what others thought. He knew she'd never contrive to accuse anyone of something they didn't do. He believed Allen McLennon had done exactly what she said. He knew sometimes the best covering could hide something rotten.

He wanted to find proof. Something that would explain why the three girls had been sent away so abruptly, disrupting four lives. That each had succeeded was a testament to their good upbringing by Margaret Nunes.

"You all didn't deserve what happened," Sam said slowly.

Fiona rolled her head to the left and looked at him. "What?"

"You and the others did not deserve to be sent away. Margaret was as much a victim as you, Fiona. Piper and Cassie, as well. We'll find out who and why, and make sure one way or another the scales of justice are balanced."

"Don Quixote, tilting at windmills. I'm not sure the scales are ever balanced. Does this mean maybe you're starting to believe me?"

"I believe you."

He flicked her a glance and saw the most amazing sight—Fiona in tears.

"Hey, what did I say?" Sam said, feeling like he'd been punched in the gut.

"That you believed me. Finally. No one did back then."

"Everyone you talk to now will. We will find out what we can and nail the bastard."

"If he wasn't caught twelve years ago, it's unlikely he'll be caught now."

"Hey, I wasn't on the case then."

Fiona laughed shakily.

It was true. If he *had* been, the entire episode would have played out differently. He valued honor and integrity too much to get caught in the trap the former sheriff had been in. To Sam, wearing the badge was a sacred trust. He was almost angrier at Sheriff Halstead for violating that trust than at McLennon for perpetrating a crime. Almost.

The sun was low in the sky by the time they reached the barbecue place outside of town. It was after seven, and the parking lot was full. They parked at the edge and walked to the crowded restaurant. The rich aroma of barbecue filled their nostrils when they entered. The noise level was only a few decibels below deafening.

Fiona looked around, an amused expression on her face.

She looked at Sam and leaned closer so he could

hear her.

"It doesn't look as if it's changed one bit. Amazing. I can't wait to get some ribs!"

It took longer than either wanted, but within forty-five minutes they were seated in a booth, a pile of ribs smothered in sauce before them.

"Heaven," Fiona said a moment later, licking her lips, then her fingertips.

Sam watched her, conscious of an attraction he couldn't deny. She looked like she enjoyed ribs more than anything. He felt a tightening in his gut.

He wanted her. He wanted to taste those lips and lick off the sauce that clung. He wanted to brush his fingers through that short hair and see if it felt as silky as it looked. He wanted to feel her against him again, as he had when he kissed her.

"What?" she asked, reaching for her napkin. "Didn't I get it all?"

Sam shook his head.

"There's a little near the corner of your mouth, and it's driving me nuts. *You're* driving me nuts."

She blinked at his words, slowly bringing her napkin to wipe away the dab of sauce, her eyes never leaving his. For a moment Sam wondered if she understood what he meant, but her widened eyes showed she did.

Then Fiona looked at her plate, putting the napkin back in her lap and taking another rib. She ate slowly, never lifting her eyes in his direction.

Obviously the attraction was one-sided. He might

not have dated since high school, but he knew when a woman wasn't interested. Too many had come on to him over the years since Patty died for him not to know that.

Blast it. The first woman he was interested in—more than interested in—and she didn't return that interest.

The disappointment hit him hard. He ate methodically, not tasting the food. Counting the minutes until he could take her home and say good night. Sam knew there'd be no good-night kiss. She wouldn't lead him on now that he'd revealed his hand, so to speak.

And obviously made a fool of himself.

The silence would have been awkward except for the buzz of noise surrounding them. At least she hadn't laughed in his face or gotten up and left in a snit.

"The thing is, Sheriff," she said a moment later, fiddling with her water glass, "I'm not good with relationships. And we don't know each other very well. You'd come up on the short end of things even if we lived near each other, which we don't. I can't afford a long-distance relationship. And what fun would that be, anyway?"

He stared at her, slowly putting down the rib he was gnawing. She wouldn't meet his eyes.

"How would we know if we didn't try?" he said, attempting to figure out if she was letting him down easily or if she would feel differently if they both lived in Bradford.

She flicked a glance at him, then quickly looked away. She turned the water glass faster.

"I'm leaving in another week. Anyway, you've been married and all and I haven't and it wouldn't be..."

She trailed off.

He glanced at her plate and his. They'd eaten more than half. Enough to satisfy hunger. "Come on, let's get out of here and discuss this."

She looked at the ceiling and shook her head.

"There's nothing to discuss."

In less than five minutes Sam paid the check and had her in his car, the door closed to the rest of the world.

He debated how to begin when inspiration struck. He leaned over and kissed her.

She responded after a second's hesitation. Fire lit between them. He pulled her closer, regretting he hadn't waited until they were at home without the constraints of the car. She kissed him back as if he were food to a starving man, and his desire shot through the roof. He wanted her in an elemental way he hadn't wanted anyone in years.

The kiss went on and on, until Sam vaguely became aware of the activity in the parking lot. He hated to end this, but he didn't want to be caught kissing in some public venue like some kid with no control. Which he almost didn't have.

"Come home with me," he said against her mouth, reluctantly ending the kiss.

Fiona pushed back and scooted to her side of the

car, putting her hands on her cheeks. Sam saw she was breathing as hard as he was.

"Goodness, Sam, I can't go home with you. What would people think?"

"Who, exactly?" he asked, already starting the engine.

"Anyone who saw us. I'm leaving in a few days, so gossip wouldn't bother me, but you have to live here. A public official has to be above reproach."

"What I do on my own time is my own business," he retorted, pulling out of the space and merging into traffic on the highway.

"Sounds good in L.A., but this is a small town where everyone knows what everyone else is doing. If you won't watch out for yourself, I'll do it for you. And for me."

"Because?"

"Because if I do get to bring a suit to court, I don't want any allegations of wrongdoing on my part, like seducing the sheriff into finding evidence for my side."

"This is the twenty-first century. I'm not going to manufacture any evidence one way or the other. If I can uncover the facts, that's what I'll do." His voice was firm.

Fiona was silent.

Sam drove, reluctantly seeing her side of things.

"If it weren't for Allen McLennon and what he did, would you feel differently?"

"I'd still *feel* the same," she said in a low voice, "but I would sure *act* differently. I'd go home with you in a heartbeat. But I think you'd be the one disappointed."

Sam looked at her. Was she saying she wanted him as much as he wanted her? All the more reason to find any evidence that would prove Allen's guilt. Never had he had such a reward to look forward to for solving a case!

Fiona slipped out of the car as soon as he stopped at Margaret's house.

"Thanks for taking me to New Orleans," she said, reaching into the back for her packages.

Sam got out of the car and came around to her side. It'd have been too much to hope he'd tell her goodbye and drive off. But she wasn't sure she was up to another kiss. They about made her forget her name.

Holding the presents for Piper and Cassie as a shield, she turned to face him.

"And for dinner. Thank you for dinner."

He laughed softly.

"Miss Margaret's manners are paying off."

She scowled. She was using politeness as another barrier, but it didn't seem to be working.

"I'll walk you to the door and say good night. No stakeout tonight?"

She shrugged. "No. I thought last night after the fair might be a good time, but I doubt anything would go down midweek. But Friday night, that might be another matter."

"And if I said leave it to me?"

"I'd say, another pair of eyes and ears are always helpful. Who knows, it might rain."

"We'll go together," he said.

"Doesn't that fly in the face of your edict that I stay

out of things?" she asked, reaching the screen door.

She could open it and slip inside without another kiss.

"Yes, but if I know you, and I think I'm starting to, you would go out, anyway, just sit in another part of the woods."

She debated telling him she wanted to talk to Janine Flowers about what she'd seen at the fair. Maybe she had been projecting and there was nothing to worry about. How silly to sit in the dark night after night if she was imagining things.

And there was Peter Johnstone to consult with again. Tomorrow would be busy. There were also any last-minute details for Piper's wedding she and Cassie would have to see to.

"I won't go out again unless I tell you," she agreed.

He cupped her face in his palms.

"When this is over, you and I have a lot of things to discuss."

Her heart caught, skipped a beat and then settled into double time. He was so close she could see the faint light from the house shining in his eyes.

"I live in L.A."

"Change that."

For a moment she was tempted. What could explode between them? She had no idea but yearned to find out.

"My job is there, my home. I never wanted to live in Bradford."

"As a teenager. You're grown now. Look at the town as it is now, not as you remember it. Wait and see."

He lowered his head to kiss her.

She knew it was dangerous to like Sam so much. His kisses inflamed her. When she was with him, she was thinking of changing everything about her, from where she lived to the clothes she wore. How pathetic was that? He wanted to kiss her, sounded like he wanted to get naked with her. But beyond that, what?

She pulled back. "Good night," she said, slipping inside before she threw caution to the wind and went with Sam wherever he wanted.

Sam watched her enter the old house. He'd just asked her to stay. Almost asked her to stay with him.

Would that be bad? She'd drive him up the wall at times, but her mouth was sweet as honey and her body had his on fire from just his looking at it. He was starting to imagine her on the porch with him after dinner, sitting and talking over their respective days.

What he wouldn't let himself imagine was their going to the bedroom together, sharing his bed, waking up in the morning together.

Who was he kidding? He didn't have to imagine it— the images came unbidden.

He feared he was falling for her and he hadn't had one crumb of encouragement. Was he heading for heartache a second time?

The next morning, after Cassie had given her a list of things to do and then departed, Fiona went to the phone directory to look up Flowers. There were three families with that name. She dialed the first one and asked for Janine.

"Janine is my brother Rob's daughter," the man who answered said. "What you want her for?"

Fiona couldn't come up with an answer, so she hung up.

She noted the address for an R. Flowers and headed out. If she remembered the town right, the street was near the high school. It wasn't yet as hot as it would be later, which made for a pleasant walk. She wore shorts and one of Piper's tops. Glad for her short hair, she was perspiring by the time she reached the street.

Walking along, she checked the numbers until she saw the old house where Janine lived. It was not as well kept as the neighbors', not that the neighborhood was upscale or pristine. There was an old car in the driveway.

Fiona walked up and knocked on the door. A middle-aged woman answered.

"I was wondering if I could talk with Janine?" Fiona asked.

"She's out back weeding. Go on around," the woman said, shutting the door.

Fiona went around the side of the house and saw the teenager on her knees near a large garden plot pulling up weeds. Fiona glanced at the house. No sign of anyone watching them.

"Janine?" she said as she drew closer to the girl.

Janine looked up, squinting a little in the bright

sunshine.

"Yeah?"

Fiona squatted down beside her, looking at the neat rows of vegetables and the pile of weeds. "Growing your own veggies?"

"Yeah, like that's something I'd do. It's Mama's garden. Gives us something to eat. Who are you?"

"Fiona Hunter. I'm a friend of Cassie Hodges."

"Does Cassie have another job for me?"

"I think she'll be calling later today about the weddings."

"I heard that model was getting married to some television dude," Janine said. "I'd love to work that wedding."

"So things are kinda tough around here," Fiona said.

Instantly Janine seemed to close up.

"We're getting by all right. My dad's been sick, but he's getting better."

"Glad to hear that. One of the nice things about a small town is how everyone rallies around when someone's in trouble."

"Ha. What century are you from? No one's helped us except the Ladies Aid from the church."

Fiona looked at the house.

"Do your folks own the house? If times are hard, maybe the bank will hold off collecting the mortgage until you're on your feet."

Janine jumped up, looking as if she was about to bolt.

"What do you want?"

Fiona rose slowly, stepped back to make sure she didn't make Janine feel threatened.

"When I was a teenager, I lived in Bradford. I had a bad experience one night, and no one in town believed me. Since I was just a foster kid, I got sent away to another foster home and was told not to contact anyone here again. I know what it's like to be a teenager and have no one believe me when I say something people don't want to hear."

Janine licked her lips. "Like what?"

"Like when some old man is coming on to me and I don't want him to."

14

"I don't know what you're talking about," Janine said.

"I saw you with Allen McLennon at the fair," Fiona said.

"So?"

"So it didn't look like a good meeting to me. What did he want?"

Janine stared at her for a moment, then dropped her gaze.

"Nothing. He said he'd make my dad pay if I ever told anyone."

Fiona wished Allen was standing there with them. She'd haul off and sock him one. She took a breath and began to talk.

"I cut school one day, Janine, and went riding with a wild boy from my class. When I wouldn't put out for him, he dumped me, in the rain, miles and miles from home. I began to walk. Allen McLennon picked me up and I thought he was going to take me home. Instead, he took me to a cottage deep in the woods and tried to rape me," Fiona said. "I fought him like a wildcat, but he was older, bigger, stronger. He beat me until I was unconscious."

Janine's eyes filled with tears. In a second she covered her face with her hands and gave way to sobs.

Fiona wanted to step in and give comfort, but she needed to find out what was going on first.

"When I finally got home, no one would believe me. Not my foster mother, not the sheriff, no one. They accused me of making it up, of some kid from school beating me and me covering up for him and trying to cause problems for the adults."

Janine continued to cry, shaking in her anguish.

"What's your story with Allen McLennon?" Fiona asked softly.

Janine tried to stop crying, wiping her eyes with her fists, but the sobbing wouldn't cease.

"My dad's been so sick. He almost died. The medical bills are staggering, my mom says. We could lose everything and be street people. She's doing the best she can. She got a job at the grocery store and works hard. But caring for my dad, and working and everything, it's not enough."

Fiona couldn't stand the pain any longer. She reached out and enfolded Janine in her arms.

"It's tough, I'm so sorry," she said, rubbing the girl's back.

"Then the bank president came by the house one day. Mama wasn't home. Daddy was still in the hospital. Mr. McLennon said he'd let the mortgage go for a few months, until Daddy was back on his feet."

"But he wanted something from you," Fiona said.

The girl nodded.

"It's been awful. I can't tell my mom—she can't take any more bad news. My daddy's too sick to do anything, and knowing that would make it worse. And if I tell, the bank will foreclose and we don't have any other place to go."

She began to sob again.

"Did he take you to that cottage?"

Janine nodded.

"Here's what we can do," Fiona said softly, not wanting to scare the girl. "We'll talk to the sheriff. Tell him what you've told me. He'll take it from there."

Janine pulled away, shaking her head. "I can't tell anyone. I can't be the one to lose our home."

"You won't be. Whatever happens, your folks won't lose their house."

Fiona wasn't entirely sure *how* she could guarantee that, but she would make sure it happened.

"No one will believe me," Janine said.

"I believe you," Fiona said.

"You don't even live here."

"But I did, and I know what McLennon is capable of. This time it isn't a throwaway teenager but a girl who has family and friends around her."

"They won't believe me. He said they wouldn't."

"Then we get to prove him wrong. Come with me to see the sheriff."

Janine hesitated, then shook her head.

"I can't."

Fiona flashed her badge. "I'm a cop. I believe you.

Come in with me and we'll swear out a warrant for the arrest of Allen McLennon for rape."

Janine looked at the badge, then at Fiona. She burst into tears again, reaching out to clutch at Fiona.

"You'll really arrest him? Really?"

"He won't ever bother you again," Fiona promised.

Sixty minutes later Fiona and Janine and Janine's mother were in Sam's office, reviewing all the statements Janine had made.

Her mother's eyes were swollen from tears she'd wept when she learned of her daughter's ordeal. Her anger was so great Fiona was afraid she'd find a gun and go shoot Allen. Not that he didn't deserve it, but the woman didn't deserve to be locked away for the rest of her life because of him.

"We'll have the search warrant in a few more minutes," Sam said. "We'll send in a team to look for evidence that Janine was in that cottage."

"Isn't her word good enough?" Mrs. Flowers asked belligerently.

"Yes, it is, for the arrest warrant. But we want to make sure this bastard never does this again. I want an airtight case against him."

Marjorie came in, carrying a couple of folded sheets of paper.

"The warrants, Sheriff. One to search the cottage and the other for his arrest." She put them on the desk. "Anything else I can do?"

Sam picked up the search warrant and skimmed it to make sure it had all he wanted. Then he rose.

"I'm going to give this to two deputies and send them out."

"You're not going yourself?" Mrs. Flowers asked.

"No. I'm going to arrest Allen McLennon."

Fiona smiled. "I'm going with you."

"No."

"I've waited twelve long years for this moment. If you think I'm going to miss this, you have rocks in your head."

Mrs. Flowers rose, as well.

"If we are finished here, Sheriff, I'm taking Janine to the doctor's. Then home."

"There will be more, of course," Sam said. "But I'll come to you when we need the next step. We have Janine's statement. That's all we need for now."

When the Flowerses left, Fiona turned to follow, but Sam caught her arm. He closed his door and looked at her.

"I did my best to investigate this case, but was never one hundred percent sure. I'm sorry, Fiona. Knowing you better now, I should have believed you from the beginning. I'm glad it's turning out this way. Justice is important to me."

"Understandable. You knew Allen, didn't know me. The main thing is justice will triump."

She felt a flare of hope with his words. And a warm glow of righteousness.

"You're darn straight on that one. Let's go."

Fiona had never seen Sam so tense as when he got into the official sheriff's car.

"You can ride to the bank with me, go inside and stand around like any other citizen, but once the arrest is made, you're on your own. You cannot ride back with us."

He reversed out of his parking slot.

"I'll just stand quietly in the lobby of the bank and not say a word," she said. "You do have handcuffs, right?"

"I know the drill, Fiona," Sam said drily.

There was a short line of customers waiting for the tellers. Several people were in the loans department, and one elderly man was talking with the new accounts representative.

Allen McLennon was standing with them when Sam and Fiona entered the bank. She moved to stand near the door, watching, every fiber of her being wishing she could go with him. But she was too good a cop to push her luck. She didn't want anything to screw up this case.

Sam walked up to Allen. He looked up.

"Hi, Sheriff, what can we do for you today?" he asked genially.

"Allen McLennon, you are under arrest for the rape of a minor. You have the right to remain silent. If you give up that right—"

Fiona matched him in her mind, word for word of the Miranda warning. But her eyes never left McLennon's face. At first he looked surprised, then angry, then he began blustering, saying there had to be a mistake. When Sam had him say he understood his rights and demanded an attorney, Sam put on the handcuffs.

Everyone in the bank had stopped at Sam's first words. They all stared at the president, stunned at the allegation. The murmur of voices began to build as Sam herded McLennon from the bank.

When they drew even with Fiona, she caught Allen's eye.

"Gotcha," she murmured.

Twelve years late, it still felt good.

Fiona followed Sam and Allen from the bank, watching as the man was put into the backseat of the patrol car and Sam took him to jail.

Slowly she walked along the street. For the first time in twelve years, she felt free. Nothing else had changed, but the truth would come out for all to know. It wouldn't change the past, wouldn't alter their lives now. But for the first time since that fateful day, Fiona walked with a light heart.

Cassie's van came down the street. When Cassie spotted Fiona, she pulled over and waved. Fiona hurried to the driver's side.

"Want a ride?" Cassie asked.

"Where to?"

"The convalescent hospital. Didn't you get the message? Margaret wants to see you."

Fiona bit her lip. The euphoria of the past few minutes dissipated. She'd have to tell Margaret. At last the woman would know Fiona had not tried to cause trouble, but had been telling the truth all along.

"I didn't get any message. Did you hear the news? Sam just arrested McLennon."

"No!" Cassie's eyes widened. "What happened?"

Fiona went around to the passenger side and climbed in.

"I'll tell you on the way to Margaret."

Cassie went in with Fiona, anxious to be with her when she saw Margaret. They'd tell her the news together. When they reached Margaret's room, it was empty.

"Are you here to see Ms. Nunes? She's down in therapy. Won't be out for another forty minutes," a nurse said, pausing in the doorway from the hall. "Was she expecting you?"

"She called earlier and asked us to stop by," Cassie said, glancing at her watch, then at Fiona. "Want to wait or come back?"

"I can wait."

"Me, too."

The nurse nodded and left.

"The room is nice," Cassie said, glancing around. It wasn't as austere as the hospital room had been. The curtains on the window and the bedding matched. There were two visitor chairs. Scattered on the tray stand were several sheets of lined paper. Cassie wandered over to look at what Margaret had been writing.

Fiona gazed out the window. She looked at the

colorful flowers blooming in a small garden. She'd missed seeing flowers in L.A. She hadn't realized it until she'd returned to Bradford and been surrounded by them all the time. Her apartment complex had grass and concrete and a small tree.

"Fiona, you should see this," Cassie said, an odd note in her voice.

"What?" Fiona turned.

Cassie was holding several sheets of paper in her hand.

"It's a letter to you from Margaret."

"Are you sure? Why write me when I see her almost every day?"

Fiona crossed to Cassie and reached for the pages.

"She can't talk very well, but she can write fairly legibly. She wrote Piper about her parentage. Maybe she felt she could communicate with a letter better than trying to talk."

Fiona began to read.

"Oh, my God," she said softly. "Listen to this

"My Dear Fiona,

Please forgive a foolish old woman. I broke your heart, I know. Mine was broken when they took you away. I loved you, dear child. You were wild and free and so full of life and energy you challenged me at every turn. But deep inside I knew you were a good girl, one who needed a mother's love more than the others. I failed you and I am so very sorry."

Fiona looked up at Cassie.

"Oh, Fiona," she said. "Is there more?"

"Yes."

"At first I believed you were angry at me and tried to break up the relationship I thought was developing between me and Allen. But in a short time, I knew that was not true. I let you down when you needed support the most. I am sorry. I tried for months to find you, to get word to you, to let you know I believed you within hours of your leaving. I should have believed you from the first. Should have been there for you slaying every dragon in our path to get to the truth. Piper will tell you how unsuited for such a role I was, but I should have.

"I know you may never forgive me, but if you can bear to visit an old woman from time to time, please know I will forever be grateful for any time you can spare. My precious Fiona, I am proud of all you have accomplished in your short life. I expect great things from you in the future. Maybe even—

"It stops there."

Fiona stared at the pages, the handwriting shaky, some of the words misspelled. Still, it came from Margaret's heart.

"She did believe me," Fiona said softly, tears filling her eyes. "Before she heard today's news, she believed me."

That was all she'd ever wanted. And today it all came.

"We'll definitely wait now and celebrate when she gets back," Cassie said, coming to give her friend a hug. "All her kids are home."

"We were her children, weren't we?" Fiona said. "She was our mother."

"I think I'd say it in the present tense," Cassie said. "She is our mother. The only one any of us has. Can you let go of the past and be all right with this?"

Fiona nodded.

"Yes. I felt so guilty earlier when I talked to Janine and found out the trouble she was in. If I had come back earlier, made people listen, I could have prevented Janine's suffering."

"Maybe, maybe not. You told the truth at the start and no one listened before. Who's to say coming back before now would have changed anything? You did no wrong. My heart aches for Janine, but thank goodness you followed up on your suspicions and stopped it from happening anymore."

Margaret was wheeled into her room about thirty minutes later. She looked happy to see them, until she saw Fiona holding the letter. Glancing at the desk, she then met Fiona's eyes, fear and worry reflected in hers.

Fiona smiled and almost flew across the room to hug her foster mother.

"Thank you for believing in me. That's what hurt the most, all these years, I thought you didn't believe me."

Margaret tried to talk, but emotions made the sounds more garbled than normal. She hugged Fiona, patting her on the back, smiling through her tears at Cassie.

"Piper should be here," Cassie said, reaching out to

grasp Margaret's hand. "All your girls will be together on Saturday, Margaret. With you. We're so glad to be home."

Home. Fiona knew the meaning of the word. Dared she hope she'd come home?

By the time supper was ready, Fiona was exhausted. She and Cassie had spent most of the afternoon with Margaret, talking and making plans for the weddings. Margaret was more relaxed than Fiona ever remembered, and by late afternoon some of her words were actually clear.

Fiona called Piper when they got home to tell her the astonishing news of McLennon's arrest. Piper wanted to return home immediately, but Fiona insisted she stay since she was scheduled to return home the day after tomorrow as it was.

"How's the visit going?" she asked.

"Fantastic. Adam's folks are wonderful, so welcoming and happy for us. You'll get to meet them Saturday. And his sister and her family are so much fun. You should see them tease Adam. Gives me a whole new perspective on the man."

"Cassie says to tell you everything is ready for the wedding. She's going shopping with me tomorrow to get a fancy dress for the occasion."

"Get something you like and can wear again. Mostly I want to marry the world's most wonderful man and start our lives together. I don't care that much about the trappings."

When they were finished, Fiona wandered into the kitchen. Matt was already at the kitchen table, watching as Cassie cooked.

"I'm going to miss your cooking when I go home," Fiona said, sitting at her regular place at the table. "I usually eat my main meal at the school cafeterias and have sandwiches for dinner."

"How long are you going to do undercover work at high schools?" Matt asked.

"I don't know. It's getting old, but there're always more drug dealers to put away."

"You can't put them all away," Cassie said gently.

Fiona nodded. Nothing would change her mother's being an addict. Nothing could change the past. She could only make the future the way she wanted.

"Fill me in on the details," Matt said.

Fiona talked through dinner, about McLennon, about Janine and about Margaret. When they were finished, she offered to help with the dishes, but Cassie said Matt would help, smiling at him suggestively.

"I'm going to call Janine, see if she wants to talk or anything," Fiona said.

She'd pushed hard, but the results were worth it. She just hoped Janine felt the same.

Before she could look the Flowers up in the phone directory, her telephone rang.

"It's Sam," he said when Fiona answered.

"Did McLennon make bail?" she asked, hoping he hadn't.

"Not yet. The judge is still deciding. I hope he makes it a million or more, just to send a message. But I'm sure he'll get out pending trial. And FYI, and only for you, I've had six calls from other women who were victims of Allen McLennon. Each thought they were alone. One tried to get help and was not believed. The rest were too intimidated at the time, but came forth today to add to the charges against him. Two are recent enough to prosecute."

"I can't believe he did that all these years and no one suspected."

"People see the outer trappings more than reality sometimes. What are you doing now?"

"I just had a most delicious meal, courtesy of Cassie, and now I'm thinking of calling Janine Flowers to see if I can offer any help."

"Good idea. Are you free in the morning?"

"Yes, why?"

"I'll pick you up at nine," he said. "Wear something that makes you look like you mean business."

"What?"

"See you then."

He hung up. Fiona slowly hung up, tempted to call him back and ask what he was talking about. Something that means business? She'd be in full battle dress if that was what he wanted.

She called Janine and spoke with the girl for a long time. It was a difficult conversation, with Fiona feeling a nagging guilt for not making sure the world knew about Allen sooner. Yet, as the others had said, she'd tried. What more could she have done?

Promptly at nine the next morning, Sam pulled into the driveway at Bradford Hall. The official patrol car told Fiona it wasn't fun and games. She walked slowly to the car, dressed in black, her makeup enough to highlight her eyes, but not too much to give a false impression.

"This businesslike enough for you?" she asked, sliding into the front seat.

"Looks like you could go undercover in a heartbeat," Sam said.

He leaned over and kissed her gently.

"How are you doing?" he asked in a low voice, his eyes looking deep into hers.

"I feel like a ton of weight has lifted. And I spoke with Margaret yesterday afternoon. Turns out she had believed me and tried to find me all those years ago. It feels really good."

He began to drive.

"Tell me about talking with Janine."

"It went well, I thought. She now feels bad about adding to her parents' worry, but I told her that was the job of adults. Kids don't have to act grown-up before their time."

"Like you did?"

"Yes, but if I could do it differently, I would have. Anyway, we talked for almost two hours. I hope I helped. I did suggest she see a therapist, but I know money's really tight for them now. Still, I hope she can get some help."

"I had a conversation with Brad Johnson," Sam said.

"Who?"

"Janine's boyfriend. He's holding together by a thread, vowing revenge on McLennon. Interesting thing, that cottage burned to the ground last night."

"You're kidding? Who? Brad?"

"He's got an airtight alibi—he was talking with me."

"Cool," Fiona murmured.

"What?"

"I don't know who did it," she said, "but I'm glad. How hard are you going to investigate?"

"As hard as I would any other crime. One of my deputies was out there this morning—no footprints, no identifying evidence at all, but the smell of gasoline was strong."

"So you look for the guy who bought a lot of gas yesterday."

"Already checked the local stations. No one filled up any cans. No one came in who didn't need almost a full tank of gas. No suspects."

Fiona smiled. She didn't believe in coincidences. Janine had friends. They were angry when they learned she'd been raped and found their own means of retribution. She didn't know who or how, but if she were in charge, she'd let the investigation lapse.

"Was the place insured?" she asked.

"Don't know. I haven't exactly discussed the situation with McLennon yet."

They were on the highway out of town when Fiona looked around.

"Where are we going?"

"Salida," Sam said. Salida was the county seat of the adjacent county.

"Why?"

"I want you to talk to someone there," he said, glancing at her.

"Who?"

"The chief of police."

"Why?"

"He's got an opening. Thought you might like having a choice about things. You think you have to return to L.A., but there are other options. If you don't like Salida, maybe New Orleans."

"Why not Bradford?" she asked, unsure how she felt about Sam's highhanded way of handling things.

"Conflict of interest," he murmured.

She stared at him.

"You can't work for me," he clarified.

"Because?"

"I want you to be more than one of my deputies."

Her breath caught. "How much more?"

"It's something we need to discuss in private."

"We're private here."

"But I'm busy driving."

"So?"

"So kisses aren't allowed when driving."

She looked out the window, afraid of where her thoughts were leading. He wanted kisses, did he? And more? Could she consider moving back to Mississippi?

She'd been dreading leaving Cassie and Piper again. And Margaret, especially after yesterday's revelation. But to return to Mississippi? Living here had never been her dream.

But that was then. This was now.

And Sam Witt was a strong inducement for staying, even without Cassie, Piper and Margaret thrown in.

She remained silent the rest of the way to Salida. Once there, Sam walked her into the small city hall and introduced her to Hal Gardner, chief of police. Then he left. Fiona was on her own.

Half an hour later she wandered out and spotted Sam sitting in the patrol car. He'd acquired a newspaper and was reading. She walked over.

"It's hot as the hinges out here," she said, getting into the car. "Why didn't you wait inside at least?"

"I wanted to make sure you knew where to find me. How did it go?"

"We need to talk."

"Good or bad?"

"What do you want from me, Sam?" she asked.

He stared out the window for a long moment, then slowly turned to look at her.

"When Patty died, I thought my world ended. We were high school sweethearts. We delayed getting married until we both finished college and I'd done time in the military. Then we started our lives together. Everything was as good as it got, I thought. Until she was killed."

Fiona nodded, not really needing to hear this. He was going to tell her something about Patty being the love of his life, but now he was ready to move on.

"I didn't think I'd fall in love again."

Her heartbeat quickened.

"But I did. And with the most unlikely woman I know."

Fiona felt her heart skip a beat. She allowed herself a small smile.

"Oh?"

"She's got an attitude that doesn't quit," Sam went on. "She dresses like a biker chick. She argues all the time, won't do as I ask."

"Ask or order?"

He ignored the provocative comment.

"The thing is, I thought about it long and hard and I can't move back to a big city. I like living in Bradford. It's a great town, not a lot of crime, and neighbors who care about one another. I know you got a raw deal when you were a teenager, but times have changed. I wish you'd stay and give us all a chance."

"I'm more interested in your comment about love," she said.

"I love you, Mary Fiona Hunter. Will you marry me?"

Fiona stared at him, stunned. She'd expected an invitation to an affair, not marriage.

"You don't know me."

"I know what I need to. Mostly, I know I've fallen in love. Deeply. I thought Patty was the love of my life, and I won't lie to you—she'll always hold a special place in my heart. But what I feel for you staggers me. If you go, I'll have to follow you. If you stay, I'll do my best to make you the happiest woman on the planet. Say you'll think about it, at least. Give me that much."

Fiona licked her lips. Cleared her throat. Looked out the window for a moment, then back at Sam.

"I've never had a relationship like what you're asking. Once I left Bradford I didn't trust anyone. It's amazing how alone I felt and yet was still determined to keep myself isolated. I couldn't get hurt if I didn't let anyone in. I'm not sure I'd be any good at marriage. I never wanted it, never expected it."

"So?"

"Until I got here and ran into you. You've made me dream dreams."

"Take a chance, Fiona. I'll do my best never to hurt you."

She licked her lips again.

"You'd want babies, I suppose."

Sam smiled slowly and nodded.

"Don't you? Playmates for Cassie's and Piper's kids."

Her heart pounding as hard as if she'd run a race, Fiona tried to wrap her mind around the magnitude of Sam's proposal.

Marriage, a family, staying in her hometown—but

with a big difference. She wasn't the scared child longing for a mother. She'd reconnected with Margaret—her real mother.

She was an adult, in love, and surrounded by family and friends. Time to take a chance. To grab hold of all that love and never let go.

"Yes," she said, delighted when he pulled her across the middle of the seat and kissed her soundly.

They headed back to Bradford Hall late in the afternoon, after shopping for rings. In Salida. Sam said he wanted to be able to tell people himself, not have the grapevine spread the word.

They stopped first to tell Margaret the news.

Fiona felt on top of the world. Hal Gardner had said the job was hers if she wanted it. She was going to get married, live with Sam and have babies. Maybe they could even get a dog. She'd always wanted a dog.

Now she couldn't wait to tell Cassie and Piper.

When they arrived at the old house, the driveway was full. It looked as if Adam and Piper, Matt and Cassie were all there, as well as the workers still finishing up the renovations.

They entered the kitchen to see their friends talking and laughing.

Piper saw Fiona and Sam first.

"Hi!" she said. "We came back early. I wanted to see you after the amazing news. Adam's folks understood."

She crossed to Fiona and gave her a hug.

"You okay?"

"Better than okay," Fiona replied, casually brushing back her hair with her left hand, the one that wore a brand-new diamond ring.

She'd never thought she'd be so girlish.

For a heartbeat no one said a word, then Piper shrieked and hugged her again.

"You and Sam?" she asked.

Fiona nodded.

Cassie flew over and hugged them both.

"I can't believe it. You're getting married to Sam? You said you'd never marry."

"So did Sam," Adam added. "Congratulations, man. You sure picked a handful, though."

"Worth it," Sam said, shaking Adam's hand and then Matt's.

"So you want the weekend after Cassie?" Piper asked. "Good grief, at this rate I'm never getting back to Paris! Wait until Margaret hears." She laughed. "Of all the people to stay in town, you're the last I'd figured."

"We already told Margaret," Fiona said.

Sam came over and put his arm around her shoulders.

"And if I'd known as a teenager Sam would be here, I wouldn't have wanted to leave."

"So *will* you get married the weekend after my wedding?" Cassie asked.

"Well, I have to get back to L.A., give notice, clean

out my apartment, ship things home," Fiona began.

She looked at Sam.

"I don't want to wait a second longer than we have to," he said. "Celibacy wears hard on a man when he wants someone as much as I want you. But it's your only wedding, Fiona. *You* decide."

Fiona's cheeks flushed.

Piper cocked her head. "You're waiting?"

"Fiona's worth waiting for. I want our wedding night to be special."

Fiona's cheeks flamed even more.

Piper stared at her.

"You're *not!*" she said in amazement.

Cassie smiled. "Good for you, sweetie."

"What?" Matt asked.

"Fiona's a virgin," Piper said. "I don't believe it!"

Now everyone stared at Fiona. She groaned and turned to bury her head in Sam's chest. Who else in the world knew a twenty-eight-year-old virgin?

"We have some champagne on ice for Saturday. Let's break out a bottle tonight," Cassie said. "This calls for a celebration. The girls from Bradford Hall have all come home."

Fiona knew her home was where Sam was and always would be.

She looked at him. "I love you," she whispered.

"Shout it from the rooftop, love," he said, then leaned over to kiss her.

Epilogue

The October sun shone through the stained-glass windows as Fiona waited for the music to change to the wedding march. The sanctuary was small and she could see Sam waiting by the altar. Cassie and Piper had taken their places, and it was time for her to walk down the aisle to meet the man she was marrying.

Margaret sat in the seat of mother of the bride, smiling. She walked to her place in the church this morning, using only a cane.

There were other friends from school days. Her ex-partner from Los Angeles had come to witness the ceremony. Sam's family sat on the groom's side. Sam had even received a warm note from Patty's parents, wishing them happiness.

She started down the aisle, alone. She'd been alone most of her life and wanted to make this last walk by herself. With a bit of luck, it would be the last time she'd be solo. She was joining her life to Sam Witt's, and after that the two of them would be a team facing whatever the future held—together.

Piper's wedding in July had gone without a hitch. Cassie's a week later had been beautiful. But Fiona secretly thought hers the best of the three.

She liked the fall colors she'd chosen for her matrons of honor.

For herself, she'd found the perfect dress, elegant yet feminine and very white and very formal. The veil gave the scene a soft haze, but she couldn't wait until Sam lifted it and all barriers were removed. Slowly she walked forward, her eyes locked with his. She felt the heat of his gaze, the desire kept in check these past months until they would become husband and wife.

Fiona had returned to California to give notice and pack up her things, then moved them from Los Angeles directly to Sam's house. When she returned to Bradford, she'd stayed with Margaret in the newly refurbished Bradford Hall.

The home for unwed mothers already had three young women in residence and they were blossoming under Margaret's care.

She loved her new job in the sheriff's department of the next county. But being near Margaret, Cassie and Sam was even better.

Cassie and Matt had rented an apartment in town until the house Matt was building would be ready in the spring.

Piper and Adam had been in Paris the past three months, flying in yesterday for today's ceremony.

The familiar music filled the sanctuary as Fiona concentrated on not tripping. When she reached the man she loved, she held out her right hand to take his and hold on for dear life. Nothing this summer had prepared her for this moment. But she was always ready to take a risk. And this was the biggest one of her life.

"Dearly beloved..." the minister began.

Fiona smiled. Everyone in this church was her dearly beloved. It had just taken her a bit longer than most to find that out.

If you liked **Cassie's Return**,
you may enjoy Billionaire's Betrothal, book 1 in the
Gold Gate Romance series.

If you enjoyed Fiona's Homecoming, please consider
leaving a review.

More books by Barbara McMahon

Bradford Hall

Cassie's Return

Piper's Discovery

Fiona's Homecoming

Golden Gate Romance Series

Billionaire's Betrothal

Her Not So Empty Nest

Dakota's Hero

One Special Kiss

Finding a Wife for Tanner

The CEO's Baby

Love Times Three

Office Charade

Cowboys of Wildcat Creek

Valentine's Cowboy Rescue

Holly's Reluctant Cowboy

Shelly and the Cowboy

A Cowboy for Eliza

Kristi's Cowboy Hero

Sweet Reunion Romance Collection

Unexpected Reunion

Unanticipated Reunion

Unpredictable Reunion

The Talmadge Sisters

Letters to Caroline

Trusting Abby

Michelle's Marriage Deal

The Harts of Texas Series

Rebel Heart

Reckless Heart

Tangled Hearts

A Sweet Clean Christmas Romance Collection

The Christmas Cop

A Teaspoon of Mistletoe

The Cowboy's Special Christmas

The Christmas Locket

A Soldier's Christmas

A Key West Christmas

Cowboy Heroes Series

The Cowboy Next Door
Cowboy's Bride
One Stubborn Cowboy
Crazy About a Cowboy
Never Doubt a Cowboy

Cowboy Marshal
Summer Cowboy
Second Chance Cowboy
Movie Star Cowboy

Tropical Escape Series

Island Rendezvous
Come into the Sun

Island Paradise

Rocky Point Series

Rocky Point Legacy
Rocky Point Reunion
Rocky Point Promise

Rocky Point Hero
Rocky Point Inn
Rocky Point Dawn

The Ultimate Billionaires

The Cynical Sheikh
Falling for the Sheikh

A Sheikh of Her Own
The Unforgettable Sheikh

Sweet Romance Stand-alone Collection

Because of You
Cowboy Charade
I'll Take Forever
Jared's Promise
Mail Order Bride
Not Really Married

Sweet Meant To Be
The Cowboy Comes Home
The Paper Marriage
Trusting Jake
The Banished Bride